I0657245

POWERLESS

John Samson

TSL Publications

First published in Great Britain in 2017
By TSL Publications, Rickmansworth

Copyright © 2017 John Samson

ISBN / 978-1-911070-27-6

The right of John Samson to be identified as the author of this work
has been asserted by the author in accordance with the UK Copyright,
Designs and Patents Act 1988.

All characters and events in this publication, other than those clearly in
the public domain, are fictitious and any resemblance to actual
persons, living or dead, is purely coincidental.

All rights reserved. No part of this publication may be reproduced,
stored in a retrieval system or transmitted, in any form or by any
means without the prior written permission of the publisher, nor be
otherwise circulated in any form of binding or cover other than that in
which it is published and without a similar condition being imposed on
the subsequent buyer.

For Anne

THE LIFT

The lift pinged softly, the sound further muted by the light green carpet that rolled away down the corridor of the tenth floor. Deon Scott, a man in his late thirties, shifted his weight to his right leg, preparing himself for the opening of the doors. He was well dressed in a black pinstriped suit, crisp white shirt and purple tie. His polished black shoes that peeked from beneath the precise hem of his suit trousers reflected the bright office lights. It was late, nearly nine o'clock and there was no sign of life in the office. Deon was tired; it had been a long hard week with very little financial reward.

He yawned and rubbed his eyes as the doors hissed open, then stepped into the car his vision slowly refocusing. A slight movement to his left startled him; he had not expected anyone to be in the lift. It was just the security guard.

Deon greeted him with an almost imperceptible nod of the head and the man acknowledged this in a similar manner then edged to the back of the car to accommodate Deon and maintain his personal space.

Both men stared straight ahead as the doors closed and Deon took in the other man's reflection in the mirror-like surface that drew across his line of vision. The guard was slightly taller than him and wore the khaki uniform that all the security personnel in the building wore, including the military-style beret. He stood straight at attention, his face devoid of emotion or thought.

Deon turned his attention from the reflection to the floor indicator above the door. Nine … eight … seven …

The lift suddenly juddered to a halt and the light snapped off, plunging the car into a deep darkness and causing the occupants to lurch. In less than a second it steadied itself and an eerie quietness engulfed them.

'What's going on?' Deon's voice pierced the dark and the silence. He groped uncertainly for the side of the lift.

'Power cut, sir.' The guard's voice had a deep resonance to it.

'Power cut?'

'Yes sir.'

The silence descended again while Deon digested the information he had been given.

'So what happens now?' his voice sounded strange, an intruder into the quiet and dark.

'We wait, sir.'

'Wait? For what?'

'For the power to come back on, sir.'

Silence.

'How long will it last?'

'Er ... maybe ten minutes, maybe five hours, sir.'

'Five hours!'

'Yes sir, five hours,' and after a long pause, 'maybe, sir.'

'You're not telling me that we are going to be stuck here for that long, are you?'

'In April, sir, we had a five-hour power cut. But maybe this time it will be short.' The voice was trying to reassure.

'Oh ja, I remember that one. Five bloody hours. At least I wasn't stuck in a lift that time.'

The memory of the power cut came back vividly to Deon. He had been with Sharon that night. They had been sitting having a glass of wine in the lounge when the lights went. Both were a little tipsy and instead of finding a torch or matches to light a candle they had opted to cuddle closer on the sofa. At first she had been quite giggly but the cuddling had led to groping and the groping led to fantastic sex. Well fantastic at least for Deon, he never knew, or really cared if Sharon enjoyed it.

'Where were you stuck then, sir?' The question jarred Deon back from his thoughts and he was suddenly glad of the darkness.

'That's none of your business,' he said brusquely. It had been a highly personal thought and he didn't like this stranger being near it. Silence fell in the lift again as the awkwardness of the abrupt reply and the way the innocent question had felt so intimate played on each man's mind. Seconds ticked by with neither of them moving nor speaking, the only sound was their shallow breathing.

Deon slowly simmered down as he realised that the questioner could have had no idea of where he had spent the five-hour power cut. But he was not going to relent and tell this stranger, this black man, about his personal life. He shuffled his feet and sighed.

'Is there no back up power for the building?' he asked eventually, partly out of a desire to break the awkward silence and partly from his frustration at being trapped.

There was a slight pause before the voice came back, 'Yes sir, there is a generator that can be used.'

'Well what's taking so long?'

'The generator needs to be turned on sir.'

'Who is supposed to turn it on?'

'The guard on night duty, sir.'

'So why isn't he turning it on?' Deon's voice was thick with incredulity.

'Because he is stuck in the lift, sir.'

6

Silence ensued as Deon realised what the guard was saying.

Eventually, 'You mean to say that you are the one who is supposed to turn the generator on, but because you're stuck in this lift there is no-one to turn it on?'

'Yes sir.'

Deon shook his head in the dark, groping around in his mind, not sure whether to choose the emotion marked 'bemused' or that marked 'angry'. He chose the latter.

'What sort of a dumb-ass security system is that?' his eyes desperately trying to see his lift companion. It's easier to be a figure of authority when you can make eye contact. The dark was unnerving him; it was stripping him of his power.

'Isn't there another guard on duty? Don't you work in pairs?'

'No sir, only me.'

'Just one of you, that doesn't make sense!'

'Maybe it is because of the cost.'

That made sense. Deon was a money man and money talked. But right now it was not saying the right things; right now the small costs of an extra security guard seemed a small price to pay for at least some time with Sharon. It was after all Friday night.

'This is just typical of the new South Africa. Nothing bloody works.'

His tirade was met with silence. Was it sullen? Deon couldn't tell. He forced himself to calm down, this was getting nowhere.

'So we wait?' he asked eventually.

'Yes sir, we wait.' The voice held no emotion, it was a voice that was used to waiting, a patient voice that did not know the mad, rushed pace of being a hotshot businessman in the city.

In a strange way Deon envied that patience. He was feeling cooped up, closed-in in this dark, small car. He wanted to move on, be doing something. There was always something to be done – he could be working, socialising, making love to Sharon. He was agitated and wanted to thrash out at the dark and the walls of the lift that confined him.

Patience was part of the job of being a security guard, Deon thought. He would have spent too many nights with nothing but his thoughts as company to be fazed by this, too many nights sitting watching the closed circuit television that told him all was well in the building, too many nights, waiting for the dawn. He envied the man's patience.

They fell silent again and the gloom closed in around Deon. He shifted restlessly and let his annoyance stew till he suddenly kicked out at the lift door.

'Damn it, what's taking them so long? What the hell are they bloody doing?' he shouted.

The noise startled the guard who had closed his eyes while standing. Deon began banging on the door of the lift.

'Help! Help! We're stuck in the lift, someone help.'

He stopped shouting for a second and listened for an answer but was not overly optimistic. Still he banged and shouted again though with less urgency. The guard smiled quietly and eased himself onto the floor where he sat in a corner and closed his eyes again. Deon heard the movement and turned round to where he thought the man was.

'Are you sitting down, huh? Come on you must help shout. Someone must hear us. We must get out of here. Help! Help!'

More banging.

The guard waited for Deon to take a break then grunted, 'It's no good sir, there is no-one else in the building, I just checked and the front door is locked. You can shout but it will not help.'

'Don't get …' *cocky with me boy.* The second half of the sentence was ripped from his vocal chords and shoved back into his mind as his P.C. gland took control. One could not say things like that anymore, not in the new South Africa.

'Don't give up so easily,' he ended lamely and banged the door again to show that he had not given up.

The guard smiled safely in the dark. He knew Deon would not see what he was doing. He didn't say anything, he would just let this stupid whitie realise for himself that banging was futile.

Deon hit the wall of the lift a few more times but it was more for show now. His mind had processed the information the guard had given him and yes, it was most likely that they were the only two left in the building. A resigned expletive fell silently from his lips, then after a final bang for good measure he slumped down in the corner opposite the guard and sighed heavily preparing himself for the wait.

Soon, however, the quiet and the dark began to gnaw at him. He was used to there being a buzz around him and light to see with. He could not stay quiet, he needed someone to talk to, but all he had was this security guard. What could he talk to him about? What could they possibly have in common? He drew in his breath, he had to start somewhere.

'Five hours. When was that again? April?'

'Yes sir. April the fourth.'

'Geez time flies hey? It feels like yesterday don't you think? You weren't stuck in the lift last time were you?' He immediately realised that he was asking the same question he had so rudely refused to answer himself a few minutes ago and cursed himself silently. But the voice seemed unfazed by this *faux pas.*

8

'No, I was at the reception, sir.'

'Did you put the generator on?'

'No, I was the only one in the building so there was no need for the generator, sir.'

The simplicity of the reply and the manner in which it was delivered caused Deon to pause. Had he been alone in a dark office block he certainly would have turned the lights on. He reflected that he would have been too scared to sit there in the dark and wait, not to mention having to cope with the boredom.

'So … er … did you just sit in the dark?'

'Yes sir.'

'Do you like being in the dark?' Deon contemplated the double meaning of what he had just said and wondered if the guard would take it the wrong way.

'Yes sir, I find it peaceful.'

'So what did you do to pass the time?'

The guard gave a slight grunt that was half a chuckle at some remembered fact and what seemed to be a half derisive laugh at Deon, perhaps because of the manner in which the question had been asked. Was this rich businessman, who strutted in and out of the building looking so smart in his suit, incapable of staving off boredom when there was nothing to do?

'I sat remembering my days as a boy,' and after a short pause he remembered, 'sir.'

'Really? What did you get up to as a boy?'

The guard smiled to himself as he was thrown back to his childhood days.

CHILDHOOD

A deep blue sky formed a canopy over the lush green hills. The two boys made their way down a narrow dirt track. In front of them a small herd of cows lumbered along, stopping occasionally to tear at the grass on the side of the path.

Hey! Hey! They chivvied the cows along, swatting them gently with their switches. 'There will be plenty of grass when we get to the grazing fields,' the older of the two boys cried at the cows. As if in response to this promise, the leader of the herd flung its head in the air and snorted loudly before ambling further down the path.

The boys walked lazily behind the cows, their bare feet padding softly on the dusty path. Every so often one of them would strike out at the grass with a swish of their whip. Both kept alert eyes on the cattle before them, but they also took in every movement of the small animals that inhabited the area.

A wild rabbit ran across the path and disappeared into the long grass. The younger one started off after it while the older laughed, 'You'll never catch it Simon,' he shouted as he watched his brother scamper through the grass waving his whip in the air and whooping with glee. He was soon out of sight and the one who had remained on the path half-heartedly urged the cows forward, keeping a wary eye out for his sibling.

After a minute the younger boy returned carrying the wriggling rabbit by its ears, a huge grin on his face.

'What do you say now Peter my brother? Am I not the best hunter in the world?'

Peter grinned fondly back. 'You are a good hunter Simon, I never thought you would catch that one. What are you going to do with it now?'

Simon looked from his brother to the rabbit and then back to his brother. The smile faded from his face and he lowered his eyes. Peter laughed quietly to himself. While Simon was a brilliant hunter, he could never kill a wild animal for pleasure. They had to be really hungry before he could bring himself to slaughter his prey and even then he would apologise profusely to the animal before slitting its throat.

'I am going to let it go,' Simon said eventually. Peter nodded kindly. Had the other boys been here they would have teased Simon for being a sissy, but Peter understood his brother and watched as the young boy set the rabbit free. It made an immediate dash into the undergrowth and was out of sight within seconds.

'Come, I'll race you,' Peter said and began running down the hill to where a muddy brown river twisted lazily along the valley.

'Hey, wait for me,' Simon shouted as he tried to catch up. Peter reached the river first and the two boys jumped in and began splashing around in the cool refreshing water. The cows followed slowly and some began to drink while others grazed along the banks.

After a time of playing they clambered onto some nearby rocks and lay naked, letting the sun dry them, but as the heat of the day intensified, they moved into the shade of a nearby tree. Simon climbed up into the lower branches while Peter sat chewing a long blade of grass watching the cows graze. His mood was changing and he was becoming melancholic.

Sensing the change, Simon jumped down from the tree and settled near Peter's feet, looking up at the serious face. He loved him dearly and would do anything for him.

'One day I will have to leave here,' Peter said, a solemn tone in his voice.

'Leave? But why? Where will you go,' Simon began to panic. He didn't want to be without his brother.

'I will go to the city, to eGoli. There I will make lots of money and send it back for you and father and mother, they do not call it the City of Gold for nothing. You will live like kings.'

'I will go with you,' Simon said. He didn't fancy being a king on his own. 'I will go to eGoli and work with you. We will both send money back for father and mother. With two of us working they will be able to live in the greatest luxury ever.'

He opened his arms wide indicating the expanse of wealth that their parents would enjoy.

Peter smiled at his brother, 'No, you must stay here, it is dangerous in the big city.'

'I can look after myself, you said earlier that I was the best hunter in the world.'

'Yes, but life in the city is very different, your skills as a hunter won't be needed there. You will need to know how to survive. Remember Silas who went to the city. He got into big trouble and came running back with his tail between his legs like a whipped dog. He did not have the right pass papers and the government will not let you stay in the city without the correct papers.'

Simon was quiet for a while, staring at the nearby cows. 'Do you think they will give both of us a pass?' he asked eventually.

THE LIFT 2

'There was so much space there, not like here in the city … in this lift.'

Simon had almost forgotten where he was and as the reality closed in around him he stopped talking.

Deon sat silently for a bit. He had enjoyed hearing about a childhood so different from his own. For the first time since the lift had stopped, the silence was a contented one, but Deon soon became restless again and needed noise so when he realised the guard was not going to talk more he asked, 'You got a name?'

'Sir?'

'Do you have a name?'

'Yes sir.'

Deon waited, but the guard was not saying. 'Well?'

'Sir?'

'Well, what is your name?'

'Oh, it is Simon.' He sat up straight and puffed his chest out slightly as he said it. He knew that he had been named after Simon of Cyrene, the one who had carried Jesus' cross. This was one of the few Bible stories he had picked up on when he occasionally attended the mission school near his family village. Peter was mentioned in the Bible too, he had been a disciple of Jesus. As a child it had pleased Simon that their names appeared in this book that was so important to the whites. As he had grown older, the sense of pride had remained.

Deon nodded in the dark. 'Simon,' he said but didn't offer his own name.

'Yes sir. Simon.'

Some of the ice had broken but they sat in silence again neither sure where to steer the conversation next. Deon was eventually the one to break it.

'Five bloody hours, is there nothing we can do? Can't we climb out the top of the lift? Like Bruce Willis did in *Die Hard*, did you ever see *Die Hard* hey? What a movie. If I was John McLean – that's the character Bruce Willis plays – I'd have found a way out of here by now.'

He stood and reached up to the ceiling of the lift, pushing and probing in the dark to feel if there was a trap door that he could use to escape through. The ceiling was solid, bar the light bulbs which were useless at the moment. He cursed and punched the side of the lift with some force, the frustration suddenly bubbling up again. The noise caused Simon to jump.

'Damn it man! This would never have happened in the old days. We

never used to have power cuts like this. Five bloody hours. Five …
bloody … hours!'

He hit the door to punctuate each word.

The old days, the days of apartheid. The days when people like Simon
were suppressed, denied a say in how their country was run. When they
were not allowed a proper education, exploited for cheap labour, made
to live as third class citizens in the country in which they had been born.

Deon slowly calmed himself after his outburst as these thoughts came
to him. He eased himself back to the floor. Should he apologise for what
he had said? Would Simon have even considered the things that he had
just thought?

He stewed these thoughts for long enough to make it too embarrassing
to comment on his little tirade without feeling foolish. He needed a new
line of conversation.

'So, where do you stay Simon?'

'Me? I live in Langa township, sir,' the reply came in the dark. And then
almost unexpectedly he went on, 'I moved there from Soweto about a
year ago.'

'From Soweto?' Deon's tone bordered on friendly. 'Why'd you move
down to Cape Town?'

There was a pause, a pause filled with thoughts of how to answer
without giving anything away.

Then, 'It became too dangerous there.' Deon noticed that Simon had
dropped the *sir*.

'Tell me about it hey. That's why I left Joeys too,' he used the colloquial
for Johannesburg with some sadness. 'Too bloody violent.'

There was another pause in which Simon shifted and thought about
going into more detail as to the real reasons for leaving when Deon spoke
again. His voice sounded distant, as distant as Johannesburg is from Cape
Town. Talk of the violence had brought back memories, memories that
were still raw and still painful.

'You see I used to live up there in Joeys, eGoli you guys call it, City of
Gold. Ja, I used to live in Rosebank. There was this …' he paused again
as the painful memories stabbed him. Simon waited patiently. 'There was
this girl that I was living with at the time.'

Why had he mentioned that? It seemed to have just slipped out, almost
as if it had been sucked from him by the dark. The mention of Joeys had
never had this effect on him before. He hadn't even been thinking of her
till suddenly she was out in the open and he felt he couldn't stop.

A lump in the throat was swallowed hard and he went on.

'She was stunning. Elise, that was her name. Man she was really
beautiful. I met her at a friend's party. Greg, he was my friend. He had

13

this huge pad in Bryanston where we used to hang out all the time, me and my buddies. There was Greg, Ian, Steve, he was mad old Steve, always up for a party, and then also Craig. We were a team – the A-Team.'

He stopped again as his group of friends from a time past, floated into his mind. He wondered briefly what they were all doing now. He had lost contact with most of them when he moved down to Cape Town. That had been more a severing of ties with the past and anything Elise-related rather than a natural going of different ways.

'We used to have great parties there, nearly every weekend. I remember the one where I met Elise 'cause it was quite subdued by our standards. There were only about twenty people that night. Elise was Danny's sister. He was one of the guys that came to the party. Danny used to work with Ian.

'She looked stunning when she walked in and all the men wanted to chat her up, even those who were there with their girlfriends. I was the cool one, I hung around outside on the verandah drinking a beer. Castle Lager of course. Hey you remember that advert on the TV?' He burst into song.

When we drink Castle
We're filled with admiration
For Charles' Brew
And how it grew
A mile high reputation.

'Charles!' Simon joined in with the toast to Charles Glass, the master brewer who, according to the well-known advert, had created Castle Lager. Deon was shaken from his thoughts and coughed nervously. Why had he exposed so much of his life? Especially something so personal and painful to this stranger who was … well, he was black. A white never spoke that personally to a black, did they? Not even nowadays after apartheid had fallen. Was it the darkness that had caused him to drop his guard like that?

Simon too realised what had happened and for a short while was silent and feeling a need to be subservient again, but something had changed in that comforting dark. There had been a small shift in the relationship between the two men, like a tiny crumbling deep beneath the earth's crust, a slight murmur before a full-blown earthquake.

Simon was the first to speak this time, feeling that the silence had gone on too long.

'I could do with a Castle Lager now,' he said in a muted tone, fearful that he was crossing lines he shouldn't.

Deon hesitated then crossed the line.

14

'Me too, nothing beats an ice-cold Castle hey.' The two men smiled, the dark making them unaware that the other was doing so, but each felt the warmth in the silence.

'So tell me more about Elise.'

Simon felt on much sturdier ground now and his question was kind and friendly. Deon gave a slight chuckle. He felt half-embarrassed to continue but now had a link with this man who was sharing the dark lift with him. He sighed as his memory was jolted back, but went on.

'Well all the men were trying to impress her so she said she was going to the toilet to get away from the crowd. When she came back she didn't go into the lounge where everyone was, but came out onto the verandah through a side door. I was standing in some shadows so she didn't see me at first. Greg's place had the most amazing view of Joeys and she just stood there at the railing looking out and breathing in the air. She had long dark hair and there was a slight wind blowing which played with it. The moon was full and bright – no I'm not making this up, it was genuinely like that. It was just so perfect man, her standing there, slim and sexy in the moonlight. Hell my heart was beating like a … like a Zulu drum.'

Deon paused, wondering if his simile had perhaps offended. Maybe Simon was a Xhosa or Sotho. Whites never could tell the difference, they were all just blacks. But he heard nothing so went on.

'It was just so perfect, you know what I'm saying. I was careful not to startle her, so I shifted my feet slightly and cleared my throat then, coming out of the shadows, I said in what I thought was a sexy voice,' and here he lowered his voice a tone or two, '"It's a stunning view hey?" Well it did startle her a bit, but she was cool. She turned round to see who had spoken and I knew she was a bit off balance there for a second so I had to strike quickly, *iron while the strike is hot*,' he quoted an advert again, 'so I said, "I saw you inside, those guys were over you." She sort of nodded and that was when the light caught her face and I saw her eyes close up for the first time. Man oh man did she have the most amazing eyes – long lashes and deep blue. I wanted to dive in and just swim in those eyes. Swim from one side to the other. Twenty lengths, no make that forty lengths – I wanted to impress this girl.'

Simon gave a small laugh.

'What's so funny?' Deon asked, 'If you had seen Elise, you would also have wanted to impress her. You would have done as many lengths of her deep blue eyes as it took.' He stopped short there. The dark and the easy flow of the conversation had momentarily made him forget that his lift companion was black. In the old days, a black man could have got beaten up for just looking at a white woman the wrong way. They were certainly not allowed to swim around in their eyes.

Simon felt the awkwardness as well and understood, but this was all supposed to be behind them now, this prejudice. He thought hard for something to say to put his companion at ease.

'I know what you mean,' he said, 'I knew a girl like that once. Thandi, she had wonderful eyes too, but not blue like a swimming pool, dark brown like the muddy rivers I used to swim in.'

This would help. The decidedly 'black' name of the girl with the muddy brown eyes would vanquish thoughts of a black man fantasising about a white woman.

Deon laughed and relaxed slightly. The differences were being acknowledged as was the need to move past these old prejudices. Black men didn't spend their entire lives fantasising about bedding white women, there was enough time taken up with trying to bed black women.

'Women hey? They have so much power in their eyes,' he joked.

'Ja,' Simon agreed, 'so tell me what did Elise say?'

'Well, as I said, I had just mentioned all the guys hounding her and she had sort of laughed. Well then she said, "Ja, it was getting a bit crowded in there." I had to be cool so I offered her a smoke. She took one and I lit it for her. Then I said something really stupid, you remember that ad on the radio for what was it now? I think it was Lexington cigarettes, anyway, I put on that deep voice like in the advert, "after action satisfaction",' Deon's voice growled the old slogan.

'I mean what a stupid thing to say, "after action satisfaction".' He shook his head at the memory.

Simon chuckled, 'That is most romantic sir. If I had said that to a girl I hardly knew I would have had my face slapped. After action satisfaction ... smack!'

He laughed uproariously and Deon joined in. Similarities were being acknowledged.

'Ja ja, you can laugh, but you know what hey? She took a huge drag on the cigarette, blew the smoke out really slow like. It seemed to take forever while I stood there feeling like a right idiot, but then she said in this like quite husky voice, "And just what sort of action are you talking about?"' He paused, then repeated, 'Just what sort of action are you talking about hey? This chick was class man. Well my legs nearly went beneath me but I was cool. Joe Cool. I just gave her this knowing look as if to say wait and see.

'She laughed then and we were A for away. We stood out there in the moonlight, smoking and talking, just general stuff at first, then we got into more serious issues, politics, religion, sex, all the taboo subjects. She had an amazing view of the world, blew my mind she did. It was the politics that got me the most. It seemed like she was completely untouched by apartheid, she had no prejudices. She didn't toe the party line, she had her own views. It was like she was my key to getting through the changes we all knew were coming in the country. She could guide me across the rubble that we thought would be left with the fall of apartheid.

'So we just clicked. I knew that this girl was the future. She was living in the rainbow nation while the rest of us were still living in braaivleis, rugby, sunny skies and Chevrolet land.'

He paused and chuckled at his analogy.

'Braaivleis, rugby, sunny skies and Chevrolet. You remember that one on the radio? It was all the things that every South African was supposed to like. Braaivleis, rugby, sunny skies and Chevrolet. Everyone liking the same things, thinking the same things. We were supposed to be like that, liking the same things, thinking the same things.'

'I've never liked rugby,' Simon said.

ELISE

Elise Swart was a very beautiful young woman, quite stunning in fact. However, this had not always been the case. She had grown up a tomboy in a town on the East Rand, a mining area just to the east of Johannesburg. Her father, Albie Swart, worked for ERPM, the local mining company that employed most of the people living in the town. He was quite a senior person in the company, and in the early seventies, as Elise was growing up, the mines were prosperous and the Swart family well off.

Her youth was carefree. She would run around the streets of the town with her friends after school. They never wore shoes, and their tough little feet were always a dirty brown. She wasn't a particularly attractive child having rather plain features and she insisted on having her hair cropped short which suited her tomboy nature. Invariably her knees were blotched with scabs from falls and red scratches criss-crossed her legs when she went running through the bushes.

Her mother, Denise Swart, was a socialite who loved the status Albie's position brought her in the town. She spent most of her life attending, or giving, tea parties for the other mine officials' wives. To her Elise was at best invisible, at worst a scruffy little urchin who sometimes invaded her parties much to her annoyance and embarrassment.

Albie was always too busy at work to spend much time with Elise and so she was essentially brought up by the family maid, Doreen. For Doreen, Elise was a surrogate child whom she loved and tried to bring up in the same manner she would have brought up her own two children had she been able to afford to stay at home and do so. As it was, Doreen only saw her own children on Sundays when Elise was scrubbed clean and forced into her pretty white dress and dragged off to church. Then Doreen would catch the slow, dirty, blacks' only bus back to the township for a brief time with her family.

Albie was a deacon at the local Dutch Reformed, a small but attractive stone church near the town centre. He also sat on the church's board of management and it was not unusual for the minister, or Dominee as they were known in Afrikaans, and his wife to be invited round to Sunday lunch at the Swart's. Elise hated these occasions. She and her brother Danny had to stay in their Sunday best until late afternoon when the Dominee and his wife left. The Dominee had no children so Elise and Danny had to sit quietly in the lounge, listening to the boring talk flit between Reverend de Beer and her dad.

'They should have shot more of them I say.'

'Maybe that's a little bit harsh Albie, they were only children and they didn't know better.'

'Didn't know better! Didn't know better than not to throw stones at the police. I'm sorry Dominee, but my dog bloody well knows better. Pardon my French. Besides which, they should be grateful for any education at all.'

As soon as the lunch party was over, Elise would race up to her room and tear her neat clothes off, throwing them on the floor for Doreen to clear up on Monday, put on her play clothes and be out roaming the streets of the town. Inevitably her school friends had been subjected to similar Sunday afternoon lunches and often none of them were around. She would walk down to the bottle store and sit on the wall outside talking to the tramps who sat there.

At first the tramps tried to discourage her from hanging out with them, the rich folk would not approve and they were already despised enough without having to make things worse. But Elise insisted and would chatter away to them about school and her friends and Doreen, but never about her parents. She would scold them whenever they produced their little brown packets and take sips from the foul smelling bottles they contained.

'Sies man,' she would say in disgust, imitating her mother, 'it's not clever to get drunk.'

This was Denise's stock phrase she used on the odd occasions that Albie did over indulge. Albie would usually just grin stupidly at Denise then stagger off to bed. The tramps, however, found it hilarious and would play games with Elise, trying to see how many sips they could take from their bottles without being caught.

Despite having fallen on hard times, the tramps were generally a good-natured bunch of harmless men. Their faces were darkly tanned and leathery. Most had at least one tooth missing, some practically toothless. A few had lost limbs, taken by mine accidents and, despite reasonable pay outs, the loss of self-esteem and respect from the community that came with their disfigurement drove them to the bottle and eventually this destitute life.

'You know what,' Terry, one of the tramps, said one day, 'if you are going to be down and out, there is no better place to be so than in sunny South Africa. Imagine having to live outside in places overseas like London where it snows in the winter. Not for me. Good old SA is the place to be.'

Ironically Terry would freeze to death during a particularly bad winter. He had taken to drinking methylated spirits which was strained through a loaf of bread to remove the poisonous blue aniline dye put in to try and prevent people drinking it. Having drunk a fair quantity of the near pure alcohol, Terry had fallen asleep without any protection from the elements.

Terry's death hit Elise hard. It was the first she had had to cope with in her young life and he had been her favourite in the group.

'Where's Terry?' she asked the Sunday after his death.

The other tramps shifted uneasily, avoiding her young inquiring eyes. It was not their job to explain the facts of death to a young girl.

'Um … he is with Jesus now,' Stoffel, an old guy with a stump for a hand, said eventually drawing pictures in the dirt with his foot.

'Well he's going to find it tough there. Jesus won't let him drink.'

The tramps smiled sadly at Elise's innocence, but behind her young exterior a mature mind mourned, not just for the passing of a friend, but also for the injustice of a society that had let it happen.

The bottle store was in a part of town that the respectable folk never went near, so no-one ever saw Elise spending time there. As she grew, the bonds she had formed with these outcasts were strong and even as a blossoming young woman she still would spend time with 'her boys'. She would smuggle food out of the house and this was shared between the men.

It was from these simple people that Elise learned about life and the human condition. She began to despise the way her parents looked down on those less fortunate and in particular was concerned about the way black people were treated in the country.

'You're not becoming a kaffir-lover?' Her dad had said one day after she had made a casual comment about the rights of blacks in the country. 'Because if you are a kaffir-lover, then you can bloody well leave this house right now, I won't have anything like that under my roof.'

So Elise left. She was seventeen at the time and something inside her snapped with that comment from her father. She climbed on the train that took her to central Johannesburg and called Danny from a tikkie box. Danny was studying at university and was living in digs near campus. He put her up for a few nights while she found a waitressing job and a room at the YWCA.

She slowly established herself, finding better jobs and a nice flat. Danny helped her out as much as he could, both financially and by putting her in touch with potential employers. He was the apple of Albie's eye and was on a good allowance from home which made things easier. Elise didn't like taking money that she knew came from her father whom she now despised, but she was a practical girl and worked extremely hard to bring about her own independence.

By the time she met Deon, Elise had become the stunner who attracted so much attention at the party, and was also holding down a decent job. She remained restless though. Things were not right in the country and she wanted to make a difference.

THE LIFT 3

Deon sat in silence for a moment, thinking what a fool he had been. Of course the majority of black people never liked rugby. Even in post-apartheid South Africa, even after the world cup win where Nelson Mandela had worn Francois Pienaar's number, the black men had never really taken to the sport. Rugby and cricket were white men's sport and soccer belonged to the blacks. There was a slow shift in that blacks were taking more interest in the white sports, but there was little interest moving the other way. Perhaps this indicated a greater willingness of the blacks to embrace the changes in the country. He decided on a different approach.

'We clicked, like a light switch going on. That's what it was like, dark the one moment, then suddenly light.'

Deon looked up at the darkness that surrounded him. 'Not like now, not like here in this lift where it was light and now it's dark. Five bloody hours. Are those guys at Eskom going to do anything to fix this mess.'

The anger grew suddenly in him and he kicked the side of the lift to vent. Was his anger directed at Eskom or at what had happened with Elise? He sat breathing heavily trying to compose himself, not wanting to answer that question.

The memories of Elise were painful, the frustration at being cooped up as well as the pressure of having to be politically sensitive were stretching him. He took his anger out on the lift and the darkness.

'This darkness in here, it's getting to me, man. There's no light, no light at the end of the tunnel as they say. Nothing to look forward to, no brightness, nothing. Bugger all.'

Simon sat silently in the dark not quite sure how to handle this outburst, not sure if he had caused it or not. White men were prone to outbursts of anger directed at blacks who could never fathom out what it was they had done wrong. He listened to Deon's breathing and wandered if that was a sob he had heard.

After a good while a composed Deon went on unprompted.

'She was the most amazing woman I've ever met. Stunning to look at, and free. Ja that's it. That was it about her, she was free. Like a free spirit I mean. She just lived life to the full, did some wild things. We hit it off at that party like I said.' Deon was back into the story, finding comfort in the telling.

'We talked the whole night. I remember watching the sun rise over

Joey's. You had never seen such a beautiful sunrise in your life, I'm telling you. Okay so maybe it was because I was with this beautiful woman who I was rapidly falling in love with, but it was still a great sunrise.

'I didn't want to part from her, but she said that she had to go get some sleep because she was dead tired and wouldn't be much use at work on Monday. She couldn't afford to lose her job. So we swapped cell numbers and headed home. I can't remember what I did that day. I think I just hung around at home, maybe went out I dunno, but that wasn't important. What I do remember is that wonderful feeling you have when you've met someone special. You know what I'm talking about?'

'Yes.'

Deon didn't notice Simon's reply. The question was rhetorical in his mind and he was too wrapped up in his story now.

'It seemed like ages till I saw Elise again. I phoned nearly every day and tried to arrange for us to meet, but she was always busy, always had something on. I began to worry that she was not interested in me, but she kept saying that ja, we must meet up, so I kept calling.'

'Do you have your cell phone with you now?' Simon's voice broke into the conversation.

'No, it was stolen two days ago and I haven't got a new one yet. Someone nicked it off my desk. Why?'

'Well, if you had one you could call someone to maybe get us out of here.'

'I didn't think of that, but then I thought we would have been out of here by now. What's taking them so long?' An idea suddenly occurred to him, 'What about you, Simon, don't you have a cell phone? Or a radio or something'

'No radio and my cell phone is in my jacket pocket.'

'And your jacket …?'

'It is on my chair at reception.'

'Ah I thought so.'

Silence fell between them again. Simon's thoughts wandered to his little desk at reception. The whole of the lobby would be in darkness, and if the moon was out, there would be that comforting blue glow making faint shadows on the walls. He thought of the peace that descended onto the building every evening. Most of the workers disappeared before he came on duty when he did nights. There would be the odd straggler who would leave after he started, but generally it was silent and Simon liked that.

He knew Deon's face well as he was usually one of the last out of the building every evening. He never said anything as he walked passed reception heading towards the lifts that led down to the parking garages.

At first it had perturbed Simon that this businessman could walk right past and ignore him. Most of the others would say goodnight or at a bare minimum acknowledge his existence with a nod of the head. But Deon gave no outward sign of being aware that there was anybody there. As time went by, Simon got used to Deon's blank expression and put it down to a white man's problem that was too big for him as a black to understand. He began to feel sorry for Deon, hoping that his problem would go away so that he could see others around him.

Every evening Simon would watch Deon on the surveillance TV, making sure he got into his car safely. A nice car it was too, a BMW.

Deon's thoughts were quickly moving back to his first date with Elise. 'We eventually managed to meet up again.'

'Who?' Simon had wandered off a bit too far.

'Elise of course. Have you not been listening to anything I said?'

'Oh ja, Elise. Sorry sir I was thinking of something else. Please go on, you managed to meet up with Elise.'

'Ja,' Deon hesitated for a second before going on, wandering if he was boring this man who was sharing the lift with him, sharing this darkness. This man who came from a different ... well a different class, there was no other word for it really. Did Simon have any idea what he was on about? Meeting a girl, falling in love? Did black people fall in love? It was a stupid thought, but one he had never actually spent time pondering. Apartheid South Africa had brought him and Simon up so differently, he somehow could not imagine black people falling in love. He had talked earlier about the girl with the muddy river eyes, but that was just lust wasn't it? Could it actually have been love?

'You ever been in love before?' he suddenly asked, his curiosity piqued and he needed time to clear his thoughts.

'Oh yes, I had many girlfriends when I was young,' he paused then added, 'Joe.'

There was surprised silence as Deon puzzled over what he had just heard and Simon wondered how much detail was required. 'Did you just call me Joe?' Deon asked.

'Yes, I thought that was your name, you said earlier you were Joe – Joe Cool.'

Deon laughed. 'Oh, no that's just an expression. When someone is cool we sometimes call him Joe Cool. I think it's an American thing. My name's actually Deon.'

'Deon?'

'Ja.'

'Deon Cool?' Simon chuckled to let Deon know he was joking and Deon laughed with him.

'Ja, Deon Cool, you can call me Deon Cool.'

'So Mr Deon Cool, tell me, what happened with Elise? Did she ever call?'

'Oh ja, she did call, but meeting up was a problem. She was always busy. What I didn't know at the time was that she was in the process of breaking up with her current boyfriend. I was a bit stupid I suppose to think that a beautiful girl like Elise didn't already have a boyfriend. She had come to the party on her own because Hennie was out of town on business. That was her boyfriend's name – Hennie. Geez did he cause trouble. When Elise tried to break it off with him he beat her up something chronic – black eyes and a broken rib. Of course she didn't want me to know about it, that's why she kept putting off seeing me, she wanted her wounds to heal first. I only found all this out much later, after she … she …' Deon's voice trailed off.

Simon waited, not sure whether to push for more or let Deon go at his own pace. The silence and the dark seemed to deepen then suddenly Deon continued. 'Anyway we did meet up eventually. It was quite fortuitous actually as I had nearly started seeing another girl 'cause I thought Elise was just stringing me along. But as soon as Elise rang to say, "You want to go out Saturday night?" I dropped this other chick, Lorraine, real quick. I felt sorry for her but the last I heard she was happily married with a couple of kids so I guess it worked out okay. You got any kids Simon?'

Simon's eyes brightened in the dark. 'I have two, a boy and a girl,' the pride in his eyes reflected in his voice.

'Oh ja, how old?'

'The boy is nine and the girl is seven. They are both doing really well at school, better than a lot of the white …' Simon paused. Had he gone too far this time? 'Better than the other kids,' he finished lamely.

Deon picked up on the uncomfortable change and, after a moment's contemplation, threw caution to the wind and said, 'Mixed schools hey? Not like when we were young – whites only in this school, blacks only in that one. Mixed schools, that's where the future of this country lies you know, with the kids growing up black and white together. Not with the likes of you and me who grew up separate, not getting to know each other, always being told that "the blacks are bad" or "the whites are bad". Were you told that at school? Probably not, a teacher wouldn't have lasted long if he was caught saying something like that to his class. Am I right?'

Simon grunted, he could not recall a teacher ever saying that. 'The teachers never did, but you heard it from family and friends,' he confirmed.

'Still hey, it's the kids of today that go to school together who will make friends. What do you think hey? It's the lighties that hold the future.'

Simon was a bit taken aback by the sudden pouring out of these opinions about the future of race relations, a topic that whites and blacks generally steered clear of when talking to each other.

But Deon had plunged in so Simon went along, 'Oh yes, my two can have a much better future than me. I always tell them to study hard as that's the only way they can get anywhere. I don't want my son to be a security guard like me. He must go to university and become a lawyer or a doctor.'

'Lorraine married a lawyer.'

'Who?'

'Lorraine, that chick I dumped so that I could go out with Elise. She married some lawyer.'

'Ja, but you got Elise. Where did you go for your first date?'

Ah, he had been listening.

'Well we went to some restaurant in Rosebank. Can't remember its name, it's not there anymore. It was an Italian one, I do remember that. The food was really good and we talked for ages. We were the last to leave the restaurant and when we got outside it was really pissing down. We didn't have umbrellas with us so I was just about to tell her to wait while I went to get the car when she says, "Gimme your car keys." Of course being a gentleman I said no and that I would fetch the car, but she insisted.

'We argued – playfully of course – for a bit then she like says, "Okay let's toss a coin. Heads I go fetch the car, tails you stay here and wait for me." Oldest trick in the book that one but I wasn't thinking straight, love can do that to you, so I agreed. It was heads, heads she goes and fetches the car. I reluctantly handed over the keys and you'll never believe what she does next.'

Deon stopped and laughed as the scene played through his mind. Nostalgia mixed with mirth and a touch of sadness.

'This crazy chick, she hands me her handbag and takes off her shoes and says, "Hold these." Then while I'm busy sorting out holding the shoes and bag, she whips off her dress and underwear and dumps them in my arms. "Hold these as well," she giggles at me and while I'm like, "What the hell you doing?" she's off and running down the street in her birthday suit.'

'What? No way sir!' Simon blurted out.

'Ja, completely naked. Remember I told you she was a free spirit. This chick laughs at me, or rather laughs at my surprise and runs off in the rain to the car which was about three blocks away. There were a few people around and they, like me were just staring. I was gobsmacked and just stood there holding her clothes really embarrassed and all as one or two of the other people around were starting to look at me funny now. I just shrugged my shoulders, what else could I do hey? I watched her body catch in the lamplight as she ran and I could hear her laughing all the way. A minute or so later she pulls up outside the restaurant in my car. I was driving a Toyota Corolla back then. You remember the ad, "Everything keeps going right Toyota"? You remember that one hey?'

'That was a good slogan, sir.' The 'sir' was an automatic reflex, distancing himself from any potential trouble for being near a naked white woman.

'Anyway, so I scheme to myself that maybe everything is going right. I mean ja, I was shocked at what she did but you've got to admit that her behaviour meant that we were going to have an interesting relationship if nothing else. She pulls up in front of me, opens the door and laughs again. Now I'm smiling and not as surprised. I had had a little time to compose myself, but I was still recovering properly. "Get in," she charfs me as she slides over to the passenger side.

'I climb in behind the wheel and just sit there looking at her. Not in a sexual way. I suppose now that I think about it I was still too shell-shocked and too busy trying to figure this chick out to have a good look. I mean I was trying to take it all in, her beauty, her nakedness and her brazenness. It was a bit overpowering all at once.

'Anyway, she just sits there grinning at me, naked and beautiful. I try to ask questions, you know like what? Why? Where? Eventually I manage to ask, "Why did you do that?"

'"Just for fun," she says then adds, "Besides I didn't want to get my clothes wet." *I didn't want to get my clothes wet*, what an answer. I mean, what you meant to say to that hey?

'So I'm sitting there staring at her and she says, "Can I have my clothes back?" The spell is broken and now I'm embarrassed so I hand over her clothes and look the other way as she dresses.'

Deon paused for a bit to give the girl in his story time to dress and reflect on how he had just come out with this tale to a complete stranger. Maybe it was the dark. It protected him, made him feel comfortable about letting these unseen ears hear his story, letting an unseen man in on a something that was quite personal. The brusque reply he had given earlier to Simon's query about the night he spent with Sharon in Kalk Bay seemed ages ago and as the dark had continued and brought the comfort of anonymity his inhibitions had weakened.

'Have you ever been with a chick who does wild things like that Simon?' he asked.

ELISE 2

Before she met Deon, Elise had suppressed most of the wild urges she had. She had often wanted to do the unexpected and outrageous, yet there had always been something holding her back. The most daring thing she had done in her life so far was to leave home. But that was not what she was after. It was a snubbing of norms, a shoving of two fingers up at the oppressive world around her that she craved. She wanted to break free of the shackles that bind one to the mundane and ordinary life.

She had felt so at ease with Deon from the start that she had begun to believe that these things were possible, that he wouldn't disapprove. Be surprised. Yes. Ask why. Yes. But disapprove. No. The beating she had received from Hennie had also had an effect. Whilst receiving the blows she had feared for her life and this perceived near-death experience had made her want to do whatever she felt like doing, to live life to the full before it was taken from her.

To her, Deon was the antithesis of Hennie. She could be herself with him and have no fear of retaliation. Her wilder side could thrive with Deon. She had not been battered into submission, but rather battered into rebellion.

Her naked escapade outside the Italian restaurant was not the last such exhibition. One evening after seeing a late night movie with Deon, she went into the ladies, stripped and then ran naked through the shopping mall where the cinema was housed. By the time Deon caught up with her at the car she was clothed again and waiting patiently behind the wheel suppressing the giggles. The lone security guard who witnessed this was at first dumbfounded, but he laughed warmly and shook his head when Elise had blown him a kiss as they drove off.

'Crazy white woman.'

Elise did not view her running around naked as anything sexual; she just liked the feeling of freedom that it gave her. She loved the looks of surprise it brought and, probably the biggest thrill, was that this sort of behaviour flew in the face of everything conservative that her father held sacred. Not that he was there to see it and he would probably never hear about it, yet she felt she was getting back at him in some way. He would most definitely not have approved and anything he disapproved of had to be good.

When she had stripped off on that first date with Deon it had been a risk and a test. It was not as impulsive as it seemed. She wanted to do something extraordinary to test his reaction. The risk was that she had misread him and that something unusual would repel him, that he was more conservative than her initial assessment of him suggested. Alternatively it could have given out all the wrong signals and had Deon groping and pawing at her in a sexual frenzy. But he had been cool. He had laughed off her behaviour once he got over the shock. He saw humour rather than sex in Elise's actions. There had been no sex on that first date, just a rather long goodnight kiss. The sex came later and by mutual consent that they were both ready.

Running around naked in public was not the only way that this new found freedom manifested itself. Her friendship with the tramps had perhaps been an early indicator that here was a person who wanted to live free of the restrictions of society. She once took off her shoes while walking through the prestigious, if somewhat stuffy, Rand Club when she partnered Deon to a work do, 'just to feel the carpets properly.' She would also have slid down the banister of a rather grand staircase at another do had Deon's boss not been at the bottom of the stairs. Despite her antics she never did anything to harm Deon's prospects as she respected and understood that not everyone was like her.

On a trip through the Karoo desert she stood up in the car with her head out the sun roof to feel the breeze on her face and sometimes she would get involved in conversations with strangers and after a short while of sensible talk would steer the talk round to some bizarre topic and watch the other person squirm as they got uncomfortable talking about artificial insemination for cows or some such obscure subject. She watched with care as the expression of her victim changed with the subject and when she finally let them go to ponder this strange encounter she would run back to where Deon was sitting giggling so much he had to help her into her seat.

When she went to parties, she would always be the first on the dance-floor and would dance with a wild abandon, not caring if people were staring. She would often be seen swaying rhythmically with her eyes closed, oblivious to what was happening around her. Each little thing she did exorcised a small part of her father and his conservative ways.

THE LIFT 4

'No sir, I've never known a woman do wild things like that. Sometimes in the bars in the townships, you know, the shebeens, the women get drunk and then they dance with strange men and things like that, but they never run around naked. I did hear once of a white girl who ran naked through Eastgate, you know the shopping centre. I didn't see it but one of the other guards did. You see I used to ...' Simon let the sentence go as a memory struck him.

Deon recoiled. His emotions were suddenly a tangled mess. He was remembering fondly the exploits of Elise, but there was always the spectre of what had happened lurking, and now suddenly Simon was too close to his life, his private life. He was glad of the protective dark as he couldn't bear putting a face to this voice. But for a different shift Simon would have seen his Elise naked. He needed to change the subject but didn't know how. The unfinished sentence from Simon dangled like a carrot in front of him.

'Used to what?' he asked, hoping the answer would somehow lead away from Elise. He was beginning to curse himself for sharing this story. Why had he done that?

'I used to be a security guard there by Eastgate sir,' Simon said wanting to leave that thought and all it summonsed up in him.

'Oh.'

Silence ensued, both men wanting to move away from their respective intimate stories, but the dark snuggled closer.

Deon was the one to break the silence. 'How long have we been in here?' he asked.

'I don't know, maybe half an hour.' Simon, feeling on safer ground, dropped the 'sir'' again.

'Half an hour, looks like we may be in for another five-hour one, what do you reckon?'

'Looks like it, they either seem to be quick or long don't they?'

'Ja, either it's like five minutes or five hours.'

Again silence fell between the two men during which Deon thought about his life with Elise and as he ran his thoughts over the events of that time he moved his story on verbalising it more for himself than for Simon's sake. In fact Simon became almost irrelevant, he was talking to the darkness.

'We dated for a while, Elise and me, but it didn't take long before she moved in to my place. She was pleased to leave the flat where she lived as it wasn't in the nicest area, and it held bad memories of Hennie. We set up together in my house. It was a bit of an adjustment having her live with me. I mean I was used to being on my own, but we settled into this new life in no time. She was just so easy to get on with. She never moaned about me leaving the toilet seat up or any of the usual things chicks moan about. "Chicks". Actually that was one thing that she didn't like and she did moan about it when I referred to women as "chicks".

"'We're not chick or birds, we're human beings," she would say. So I stopped calling women that, although I never stopped thinking of her as a chick. Not the sort of sexist version of chick, but rather it was the softness of her skin and the almost child-like glee she took in living that made me think of baby chicks running around. I mean sometimes I felt a bit like a mother hen trying to get her to behave.'

Simon gave a friendly laugh.

'Anyway I suppose it's not really politically correct to call women chicks anymore. It is sort of a seventies' thing. But that's what I grew up with, that's the slang of the day. It was harmless, nothing was really meant by it. But the word just stuck with me. I suppose it's a bit like kaf …'

Deon suddenly remembered that Simon was a black man. He had been going to say 'kaffir', a highly offensive name for black people, yet he used it quite freely when talking to his white friends. He did have a bit of a conscience using the word but as those around him always did, it had slipped effortlessly into his language because he wanted to fit in. Not that that was a good excuse, he felt, but the need to be accepted with his mates was greater than his conscience about this. Besides which, if there were no blacks around when he said it, was he really offending anyone? He wandered how many of his friends also didn't like the word, but used it just to fit in.

Simon realised straight away what Deon had been going to say and he tensed up. He had enjoyed talking so freely to this white man, getting to hear a personal side of how the other half lived. But the almost use of *that* word sent a barrier crashing down between them. With the fall of apartheid had come a time when he was no longer called that to his face. There were the odd occasions when he had heard, usually overheard rather than a direct insult. But here it was rearing its ugly head again and in an environment he had least expected it. This was an office, a place frequented by professionals. They tended to be more politically sensitive, or was this just a façade erected to ensure the smooth flow of money? In the new South Africa, a businessman could not be seen to have any racial prejudices.

Deon coughed to cover his embarrassment and then realising that Simon knew what he had been about to say quickly apologised, 'I'm really

sorry, I didn't mean to…you know…well I was going to say … but I …
er …' He fell silent. He was beginning to sound, and certainly was
feeling, foolish.

The silence expanded. Simon was not interested in talking to this racist
anymore, while Deon sunk into the quagmire of his shame. He was once
again glad of the darkness so that he didn't have to face the man he had
just insulted. Like that day with Elise, Deon felt powerless again. He
couldn't do anything, couldn't say anything. He just wanted to be out of
here, out of the lift, in his car heading home, or better still at home with
Sharon.

He desperately felt the need for Sharon's arms around him. The
memories of Elise had jarred him from the comfortable tiredness he had
left his desk with and he was desperately trying to work through them
when he had offended the person who was listening, and this now jarred
too. He sat quite still, feeling sorry for himself.

Twice he attempted to start talking to try and break the quietness and
awkwardness that now lay thick and heavy in the lift. He drew in his
breath, willing the right words to form in his mind, words that would heal
the wound that had been ripped open between him and his friend, the
voice. But nothing came.

Simon sat silently in his corner; he had shut his eyes tight. That one little
word had had a powerful effect on him, bringing back his own painful
memories. Memories of apartheid times, times that had torn his world
apart. Wounds he thought had healed were being opened again in his
mind and he wanted to scream out to make them go away.

Deon moved his thoughts to concentrate on Sharon. These were more
pleasant. He welcomed them into his mind which had been in turmoil
with everything else that was going on. Sharon. Ja, Sharon. She had been
a godsend. After what had happened with Elise he had been a complete
mess and in danger of doing something stupid.

Had Sharon ever called the blacks kaffirs? He pushed hard against that
thought to get it out of his mind. The answer was yes, and his guilt was
mounting as he remembered that Elise had never used that word.

SHARON

Sharon van Tonder was the opposite of Elise in many respects. Where Elise had broken free of the shackles of conservatism that gripped many like her in the country, Sharon had embraced them and worn them as a protective blanket. Moving in with Deon without getting married first had been her most radical step to date, but in post-apartheid South Africa, this was becoming slightly more acceptable to even the most conservative families. It did still cause consternation amongst the older van Tonders, especially her grandmother who was only now, nearly two years on, deigning to acknowledge Deon.

Sharon was a very domesticated woman and saw it as her duty to look after her man. She would rush home from work every day, shower quickly, then arrange a good meal for Deon and still leave enough time to apply a fresh mask of make-up and generally ensure that her appearance was immaculate. All her spare time was spent working on ways to please her man and keep him happy.

She lovingly baked koeksusters on the weekends, believing that the syrupy twisted twirls of deep-fried dough could find a way to Deon's heart via his stomach. Unfortunately it was only the cholesterol that was making the journey so far.

After what happened with Elise, Deon had sought comfort in this domestic bliss rather than love. He knew that in the long-term it would not work, he would want to break free from this relationship and that was why, although he had convinced Sharon to move in with him, he had so far resisted the pressure from her family for them to marry. This was something else he was not proud of. He knew he was using her, but felt that his own need was greater than that of Sharon's. She would easily find another man when he finally got round to moving on.

For her part, Sharon was convinced that Deon would one day pop the question and until then she would continue with her subservient role because that was what she had been brought up to believe would win her a man and winning a man was her main goal in life. To not succeed in this would, in her eyes and those of her family's, be a huge failure.

She knew nothing about Elise and what had happened. Deon never mentioned any of this to her. He had hidden all his problems when they had met. At the time Sharon was the secretary of a good client of Deon's. He had begun by flirting with her on the phone when making appointments to see Clive. He knew it wasn't overly professional, but he liked the comforting motherly tones he heard in the voice on the other end of the phone and she wasn't bad looking in the flesh either.

She had seen through his professional veneer and had fallen for the 'little boy lost' that would come into the office every now and then and her maternal instincts told her this was someone who needed to be loved and cared for.

Clive was not too impressed at first when Deon broached the subject with him.

'Clive, I am thinking of asking Sharon out. Like on a date,' he had said after the business part of the meeting was over.

'What? You mean Sharon?' His inclined head indicating the outer office.

'Ja. Do you mind?'

'Hell Deon, it's not the best thing for business. I mean what happens if things don't work out huh? Will I lose a good secretary or worse still a good business relationship?' A shake of the head accompanied this.

'It's just a date Clive. If we don't click then it's not a train smash. We're both professional.'

Clive pushed his chair back from his desk a bit, clasping his fat fingers together over his rotund belly. He sighed.

'Well it's a free country I suppose. I can't really stop you, but just make bloody sure I don't have to suffer from any fallout if things go wrong.'

'Thanks Clive,' Deon stood to leave.

Once he had gone Clive sat back and smiled. Despite his grumpy exterior he had a soft heart and had secretly been hoping that Deon would ask Sharon out, they seemed well suited.

So began this relationship of convenience for Deon and of hope for Sharon.

THE LIFT 5

Deon cleared his throat. He knew what he had to do. He had to re-establish a conversation with Simon. It would be mind numbingly boring to sit in silence for however long this power cut might last, but more importantly, his conscience wouldn't let it lie. He needed to make amends, he owed it to Elise. Simon may have no problem with doing nothing but giving his thoughts a run out, but Deon knew he could not do so himself.

'Er, look Simon?' he hoped that he had remembered his companion's name correctly, 'Simon?' A slight snort told Deon that Simon had been dozing and he had woken him. Despite his earlier anger, the dark had soothed him quickly into a light sleep, almost as a defence against the unwanted word.

'Yessir.' The phrase was a reactionary one and as his mind focussed again he was annoyed with himself for using the subservient *sir* as the power of *that* word hit home again. He did not need to be subservient to that sort of thing anymore, he told himself. This was the New South Africa, the blacks were in charge. He no longer had to tolerate being called a *kaffir*. He should say something, strike back. What could this white businessman do to him? The law was on the side of the black man now.

But he struggled to find the words to fight back with. The years of suppression that apartheid had subjected him to still shackled his tongue and all he could manage was the demeaning, *Yessir*. He hated himself for not having the courage to speak out.

Deon would have welcomed a tirade. He would have liked to have been chastised; it would help ease the guilt.

'Look Simon, I'm really sorry about ... you know ... about using that word. I know I'm not supposed to use it, in fact I never liked it.'

Simon was taken aback by this admission. Was Deon being genuine when he said this? There had been too many lies from the whites in the past. Was this just another one? But there was something in Deon's tone that made Simon listen on.

'Under apartheid everybody I hung out with used it and ... well, if you didn't use it ... you know what I mean. Look I'm not really good at this, but I am really sorry. Things like that were sort of drilled into us whities. Not like a deliberate indoctrination, but a more subtle thing. Indoctrination by environment if you like. Ja, that's probably the best way to describe it. Because of the environment we lived in, certain things were perceived as being normal. Like using that word and others like it. I mean as we grew up some things were just taken for granted as being the way they were. I know this is no excuse and all I can do is say I'm sorry, but apartheid messed up us whities as well you know. Do you understand what I'm saying?'

Simon stared hard into the darkness at this faceless voice. What was it saying? What was he jabbering on about? He was apologizing, but at the same time he was making excuses. Did his arguments make sense? 'Indoctrination by environment', what the hell did that mean? He tried hard to put his mind that had slipped into neutral, back into gear. He needed to say something, challenge Deon, or berate him.

'Sir?' was the best response he could muster and he hated its weakness.

Deon sighed inwardly. It was going to be difficult to try and explain this emotive issue. He wished he was better at verbalising what he felt sometimes.

'Simon, I'm just apologising for what I said earlier, you know when I nearly used that word,' he paused before saying it, 'that word *kaffir*. I was trying to blame me saying it on apartheid. Like … like you know, you guys were brought up to distrust and hate the whites, and it was like that for us too. We were brought up to mistrust the blacks, be scared of them even. There must be something you feel about the whites that you know is not quite right, but it has become ingrained into you by the system. I mean we're all human beings with feelings and all that, but that stupid apartheid system made us hate each other. "Sir", that's one of the stupid things.' Deon had hit on an idea and he floundered towards this straw.

'Sir?'

Was that questioning the validity of *sir* as an argument or saying *sir* because he was confused?

Deon ignored the question his mind posed and pressed on, desperate to dig himself out of the hole he had dug.

'Ja, that's one. Sir. You keep calling me sir, but a little while ago when we were just talking normally you stopped saying it. We were just two people then; there were no barriers between us, no black, no white. We were talking like friends, just one man to another. But now when there's some pressure on us we revert to the old bad ways. It's like instinct, you calling me sir and me using that word. I'm really sorry, but look I am trying. Okay?'

Deon waited for a bit, then went on gently, 'Please call me Deon, not sir. And I won't use that word again. We're just two people talking. No black, no white, no apartheid, apartheid is dead, but its spirit still haunts us.'

Simon began laughing, a deep booming laugh. It was infectious and

Deon joined in nervously, although not quite sure what it was he was laughing at.

'No black, no white,' Simon managed to get out between his laughs, 'no black, no white. Deon ...' he paused. Using this man's first name suddenly tasted weird in his mouth, not like earlier when he had joked about Deon Cool, that was just a joke. He was now addressing the man, using his name in all seriousness, as a friend even.

He went on, 'Deon, with no lights in this lift, both you and I are completely black.' He howled with laughter.

Deon joined in, feeling the relief flow through his body.

'Ja, you're right,' he said, 'we're both black in this darkness. The only problem is this black man can only say a few words in Zulu and one or two in Sotho. I am not a very good black man.'

Simon laughed uproariously at this and Deon joined in again. Barriers had been lifted again.

'You know it's quite ironic,' Deon said as the laughter eventually subsided and a seriousness settled on him, 'that word originates from the Arabic for non-believer. Apparently the early white missionaries used it to describe the blacks who were not Christians when they came here. But nowadays the whites are leaving the church while it seems the black churches grow bigger and bigger. If you look at it in those terms, then it's more the white man who is the ...,' Deon paused, but then re-assuring himself that the word was being used in a politically correct context, went on, '... I mean it's us whites who are the kaffirs, the non-believers now. We're the white kaffirs.'

Simon struggled to believe what he was hearing. White kaffirs? Now that was a novel idea.

He chuckled, then said, 'I suppose you wouldn't be too happy if I called you a kaffir would you?'

The word hurt as it slid off his tongue. There was too much history attached to it for it to ever be comfortable to say.

Deon thought for a minute. 'No, you're right, I wouldn't like it. It's got too much baggage that word. It's loaded with hate and intolerance. Still I suppose I couldn't complain if you were to call me one. We whities deserve it I suppose.'

There was a slight pause while Deon half hoped that Simon would call him a white kaffir. In some ways it would ease the guilt he felt generally about his own use of the word, and specifically about using it in front of Simon.

Simon paused, contemplating calling Deon a white kaffir, but quickly dismissed it as the sharp pain it had caused his tongue returned to his mind.

'I don't think I could ever call you that,' he said eventually. 'I never liked being called by that name so it would be wrong of me to use it on you.'

Deon nodded acceptance, unseen by Simon, then said, 'Look I'm really sorry about earlier.'

'That's okay Deon,' Simon said, 'I think I understand what you are saying. You know it took forty years of apartheid to mess us up. It's going to take a while for us to recover from it.'

Deon nodded in the dark. 'Friends?' he asked.

'Friends,' Simon agreed, although this did not feel quite right on his tongue.

The two men fell silent again feeling the euphoria of the laughter drain from their bodies. Deon started moving his thoughts back to Sharon when Simon said, 'So what happened with Elise? You guys moved in together, then what?'

Deon hesitated for a second to redirect his thoughts. The question threw him back to the story of Elise and the pain it brought.

'Well, like I said, we moved in together. We were really happy. I loved the way she seemed to be so free from all the nonsense that apartheid brought. She wasn't in any way a racist. You know how I was saying earlier about the way the system affected us? Well it had no effect on her. I don't know why she wasn't affected by apartheid, but somehow it didn't get to her. She just didn't see people as black and white, not even subconsciously, she just saw people. I used to think it was because she was a bit simple but as time went by, I realised that she had somehow by-passed all the indoctrination. She let it pass over her, like water off a duck's back, as they say. I've never met anyone else who was like that. I guess there are others out there like her, there must have been, but I never met any.

'You would have liked her, she had respect for everyone, never looked down on a person.' Deon paused for a second, wondering again how it had been possible for Elise to have come through an apartheid upbringing unscathed. It was as though she had held on to her childish innocence where there was no colour in people. He knew nothing of the tramps and how these social outcasts had helped form the views of the woman he had loved.

'She sounds very special,' Simon said imagining this white woman who didn't see colour, a rare person indeed. He struggled to picture a white person who didn't look down on him, but couldn't see it. He had spent too much of his life being second class to the white. Even now, years after the fall of apartheid he still felt inferior. Perhaps there was something in what Deon was saying – indoctrination through environment. He had always been treated as inferior, so always felt inferior.

'Ja she was special. You know she used to work at an Aids orphanage in Soweto. She heard about what was happening there and she just volunteered. I was pretty cool with her working there 'cause it was something she was passionate about, but I did worry. I mean this was in the early nineties when all that violence was happening in the townships. You must have known about it first hand. You were living up there then weren't you?'

'Yes … Deon,' the name still felt strange to use, but stranger still were the emotions that talk of the nineties and Soweto stirred up in him. 'I was there then. Not a good time as you have said. There were things happening then that were scary. I … I don't really like to think about them, it's all in the past.'

'Ja, it's all in the past now,' Deon sighed and went silent for a bit. It wasn't the political problems that he had been referring to. 'The past,' he eventually said, 'it has a nasty habit of creeping up on you in the present.'

Simon nodded in his corner of the lift unseen by Deon. The two men were again quiet.

All in the past. Simon contemplated the phrase. The whites seemed to like that, they wanted to sweep everything under the carpet. 'Let's just forget about it can't we? Let's just get on with the present, no need to hold a grudge, let's move forward,' the phrase seemed to say. But how could he forget the past, the pain and anguish it had caused him. There was no carpet big enough to sweep it under.

'Powerless.' Deon broke the silence and slammed the carpet down on Simon's thoughts. 'Powerless against the past, powerless in the present, who knows what the future will bring.' It was a sudden heated outburst. He was angry about the past, the memories it brought; angry with the present, the confinement it brought; and despite his somewhat liberal views he was angry with a future that stretched out forever in front of him where a comfortable life as a white male was now no longer something that could be guaranteed, they had relinquished power in 1994.

He thought of his future with Sharon. It was a doomed relationship and he knew it. She didn't know it, she was happily playing the role of good little housewife and thoroughly enjoying it.

YVONNE

Soon after moving in with Sharon, Deon met Yvonne. She was a relatively plain looking woman, neither attractive nor ugly but what she had was a sense of humour. She was the wife of one of his team mates at the local cricket club. Deon had enjoyed their chats while watching her husband, Trevor, bat and she reminded him a bit of Elise in the things they spoke about. Trevor was a good batsman so he spent a fair amount of time talking to Yvonne, but it was when he rang up to inform Trevor of the details of the Saturday fixture that things moved forward. Trevor was not in and he ended up talking to Yvonne for an hour.

During that hour things shifted in the relationship and Deon soon found he was calling Yvonne up when he knew Trevor was out. He enjoyed the banter they had and eventually plucked up the courage to ask Yvonne to meet up with him. He was nervous as it was a double deceit – he was cheating on Sharon and about to cheat on a friend.

Despite his nerves he had no conscience about it. His nerves stemmed from a fear of being caught and having to give up both women as well as lose Trevor as a friend. His motive was purely selfish. After what had happened with Elise, he felt an acute need for the kind of conversation he had had with her and Yvonne was his best substitute.

Yvonne on the other hand was pleased with this distraction, for that was how she saw it. She was bored with Trevor, but at the same time comfortable. Trevor offered her financial stability and was a good father to their two children – David and Gillian. Seeing Deon gave her a break from the monotony of being a housewife. It brought excitement and she wallowed in the joy of being noticed again. She was determined to ensure that the relationship with Deon remained platonic, but sort of knew deep down that if the opportunity arose she would go to bed with him. He was after all pretty good looking.

Being male, Deon definitely wanted the relationship to end up in bed, and from their first clandestine meeting began steering things in that direction. He slowly broke down Yvonne's minimal resistance and one Saturday when Trevor went off for a cricket match which Deon had excused himself from citing business commitments, Yvonne packed the children off to her sister's to play with their cousins.

They arranged further clandestine meetings and Yvonne was surprised by the way she abandoned herself to his body. But her sane side started to send warnings to her. Being reckless in bed could lead to being careless about keeping her deceit from Trevor and this played on her.

Tension grew as she began to fear being caught. The sense of humour that had been the initial attraction for Deon began to be replaced by paranoia. Deon struggled with this, telling her brusquely to relax, but this further aggravated the situation, eventually causing him to drop his guard and he went hard at the lovemaking, feeling that he was losing the traces of Elise in Yvonne. In this impassioned state he called out Elise's name, trying to summons her back.

Yvonne was surprisingly calm about this. She had sort of figured that if Deon could be unfaithful to Sharon whom she knew about, it was not unrealistic to believe that he was stringing along any number of different women. She also knew that she couldn't point fingers when she was being unfaithful to Trevor. So she just lay there pretending not to have heard, the recent orgasm aftershocks quickly evaporating.

The effect on Deon was profound. Blurting out Elise's name had opened up old wounds. He had tried to bury the memories of her deep in some inaccessible part of his mind and the realisation that this was not possible hit him hard. He started trying to apologise, then looking at Yvonne he saw that she seemed not to have realised what he had said, although a slight grimace on her face left him in doubt.

The couple lay in the bed for a while in silence, each consumed with different thoughts. Eventually Yvonne glanced at the bedside clock and said quietly that he had better go as Trevor would be coming back soon. Deon climbed quickly out of the bed, almost grateful for being told to leave. He washed quickly, then drove off a bit too fast, nearly misjudging the corner at the end of the road before forcing himself to calm down. Yvonne showered once Deon left, feeling grubbied by the encounter and wondering how to call the affair off. When Trevor had arrived home, she lavished him with attention as a penance for her infidelity.

The affair wasn't called off so much as it just fizzled out with neither party making the effort to arrange time alone together. Deon remained physically faithful to Sharon from then on, but more out of a sense of devotion to the memory of Elise than a loyalty to Sharon. The mention of her name while in bed with Yvonne had shaken him badly.

THE LIFT 6

The nineties in the townships was a time of great upheaval. The late eighties and the early nineties had seen the country move slowly towards anarchy, then the miracle occurred. The ANC was unbanned, Mandela was released, free and fair elections were held and suddenly the black man was in charge. It had been coming – a lot of whites foresaw it – many believing that it was inevitable, but how much blood would have to be shed before it occurred was the unknown and the frightening. They now faced the question of their own future on a continent that had slowly rejected their presence and, in numerous cases, done so in a quite ruthless manner.

South Africa was the last bastion of white rule on the continent and this had been maintained in a heavy handed and at times brutal manner. Reprisals seemed unavoidable, almost a necessity. But it never came to that.

For the black man, there had been mixed emotions. There was the euphoria of finally gaining the freedom that they had fought so long and hard for, but with it came a lawlessness and violence in the townships that made life dangerous for many. The bitter irony was that the climate of civil unrest which was such a powerful tool in bringing apartheid to its knees also turned inwards and became a real issue for those it was meant to help.

The whites lapped this. *You see, they are barbarians. They'll kill each other if we're not in charge to protect them from themselves. It's all tribal you know.* Few whites would accept that a lot of the violence was being stoked up by government agents trying to divide and rule. Talk of a *third force* designed to set ANC against Inkhata become more prevalent.

'She loved the work she did at the orphanage. Those kids melted her heart. She was forever talking about them, knew every single child's name. I remember some of them that she used to talk about – Sipho, Jacob, Miriam, Mary, Margaret, Sophie and little James. He was her favourite, James. She brought him home once, as a special treat. He was a cute little boy. Never said a word, just sat there staring around the place, his eyes wide. Must have been about three of four years old. We gave him ice-cream. Boy did he love it. Got it all over his face. I can still see Elise cleaning him up. He looked so serious, but just stood there obediently. I remember looking at Elise just then and there were tears in her eyes.

'I didn't know what had caused that reaction. Was it that she was wanting kids of her own, or was it sadness at the plight of this little kid. Maybe they were tears of happiness at the obvious pleasure James had got from the simple act of eating an ice-cream. I never found out. We couldn't talk about it at the time, not in front of the kid, and by the time she had taken him back to the orphanage I had forgotten about it. I only remembered after she …'

Deon paused for a long time then added, '… when she wasn't there anymore.' He left the sentence hanging. All this talk of Elise was taking its toll. He felt the weight of those events press down on him and he wanted to back out of his story, go back to having a rant about the electricity company or something like that. But so far he had spoken more about Elise to Simon than he had to anyone else. He had never divulged so much before. Not to Danny, Elise's brother and his closest friend. Not even to Sharon, the person who was the closest to him these days.

It must be the dark, he thought, this is the only way I can talk about it, face to face with the dark, the dark with a voice. A voice that seems not to really understand or relate, but it is something I need to talk about to someone and what better person to talk to than a faceless voice. There won't be any judgmental looks, or worse still those looks of sympathy that I hate. It's just me, the dark, my memories, the voice and those unseen ears.

He went quiet again and Simon waited, unaware of the significance of his ears and the status the dark gave them. But he had his own thoughts to occupy himself. 'After she wasn't there anymore'. Those words had struck him hard and he forced himself to think in the opposite direction, trying to dislodge his own painful memories from his brain.

After a while the quiet began to close in on Deon and he needed to talk again.

'You know I think that maybe it was all those reasons why she cried like that. She wasn't one to cry easily but maybe the combined whatchama-callit, oh ja, maternal instinct thing and seeing that little kid, James, looking so bewildered and happy at a simple act of kindness was a quite intense moment for her I guess. You see I wasn't ready for kids back then, not at that time in my life, but she was hinting at having some. I always changed the subject whenever she started talking about it.

'I mean I was young, I wasn't ready. I was just getting over the whole apartheid nonsense and getting my life on track, building a career, finding my place in the New South Africa and all that. I didn't have time for kids. There were bigger fish to fry. I was going places. I didn't want kids holding me back. It's not like I have anything against them. I mean, I did want to have some eventually, but not just at that time.'

'So have you got any now?' Simon asked.

'What? Oh no, no. I'm a bit old fashioned. I want my kids to be born inside wedlock and I'm not married.'

'Not married, a good looking young man like you!'

Deon gave a small laugh at this, he liked flattery. He thought of asking Simon how he knew that he was a good looking young man. They had hardly glanced at each other when he had stepped into the lift and for his own part he had no idea what Simon looked like. He felt a bit guilty suddenly as he realised that he probably walked past this security guard every evening without ever noticing him, yet Simon seemed to know his face.

'You should be married,' Simon continued, oblivious of Deon's thoughts. 'You never married Elise?'

That hurt. It was an entirely innocent comment, but his lift companion had not picked up on his emotions about the whole Elise issue. Deon swallowed hard before saying, 'No, I never married Elise,' his voice sounded cracked. 'You see she …' this was hard, but he needed to say it, he needed to talk to someone about it, '… she died.'

There, he had said it. Said it to the dark, said it to those unseen ears. He waited, expecting some sort of huge cathartic release, but it never came. Instead he heard Simon suck his breath in sharply.

'Hau! I'm sorry Deon.' Simon searched for more to say, but couldn't find any words. He sat helplessly in the dark, wanting to offer more comfort, but didn't know how. He had started to like this girl Elise whom he had been hearing about. She had sounded nice, a kind person, someone who would not have looked down on him as just another black man, another security guard. Rather she was someone who would see him as a person, someone whom he could talk to about those things in his life that hurt like Deon was hurting now. He felt a sense of loss at the news that Elise was dead, cheated even.

His thoughts were interrupted by what sounded like a sob. He stopped thinking and listened. Yes, there it was again. Now what to do, this white businessman was crying. Simon felt awkward, caught between ignoring it and perhaps looking foolish for doing so, or reaching out to comfort and risking a harsh rebuke – *Don't touch me kaffir!* He could almost hear the unsaid words. He shifted uneasily in his corner of the lift.

Deon heard him shift, but he couldn't help himself sobbing, the catharsis was starting. He drew his knees up and hugged them. He needed human comfort and all he had was his knees.

Simon reached out a hesitant hand in the dark, taking the plunge. He waved it about as he sought his lift companion. After shuffling a little on his backside he found Deon's arm which he rubbed gently in an act of sympathy, a mother comforting a child. At first Deon flinched. He was tired of the sympathy. He needed more, he needed someone to say something, he needed to talk more about it.

Simon felt the flinch and started to remove his hand, but Deon suddenly reached out and put his own hand over Simon's, holding it for a few seconds, acknowledging the sympathy. Although he wanted more than a pat on the arm, he still had enough wits about him not to alienate a possible source for what he craved. He had already done enough damage with words; he didn't want his actions to be guilty too.

He patted Simon's hand and after swallowing hard, muttered, 'Thanks.'

Simon nodded, unseen in the dark, and slowly withdrew his hand. The gesture had been made, no need to prolong it and turn it into something it was not.

Deon sniffed quietly. This was not working. He hadn't moved on. Just the same old gestures and words.

'How did she die?'

Deon started. No-one ever asked him this. They all waited for you to tell them and if you didn't they never felt they could ask. That was the way people were. They were all afraid that they would open up old wounds, cause more hurt where there was already enough. No-one ever seemed to think that this was exactly what Deon wanted. He wanted to talk about how Elise had died. He wanted that release, and now suddenly here it was, someone wanting him to talk about it, a voice urging the story out of him. He wasn't prepared for this. Not now, not here. But this voice in the dark was probing. He was taken aback but didn't let this show in his response.

'I don't like to talk about it.'

Simon shook his head silently, 'But you must talk about it,' he said, wondering if he was pushing too hard. 'If you don't talk about things, then you keep them inside you like Coke in a bottle that's been shook up. It all builds up till eventually someone opens it, then pssshhheww! all over the place. Then it gets messy. You need to let it out, but do it slowly, then you have no mess.'

Deon had to smile. A number of his friends had told him the same thing before, but not in such language, not with such a colourful metaphor.

'Things go better with Coke,' he said and chuckled. Simon laughed a deep booming laugh.

'No they only go better if you don't keep it in the bottle. A bottle full of Coke is no good when you're thirsty unless you take the top off and drink it.'

Deon laughed again as he was struck by the wisdom Simon showed. It was true, he needed to let off some steam on the whole Elise business, but had never found someone to do it with. Could he do it with Simon, this unseen voice in the dark? He wondered about this for a few seconds then thought, what the hell, it's not like I have to face him every day like I do Sharon.

Had Simon been privy to this thought he would have laughed and shaken his head sadly, realising again how little notice Deon took of him as he walked past the reception desk every day. However, thoughts are private and both men were spared any embarrassment.

'I'd like to buy the world a Coke and keep it company,' Deon suddenly sang the jingle from the old advert, buying time. He knew he would tell Simon how Elise had died, but he wasn't quite ready for that, he hadn't adjusted his mind enough.

'That would cost a lot of money, are you that rich?' Simon smiled.

'Hey I'm not that rich,' Deon said not thinking, 'I'm struggling to pay off my mortgage you know.'

'I wish I was paying off a house, I just pay rent for my place.'

Deon felt as though he had been slapped. Damn! He cursed himself silently. Without thinking he had once more been insensitive. A bond on a five bedroom house where two people lived and he was moaning, yet this guy here with him could hardly afford a what, maybe two room shack if he was lucky.

'Well,' he drew the word out, 'a bond is not all it's made out to be you know. It traps you into a job just to keep a roof over your head.' He was making it worse and he knew it. 'Okay, that sounded lame, it's not that bad and I shouldn't moan I suppose. I'm lucky to have a nice house.' This felt uncomfortable. How had things moved so quickly on to this? One moment it was 'How did she die?' and all of a sudden he was feeling guilty about being rich. He wanted out of this conversation but had nowhere to turn in the darkness.

'How big is your … your shack?' Talk about digging your own hole, he thought.

For his part Simon sat grinning as he heard this white businessman disappear slowly into the quicksand of his own making. He decided to play things up a bit. 'Well sir,' this time the sir was on purpose, 'my shack is very small, just the one room where we live, five of us.' It was actually a small three bedroom house that Simon had obtained as part of the housing programme introduced by the government after apartheid had fallen. 'Yes sir, me, my two children, my girlfriend and my mother, we all live in the one room. We have to put down a mattress for the children every night and then fold it up in the day.'

In reality, Simon and his girlfriend, Lucy, shared a room, the two kids shared one and Simon's mother had one to herself. It was a clean little house that Simon's mother kept tidy. She was a retired housemaid but her habit of cleaning had not died when she stopped working. As a house-proud woman and doting mother, she took great joy in looking after her son, fussing over him and Lucy whom she had taken to and treated like a daughter. However it was her grandchildren that benefited most from the outpouring of love that this old woman gave.

'Really?' Deon was buying the story and feeling quite terrible. 'Geez I don't think I could cope like that. How do you do it?'

'Oh we manage,' Simon said offhandedly. 'When you've always lived like that it is normal. I think it would be difficult for me to live in a big house now. My family is too close, we wouldn't see each other if we had a large home.' Had he pushed things a bit too far?

He waited, but nothing was forthcoming either way. 'It's always been like that for us,' he concluded, now feeling a little guilty at his deception.

Deon nodded. He was still uncomfortable and wanted to change the subject but wasn't sure where to go with it. 'I guess some things don't change, hey?' Maybe they could move on to talking about the changes that had happened since apartheid fell. 'I mean us whites still living in our big houses and you guys still living in shacks.' He was hoping for some agreement that things had not got any better since a black government had come in. It would sort of vindicate the whites for having oppressed the blacks, reaffirm the white man's belief that blacks had a better life under white rule. But they needed to hear from the lips of black people. It helped with the guilt, somehow made it okay that they supported the apartheid system as everyone was better off under it.

Simon was not going to rise to the bait.

'Actually it's not that bad now. I have got a very nice three bedroom house. I used to live in a one bedroom shack but things are much better now.'

'Why did you lie then?' Deon demanded a fair bit of venom creeping into his voice.

'Because you were making me feel bad with your big house, so I wanted you to feel bad too.' A sudden anger surged in Simon in response to this attack. 'You white people, sometimes you have no idea what it's like for us. You live your protected lives in your big houses with high fences and barbed wire to keep out the blacks. You think we are all criminals.'

There had been something in Deon's voice that had caused Simon to lower his guard. He had never had an outburst like that before. But the fire of his memories had been stoked up and his nerves were suddenly raw and the long pent up frustrations of apartheid bubbled to the surface. Then the old ways took hold again. How had he dared to speak to a white man in such a voice? It went against the way he had been brought up and

47

he bit his tongue, hating himself for doing so.

Deon was taken aback by this tirade. He was not used to people speaking to him like this, black or white. His position and skills at work commanded respect from both his subordinates as well as his seniors. He prepared to launch a response, drawing a big breath to give room for his riposte when suddenly Elise's face appeared in his mind's eye. She had that look he knew well, it berated yet did not judge, rather it understood. She was telling him to calm down, consider his response. The vision caused him to stall.

Elise would never have got herself into such a conversation. She would never have been insensitive like he had just been. He blew out the pent up air loudly and with it went his anger.

Then in almost a whisper he said, 'I'm sorry.' And he really felt sorry now. The little time he had spent with Simon had shown his lift companion to be a good man, and if he was honest with himself, Simon's little joke at his expense was quite funny.

He waited a while, then said it again, this time with more confidence, 'Look, I'm sorry ... again. I don't know, I just wasn't thinking, I was just talking like I would with my friends. I realise we live in different worlds but you know in the dark here we are both the same, blind and powerless. I'm blind to your situation and I can't really do anything about it, and you are like that too, you will never know what it's like to be me, to live with the problems I've got and there's nothing you can do to help me with my problems. And I guess there is nothing I can really do to help you with your problems.'

He sighed a huge resigned sigh as if that was it, that was the end. There was nothing more that could happen, they had reached the end of everything. He stared into the darkness and banged the back of his head gently against the lift wall, a slow rhythm trying to knock the nightmares from his mind.

Simon stared into the darkness. He had his problems, some that Deon could guess at but others that Deon would have no idea about. He didn't know what to do or what to say. Deon was right he was powerless. They were powerless. Neither could do anything to help the other.

LUCY

Simon climbed into the mini bus, hunching his shoulders as he struggled into the back seat. He nodded to the woman next to him, a politeness reflex. Apart from that he hardly noticed her. The sun's warmth and the long day made him weary and the funk of the compressed bodies in the taxi deadened his senses. He closed his eyes, trying to shut out all that was unpleasant about his daily commute. The taxi engine throbbed and he felt its heat seeping up through him as they eased their way into the homeward bound traffic.

The taxi gathered speed as they headed onto the highway and Simon opened his eyes letting the cool breeze that came through the open window refresh him. He let his mind visit some familiar daydreams, dreams of wealth and life outside the townships. But suddenly they were wrenched from him as he felt the taxi lurch and watched in horror as it mounted the grassy ridge at the side of the road. Instinctively he reached out for something to hold on to and grabbed the leg of the woman next to him. The vehicle began to slow as it climbed the verge, lost its balance and lazily fell over onto its side.

There was a scrambling of limbs as people fought against gravity while the taxi hit the ground with some force, slid for a few metres then stopped. Simon was dumped unceremoniously on top of the woman who had been screaming. His weight cut her scream short in a whoomph of air that was forced from her. Later they would joke about how he had taken her breath away.

The two others in the backseat pushed down heavily on Simon as he tried to manoeuvre himself so that less of his weight was on the woman underneath him.

Slowly as a calm descended people began to pick their way out of the wreckage.

'Are you okay?' he asked the woman beneath him. She managed a frightened nod.

'Hold on, hopefully we can get out soon.'

She nodded again still gasping to replace the air lost from her lungs. There was a strange intimacy between them and they both sensed this.

Simon felt the relief as first the one, then the other passenger on top of him rolled out of the emergency exit. He gently eased himself up, trying not to put any extra pressure on the woman. Once free he reached back inside to help her out.

The other passengers were milling around, somewhat dazed.

'A tyre blow out,' said a voice.

'Hau! These taxis are a nightmare,' came another.

Simon helped the woman to sit down on the grass, then noticing a small cut on her forehead, took out his clean handkerchief.

'You're bleeding a little bit, may I?'

She nodded, still shaken and bewildered although her breathing was becoming more regulated.

His hands were gentle as he carefully dabbed at the cut and she smiled. Simon grinned back wondering what to do next.

'I think everyone is okay. How is your wife?' The driver was checking up on his fares.

'My …?'

'We are okay, I think my husband may get a bruise here.' The woman's hand brushed gently against his cheek and a shy smile flashed over her face.

The taxi driver nodded and moved off to check on the others. Simon stared quizzically at the woman seeing her beauty for the first time. He guessed she was a few years younger than he was.

She giggled at his surprised look. 'If they think that we are married we may be allowed on first when the next taxi with any space comes along,' she explained and a grin grew on Simon's face as the logic of the simple plan began to make sense.

'I had better know your name then.'

'I am Lucy.'

'And I am Simon.'

They sat giggling slightly and talked in quiet conspiratorial tones.

'Shouldn't I hold your hand or something?'

Both knew this was not necessary. Physical contact in public was not something their generation did. The youngsters were not so constrained by this custom, but Simon chanced his luck, flirting even.

Lucy smiled.

'Okay, but make it like you are comforting me.'

She tentatively stretched out a hand, her heart pounding. She had not been this intimate with a man since her husband had left her ten years ago to go work on the mines in Johannesburg. She had never heard from him again.

It was not too long before a relatively empty taxi arrived and Simon and Lucy were allowed in first as Lucy had predicted. They talked all the way back to Langa where the taxi stopped near Simon's place before heading on to the area where Lucy shared a small house with a friend.

'Come to my place for a cup tea first, then I will make sure you get home,' Simon blurted out before he had even had a chance to think it through.

'I … I … can't,' she replied hoping that he would insist.

Simon paused for a second, not sure if he should try again, but then took the plunge.

'Please come in, just for a cup of tea. I know my mother would like to meet my wife.'

Lucy laughed warmly, then with the left over smile on her face she nodded.

'Okay, we don't want to disappoint your mother. But it must be quick, I do need to get home.'

The following morning, Lucy washed quickly, then hurried home. A few weeks later she moved in with Simon, his mother and the two kids. She quickly settled into the family set up, immediately being accepted by the children whom she treated as her own. The love they responded with helped fill the hole that had been left by the death of her son who had died of pneumonia a few years earlier. Simon's mother accepted her as a daughter.

With the added income from Lucy, the newly constituted family could afford to move into a bigger and better house which they did at the earliest opportunity. Aided by a post-apartheid housing initiative they found their new home and settled in.

For Simon, Lucy moving in was a huge blessing. He now had a mother for his children and he was particularly pleased with the way that Simon junior and Sibongile his daughter took to her. The mother of Simon's children had run off with another man while they still lived in Soweto outside Johannesburg. But they had a new mother now, one whom Simon felt sure would not leave.

THE LIFT 7

The soft banging of Deon's head began to annoy Simon and without thinking he commanded, 'Stop that!' Deon stopped immediately and Simon marvelled at the fact that not only had he actually issued a command to a white man but that it had been obeyed.

Deon didn't think much about this. The emotion of the memories and the fatigue of the week's work were catching up with him and the dark meant he had no reminder that Simon was black. He was too tired even to take umbrage at the command that came from someone whom a few years back would never have dared to be so bold, and even now, surely the social divide would have made a difference. Deon could have this guy fired for his insolence. Or could he these days?

He rested his head against the wall of the lift and closed his eyes, sighing quietly. It is pointless closing my eyes, he thought, it's just as dark with them open. Still he kept them closed and began to relax his temples which had begun to ache with the tension that had been building up. His mind slowly relaxed while he tried to think of more pleasant things than the offence he had caused Simon and even more so, he needed to think of something other than the death of Elise which had ripped his world apart.

He was back to square one. In the dark, powerless with a huge barrier between him and this man he had come so close to telling about Elise. He sighed again, this time slightly louder.

'*Ja swaar*,' he breathed out emulating the TV advert where two yokels bemoan the heat and boredom of living in small town South Africa. He thought about what he had said. 'Swaar' in that context meant brother-in-law, but could also mean heavy. In the ad and colloquially it had come to mean friend.

Simon had to stop himself from laughing. His anger had been short lived and to be honest was not really directed at this particular white man sharing the lift with him. It was more an anger at a system that had deprived him of the life of luxury that he perceived Deon to have. All the anger and suspicions that had come about under apartheid still lingering as the Rainbow Nation ploughed forward. And here they were, a black and a white man sitting together and the white guy calls the black man friend even though they had just been fighting.

'*Yebo Gogo*,' Simon responded to Deon's '*Ja Swaar*' with another quote from a different advert. *Yebo Gogo*, yes old man or grandfather. The post-apartheid ad itself had poked fun at the way the whites still treated the blacks and Deon was aware of this. He smiled in the dark, they were back on talking terms, but he had to be more careful in what he said.

'Hey, you remember that Coke ad I was singing earlier *'I'd like to buy the world a Coke?*' Deon sang the line again, looking for something to talk about that didn't involve Elise.

'Ja, I remember it,' Simon was also glad they were talking again.

'Well apparently when they came to show it in South Africa, they wanted a version where there were no black people in the advert. I mean really, like the old government thought that maybe if we saw the ad we would all run out and buy the nearest black person Coke and this would somehow cause the fall of apartheid. Some of the things that government did, geez they were really weird.'

'Hau! Did they really want a version with no black people? Didn't black people also drink Coke? If I had known that I would have stopped drinking Coke.'

'It wasn't Coke that wanted a whites' only ad, it was the government. Coke in America insisted that the advert had blacks in it.'

'Oh. Still, my favourite is not Coke but Iron Brew or Stoney Ginger Beer,' Simon smiled.

'Do you know that at one stage more Iron Brew was sold in South Africa than Coke. We must have been one of the few countries in the world that sold more of a local cold drink than Coke,' Deon added the trivia, glad of the distraction it brought. It did have a slight political undertone, but was harmless and he felt his mood lighten.

'Really, I did not know that,' Simon too was starting to relax again. Deon smiled in the dark, but then struggled to think of what to say next so lapsed into silence. Simon's thoughts turned back to Elise. He wanted to hear what happened to her, to see the story through to its end, but didn't dare raise the topic.

The silence expanded and started to depress Deon. His thoughts turned back to Elise and he began to speak again. He had to get the story out, he could no longer keep it in. It felt as though something was pulling at it, dragging it out into the open.

'They just killed her.'

This time, because he had also been thinking about her, Simon knew exactly who Deon was talking about.

'She had gone to the orphanage as usual, just another ordinary Saturday. I'm told that she was particularly cheerful and played with the kids more than normal. She had also given them all a big hug before leaving, something she had never done before. It was as though she knew what was going to happen, like she had some sort of foresight. In fact some of the other people from the orphanage said that to me at the funeral. But it wasn't that, it was something else.'

He paused and swallowed hard again.

'Anyway,' he continued, brushing over the *something else* and continued. 'She got back home a bit late as she had stopped at the shops to pick up some stuff, you know like milk, bread. Stuff like that.

'I remember hearing the car pull up. You could not mistake the engine, it was a Volkswagen Beetle, those cars have a distinct sound. So I went to the window to wave to her. She was busy scrambling in the back seat of the car for the groceries then straightened out and noticed me watching her. She smiled and that was when I saw them.'

'Who?' Simon was at the window with Deon, admiring this beautiful woman who did not see colour.

'Three of them. I dunno, tsotsis, gangsters. They had balaclavas on, I never saw their faces, it all happened so fast but yet so slow. They jumped out from behind the bushes at the side of our driveway. She never heard or saw them. They just ran up and killed her. One shot to the back of the head. BANG!' Deon flinched at his own sound effect.

'She was dead before she knew she had been shot. There was not even any surprise on her face, she just kept smiling. It was like she knew something no-one else knew, a wonderful secret.'

He drew in a large breath, but cut it short as it threatened to spill over into tears.

Once he had recovered he went on, 'I couldn't do anything it all happened too quickly. I didn't even have a chance to call out to warn her. I was powerless to help, she was dead before I could even lift a finger.

'They jumped into the car and sped off while I ran out to her, but I knew there was nothing I could do. There was blood everywhere. I couldn't believe it. This woman who had been so full of life, so full of goodness, was now lifeless, killed by such evil. And for what? A car. A bloody car. I would have let them have the car if they had just let Elise live.'

He sighed, feeling safe from the embarrassing tears now and drew in a deep full breath. He needed to re-stock his body with new air, air to replace that which had been purged by the telling of his story. But the air in the lift was stale, recycled.

'I don't remember much after that. I must have phoned the police, or maybe a neighbour did. Later someone told me that they had found me sitting with Elise's head on my lap, stroking her hair and just staring into space. The ambulance men had trouble getting me to let go of her. I just wanted to hold on. I was scared that if I let her go she would never come back. A stupid thought I know. She was already gone, but I didn't want to give her up.

'I didn't really comprehend what had happened till the following morning and even then I refused to believe it. I kept thinking that Elise would walk in through the door with a big smile on her face. But it never happened. After a few days, the dreadful truth began to sink in and I fell into a huge depression. It was even worse when I went to see the coroner to sign off some of the papers. He then asked me if I had known that Elise was pregnant.'

'Hau! Oh no, that is terrible.' Simon was shocked. Why would anyone kill a woman who sounded as good as Elise, especially as she was pregnant? He thought about the unborn child and a tear ran down his cheek, hidden by the dark of the lift. He wiped it away with the back of his hand.

'Well of course I had no idea. I was dumbstruck. Elise had been pregnant and she hadn't had the chance to tell me. Maybe that was why she was smiling when she got shot, maybe she had just found out and was going to tell me when she got in. Hell I dunno how I would have reacted had she lived to tell me. I wasn't really ready for kids back then, and possibly that's why I think I am even less ready now. I have never told Sharon about any of this. She's far too conservative and would never understand.'

'Who's Sharon.'

'Oh she's my girlfriend. We live together in Kalk Bay.' He was offering up more personal information. It was okay to talk about Elise, that was the past, but Sharon was the present. It was almost as though he was inviting Simon over to his place. Could he ever do such a thing? Could he break through these barriers that still stood between black and white and ask Simon to come visit. What would Sharon say?

There was no way he could ask, and he knew this deep down. Even if he was living on his own could he bring himself to have a black man come visit as a friend? Talking about personal issues in the dark where Simon was unseen was fine, but in his house? He tried to imagine him and Simon standing round the braai, beer in hand. No it could never work. Besides, Sharon would never allow it.

'Your girlfriend? And you never told her anything?'

'No.'

'Never told her anything about Elise like you are telling me now?'

'She knows nothing about Elise.'

'Why have you never told her? You have bottled this up for so long.' There was almost a demand in there.

'I don't know,' Deon was on the defensive. This onslaught of questions muddled his brain. What did it matter to Simon whether he told Sharon anything or not. He focussed his thoughts and prepared a counter attack, a slight anger rising in him. But as quickly as it rose, he hammered it down with sensibility, memories of his recent *faux pas* with Simon helping him.

'I guess I just felt she would never understand.' It was dismissive, deliberately so.

'You see she is quite conservative. She would never have understood about Elise being pregnant. In fact she would probably have a problem with me even having had a girlfriend, she's a bit old fashioned that way.'

'She is a fussy one this Sharon.' Simon shook his head in the dark, smiling at how women were the same no matter what colour they were. He was lucky that Lucy had been so open minded about his ex. Most other girls that he had tried to date before meeting Lucy would run a mile when they heard that he had kids.

Deon was also smiling. Sharon could be fussy, but her heart was in the right place.

'Did they ever find the guys who did it?'

'Did what?' Deon had wandered off too far.

'Killed Elise.' It was blunt, but this time Deon didn't flinch. The smile did, however, leave him.

'No, you know what it's like these days. So much violence, the cops can't keep up with it all.'

'Were they blacks?' There was no political undertone here, just interest.

'Ja, they had balaclavas on, but their hands were black. It's strange how a detail like that sticks in the mind. They found the car in Alexandra Township a few days later. It was burnt out. No fingerprints, but even if they had found fingerprints they would never find the guys who did this.

'I wish they would find them, then I could tell them that the woman they shot was not their enemy. She was on their side, helping the Aids orphans and everything. She always tried to help the black man, during apartheid and even afterwards.'

Deon paused for a second. He had never quite been comfortable with Elise's inability to see colour. It clashed too much with his own upbringing and the environment he was brought up in. Morally he knew he could not argue against it and had never tried. He always thought of himself as being a moral person, but Elise's behaviour made him feel inadequate in this department where he had usually felt slightly superior to his other friends. Was it made more acute by the patriarchal society in which he was brought up, could it be he hated being outdone by a woman? He shook his head to clear these thoughts, then smiled slightly. Despite these feelings, here he was boasting of Elise's goodness.

'They killed someone who would have done anything to help them if they had only asked. I mean what sort of people go round killing innocent white women?'

'I killed an innocent white woman once.' The words were out there before Simon could stop them.

MARIE STANDER

Marie cried on her last day of school. It was not only for the passing of an era in her life that the tears fell, but also for the fear and dread she had that her boyfriend Wessel would not return from the army. They had a month from the close of school before he was due to report, along with thousands of other young men, to go off and defend their country. He left with a promise to return and marry her.

She cried again when she heard that he was due to go up to the border where the war was. They were guilty tears for while she feared for the life of her man, she knew that he was going out there to keep her and all the whites in South Africa safe from the marauding black communists.

She cried again when news came through that Ryno, the boyfriend of her close friend Tanya, had stood on an anti-personnel mine and would not be coming back. She prayed harder that week for Wessel's safe return than at any other time during his tour of duty.

She cried when she listened to *Forces Favourites* on the radio, taking little comfort in the fact that she was not the only one sending in requests for loved ones in the army. *Vasbyt, min dae.* Hang in there, not long now.

And at last she cried tears of relief when Wessel returned seemingly unscathed. The official proposal and acceptance followed quickly, but Marie soon noticed the change in Wessel. He never spoke about what happened there, always changing the subject when she would probe. *This is not the sort of thing a woman needs to know about,* he would say closing the subject.

Marie tearfully confided her concerns to the dominee who was going to marry them.

'I don't know dominee, he's not the same Wessel that I knew. I'm worried that something horrible happened to him up there on the border, but he won't say anything, he just gets annoyed when I ask him about it. It's like he doesn't trust me anymore.'

But the dominee sided with Wessel. 'He has been through a lot, seen many things that a woman mustn't know about. He just needs time to adjust. All the men who go to the border go through this. They all come out okay in the end.'

She accepted this. It must be true because the dominee had said so.

The new Mrs Marie Stander soon found other challenges in her relationship. Wessel did recover from his army stint and, although he still did not talk about his time there, he returned to being the cheerful and caring Wessel that she had fallen in love with. But he needed to make a living and the best way to do so was to get some sort of qualification. Marie now found herself competing with textbooks for attention. She had been raised with a *stand-by-your-man* mentality and hung in there hoping things would get better.

There were nights though, when she would lie awake, her body aching for his touch and he would not come. Eventually he would crawl into bed exhausted from his day's work and evening studies. Marie would get a perfunctory kiss before he would roll over and fall asleep. She began to wonder if all this was worth it.

Then one day the news came through, 'Wessel, I'm pregnant.' It was timid, bordering on frightened, how would he react, were they ready for kids, how would they cope?

He was fine, pleased even. He took the evening off from his studies and they went out to dinner to celebrate. The next night he was back at the books. *I've got to get this assignment done, my love* he said, putting as much feeling as he could into the term of affection. She had nodded, smiled sadly and headed off to bed.

It was a boy, just under eight pounds. *His name is Jan, pa. Just like yours.* Wessel's dad was proud. He now became Grootjan (Big Jan) and the new edition Kleinjan (Small Jan). Kleinjan filled the gap that Wessel's books had created in Marie's life and she devoted herself to his upbringing.

Wessel I'm pregnant. It was more confident. They had survived the first and he was now earning a semi-decent salary. Also final exams weren't far off.

We've decided to call her Annette, we like the name. Wessel's mom was disappointed but said nothing. Marie's mom was hurt, but said nothing.

Wessel I'm pregnant. A third time, and this one was almost dismissive. He was going places, money was no longer an issue and the degree hung proudly in the study. Seven pounds became Sannie. Wessel's mom was hurt but said nothing, Marie's mom was ecstatic. Marie hated herself for giving in to the unspoken pressure about the name.

THE LIFT 8

Deon froze. Was this man sharing the lift and the dark with him a tsotsi? He didn't seem the type. There had been no real animosity about him so far. In fact he had been quite civil. There was no way he could be a gangster. Maybe he was a reformed gangster. These things did happen didn't they?

He had said it quite casually – I killed an innocent white woman once.

Deon was shocked away from any reminiscing about Elise. How could he respond to such a comment? Surely Simon had not been joking. It would be a very sick joke if he was. Deon cleared his throat feeling he needed to say something, his mind desperately searching for the right words.

Simon left the statement hanging, shocked that he had just come out with it – I killed an innocent white woman once. It was something he never thought he would talk about, something he didn't want to talk about, but it was suddenly out there. *I killed an innocent white woman once.* The sentence threw him back to the day of the killing, that sickening day.

He knew he should say more, but didn't know where to begin, what to say, or even how to say it if he could find the words. He decided to try and avoid the issue.

'Yes, but that was a long, long time ago. It was another lifetime, things were different then.'

He was not sure if that made it sound better so he tried to move the subject away from what happened. Sighing he went on, 'Too much violence. First we had the violence of apartheid and the struggle for freedom, now it's just criminal violence. When will it stop?'

He leaned back closing his eyes and shaking his head, trying to erase the memory of the killing from his mind. He clenched his fists into tight balls, he wanted to squeeze that incident from his life, but it would not go.

Deon sensed his companion's distress and decided to leave him alone for a bit. Besides, he had his own demons to deal with. He was beginning to feel a slight sense of release from the whole Elise affair. His mind was slowly building a fence around it, cordoning it off. He reflected on this and smiled slightly as the thought struck him that this was how white South Africa was now living – high walls and fences designed to protect them from the violence outside. People were creating these little cocoons that they felt somewhat warm and safe in.

The little cocoon that he was now trying to create in his mind did not hold a rainbow-coloured butterfly that would emerge one day, but rather a scorpion that must be kept captive in those silky chains, locked away for good. He should focus on the positive. That was a good business term – focus on the positive, remember the good times with Elise.

He deliberately tried to bring up the image of Elise's face just before she was shot, that last fraction of a second of her life where she seemed so happy, the slight smile playing on her delicate lips. Was she going to tell him about her pregnancy that evening?

He tried to imagine what their child would have looked like. He never found out if it was a boy or a girl. Could they have told him so early on in her pregnancy?

He was surprised that these thoughts no longer caused the deep biting pain that they normally did. Usually the pain would ensure that he kept well clear of such memories. He was surprised too that Simon's confession had not caused him more pain. In fact he found himself hoping that the power cut would not end. He was beginning to feel safe within the dark, talking to and listening to the voice of an unseen companion. The dark that had seemed so threatening at first now comforted. He also wanted to hear more of Simon's story now that he was no longer so engrossed in his own pain.

But how to approach Simon to extract the story? He sensed the reticence that he himself had experienced earlier and shifted his weight slightly on the floor. It was hard and he was getting a bit numb so he climbed rather stiffly to his feet as he tried to think, stretching and yawning.

Simon opened his eyes, a useless gesture as it was still pitch black in the lift, he could not see a thing.

'Do you think this power cut will go on much longer?' Deon asked, still trying to think of a way to get Simon to tell his story.

'I don't know,' Simon felt a little better that the conversation was moving away from him. 'It must be nearly two hours now.'

Following Deon's lead, Simon decided to stand as well. He bent his knees slowly once he was up, easing the slight ache that had set in.

They stood for a bit longer in silence then Deon said, 'It's funny how when you've been sitting for ages you think you can then stand forever, but my legs seem to get tired more quickly and all I want to do is sit down again.'

He sank back to the floor and his mood went with him.

'You know you're right. We have had too much violence in this country. It is such a beautiful place and generally speaking, the people are friendly. It seems strange that with all that, we still cannot live together peacefully. Do you think it will ever come right?'

Simon, whose legs had also tired quickly sat down again and answered, 'Ja, it must do someday. There is no longer the politics in the violence. The government must just make sure there are more jobs, and you whities must do more to share the wealth around.'

It was a bold and direct statement, one that Simon would never had dared to come out with a few minutes' earlier.

Deon was annoyed by the response. Not by directness of it, but rather by the inner conflict it caused within in. Yes, Simon was right, the whites could and should do more to help. They had, after all, exploited the blacks for many years under apartheid, used them as cheap labour. But, on the other hand he did not want to give up any of his wealth. He had worked hard for it, why shouldn't he keep it? He decided to press the subject of the government doing more.

'Ja,' he said, 'the government don't really help much do they?' Again he was fishing for agreement that the black man couldn't govern as well as the white.

'Oh, the government has already done a lot in the short time since apartheid, we are much better off. I have a house now, but there is still a lot to do. They must just keep on building the country up.'

Simon's response didn't appease Deon's desire to be proved right, but he gave a wry smile this time. He hadn't really expected the answer he wanted and berated himself inwardly for hoping otherwise. Elise could see that the blacks were better off under black rule so why couldn't he accept it?

He suddenly found himself thinking about Yvonne again, the short-lived affair he had had with her. He couldn't remember her ever having been touched by violence. That was strange as at that time just about everyone was affected, either directly as he had been, or indirectly by knowing someone who had been affected. Had she ever talked about the violence? He couldn't recall any conversation he had had with her on the topic. Maybe she just never spoke about it, maybe she had been so traumatically affected that she, like him, had found it hard to talk about.

Even Simon, who shared the lift with him, had experienced the violence first hand, but as a perpetrator rather than a victim. Deon preferred to think that Yvonne was actually one of the few lucky ones not to have been affected and clung to that belief in a way that gave him naïve hope. He wondered what it must feel like to be so innocent in this land where violence had played such a role.

'Not everyone has been caught up the violence,' he said, trying to convince himself and offering comfort to Simon who still seemed agitated at his own memories. 'I knew this one woman, she never seemed to have been affected, she never told me stories of people getting hijacked or mugged or anything. Yvonne was her name, nice woman.' He suddenly felt the warmth of Yvonne's naked body next to his in Trevor's bed, and shuddered pleasurably.

'Was she another of your girlfriends?' Simon asked, glad of the opening he had to move away from the question of violence and killing.

Deon was again shocked away from a thought by what seemed like an intimate intrusion, but he was more sensitive to things now so he just chuckled.

'No,' he lied, 'she was the wife of a friend, we used to play cricket together. No, not me and Yvonne, me and Trevor, Yvonne's husband. Trevor and I used to play cricket together.' He added the last bit as he realised that the way he had said things may have led to Simon getting the wrong end of the stick.

Despite his friendly reply he was a bit agitated as he wanted to slip back into bed with Yvonne, but Simon was pushing on, trying to move the conversation further away from where he didn't want it to be.

'What about Trevor, did he ever talk about the violence.'

Deon thought hard.

'No, you know what, he didn't either. Neither of them did. They were a lovely couple, always friendly. I don't see them much anymore,' a touch of sadness clouded his voice, 'but no, they don't seem to have suffered from the violence. They must be among the lucky few.'

Simon nodded in the dark. He had other thoughts coming in which he didn't want surfacing again. He sucked in his breath quite sharply, then expelled it in a long gust along with his thoughts.

'Do you want to talk about your killing the white woman?' Deon forced the thoughts back immediately. 'It may help. Like you said earlier, don't keep things in your Coke bottle 'cause when you open it psssssttt's all over the place.' He tried to keep his tone as kind as possible. 'Have you ever talked about it to anyone before?' Deon went on after a pause in which Simon remained silent; there was not even a laugh at his repeated comments of earlier.

'No.'

A two letter word yet in the tone it was delivered, it conveyed a huge amount. Simon needed to talk about it. He knew that, but he could never bring himself to say anything. Not to his mother, nor to Lucy. He could not talk about his feelings. He was the man of the house and he feared breaking down in tears should he ever start talking about this. Men don't cry.

Deon waited for a while then said, 'You know what, for me it has been really good talking to you. In a strange way the dark helps. You see when I was telling my story, you were just a voice and some unseen ears. It somehow made it easier to talk about it when I couldn't see you. Does that make sense?'

Simon thought about this for a bit. Maybe this white guy was right, maybe he could talk to unseen ears. Perhaps it would be all right to cry even in the dark. He drew in his breath again.

'It happened in Joey's.'

LUCY 2

Lucy knew that Simon had killed someone, but she did not know the details of what had happened. Simon's mother had mentioned it one day when Lucy was asking her advice about another issue.

'There is a gang of tsotsis causing havoc where I used to live, so far no-one has been killed but tensions are rising and I am so worried about my friend Anna, she still lives there. She wants to move away because there is going to be trouble soon. But Anna has nowhere to go. Do you know of anywhere round here she can move to?'

Simon's mother was a well respected woman in the community. She was an unelected leader of the people who lived in their corner of the township. Women came to her for advice and help with their children's illnesses, young men would be seen talking to her about prospective girlfriends or wives and the old men would sometimes flirt with her. The latter would usually end in huge smiles and often roars of laughter as the good natured banter flew back and forth.

She listened patiently as Lucy talked of her fears, waiting for her to finish. Then she patted Lucy's hand and said, 'Don't worry my daughter, I will talk to Jonas Tshabalala. I think he has a small room to let in his house. It's such a big house and he is there on his own now that his son has gone to University in Johannesburg. He is a good man; Anna will have no cause for worry staying there. He will not touch her.'

A tear squeezed out of Lucy's eye. 'Thank you Mama, you are a good woman. You are like a mother to me.' She smiled through her misted over eyes and the old woman nodded slowly. 'You also have a very good son,' Lucy went on feeling a little emotional about the whole Anna thing.

The smile faded from the old woman's eyes. 'He is a very good boy,' she said with some sadness, 'but he has too much on his mind all the time. He worries about things and he never talks about them. Like the time he shot that white woman. I can see that it is eating him up inside, but he never says anything.'

'He shot a white woman!' Lucy's hands flew to her mouth as if to stop this shocking news from escaping. 'When? How? What happened?'

'He never told you?' The old woman's question was more a statement. She seemed to have already known the answer. 'Of course he wouldn't have told you,' she went on, 'he never talks about it. It happened a long time ago, long before he met you. When he was there in eGoli.'

Lucy sat stunned. She thought she had got to know Simon quite well, but now she was hearing about a part of his life that he never spoke about. She had often felt that he was keeping part of himself from her, but usually blamed herself for the feeling and put it down to loving the man too much, almost wanting to know more about him, even wanting to know beyond what was actually him.

'No, he never said anything to me about it,' she said. 'Do you know any details?'

'No,' the old woman replied sadly. 'Simon does not talk about these things. He just came home one evening from work. I could see he was very worried about something but he would not say what. He just sat staring out the window for a long time, he didn't even eat his supper that night. I tried asking him again what was wrong but he wouldn't say. That night he went out to the shebeen and came home very drunk. You know Simon and he never gets drunk, but that night … Hau! It was terrible to see my boy so upset. He came home and went straight to bed. I had trouble to get him up for work the next day. He just lay there holding his head and moaning. Eventually he said that he didn't have to go to work because he had shot a white woman. He never said anything more about it.' The old woman sighed sadly.

'I tried to read the story in the papers, but he threw them into the fire before I got the chance. He didn't want me to see. He was ashamed. People here said it wasn't his fault, but no-one knows the full story. I can see that he still thinks about it, even though so much time has passed. I wish he would talk about it, let the demon out.'

Lucy sat holding the old woman's hand and nodding.

'I will try and get him to talk about it,' she said eventually, 'it is not good that he is like this about it.'

THE LIFT 9

'You remember I said that I used to be a security guard at Eastgate?'

'Ja, that was where Elise did her … well you know.'

'Ja, it was my friend Samuel who saw her. It is a small world, isn't it?'

'Tell me about it. Who would have ever thought I would be stuck in a lift with someone who was connected with my life.'

Deon paused slightly to contemplate what he had just said. Was it fate that had somehow brought them together in this lift? He never really believed in fate or destiny or any of that stuff. He had been brought up in a Christian household, but his parents were never devout and would only occasionally drag him along to Church and Sunday School. None of what was said there made any real impression on his life and after he left home he never went back into a church other than for Elise's funeral.

This thought process took him back to the day of the funeral and it jerked him out of the comfort zone that he had built up by thinking that the cathartic moments earlier had done the trick. Now he didn't want to hear Simon's story, he wanted to talk more about his own story, about his emotions at the funeral. But where to start? They were moving down the road toward Simon's innocent white woman. Was it fair to side-track Simon to finish his own unfinished business? Did his lack of real release warrant possibly denying Simon his chance to unburden himself?

Simon was preparing himself to tell his story. He had never spoken to anyone about it before. Yes, he had had to deal with the police and his boss. He was fortunate that due to his colour he had not had to face the intimate glaring eyes of the press. There was that one journalist who had tried to do a story on him, even going so far as to find his address and venture into the then no go zone for whites in Soweto, but Simon did not talk to him. Rather he told the guy to 'talk to my boss. That is all I am allowed to say.'

He cleared his throat to start but was interrupted by Deon. 'Do you believe in fate?'

'What?'

'Do you believe in fate?' Deon was working the conversation round to talk about the funeral using the exact same thought process he had gone through moments earlier.

'You mean like where God makes things happen in a certain way?'

'Well, God or something. Destiny. Something like that. Do you believe in God?' This was going well for Deon.

'Of course I believe in God, don't you?' Simon was amazed that Deon may not share his belief.

'No,' it was a simple blunt answer. 'I never have really. I went to church a bit when I was small but haven't been since ...' he paused now, not wanting to be too obvious about how he had manoeuvred things round to what he wanted to talk about, '... at least not since Elise's funeral. It was quite a strange thing her funeral.'

The conversation was now where he wanted it to be. Surely Simon was hooked and wanting to hear more about the funeral. Talk about killing innocent white women had been banished, at least for the moment.

'Strange, in what way?'

'Well, obviously there were quite a few of her friends there and some of mine. Hers were there to mourn her passing, mine came to comfort me and I guess to mourn her passing too, although once I started going out with her, I seemed to see less of my mates. Anyway her brother Danny was there, but neither of her parents came. I was surprised at the time, but later Danny told me all about how Elise had left home after her dad called her a kaf....I'm sorry but they were his words, he called her a kaffir lover and that if she wanted to be one she had to leave home, which she did.'

'Hau!' Simon liked this mystical girl Elise even more now. She was a woman of principle, leaving home because she could not abide by her father's racist wishes. 'She was a good woman. She did not deserve to die.'

'Danny also told me that his mother had wanted to come to the funeral but his father had forbidden her from coming. "It's not like she wants to mourn Elise's death, she just thinks she looks good in black. Besides, it would mean that all those mine aunties would fuss over her. She likes that." That's what he told me. Imagine that, not going to your own daughter's funeral, or only wanting to go because of the attention you'd get.

'When Danny told me this I was pleased that they had not come. I wouldn't have liked to meet them knowing what they were like. Elise never talked about her parents, she would always avoid the subject or just say, "You don't want to meet them." I was half hoping they would be there so I could see for myself what it was that would make me not want to meet them, but when Danny explained what had happened I was glad they didn't come.

'There were also some of the women from the Aids orphanage, six of them, all blacks. They sat together away from the rest of the people in the church, or rather I should say the others sat away from them. It's weird how we still like our little bit of apartheid.'

Simon nodded his agreement, he knew the score. In post-apartheid

South Africa, in a situation where you are a minority of one race among another, you still stuck together, even if you didn't know each other. It felt more comfortable to be with people whose ways you were more familiar with. It was the natural thing to do.

'Danny had made all the arrangements for the funeral which was good as I was such an emotional mess that I couldn't have done anything. He was a blessing was old Danny, he just got on and did things. It was like he knew Elise would die young. He was not even surprised when I told him that she had been pregnant. He just nodded sadly and moved on. There were many days when I wished I could move on like he had, but I guess we all cope with death differently.

'So anyway, there were these six black ladies and they had asked if they could sing a song. Of course we had no objection. When the time came for them to sing they walked quietly up to the front of the church and started singing. It was a funeral song so it was quite mournful, but they had amazing voices and the harmonies were just superb. The one who was leading the singing put so much emotion into the song. I didn't understand the words, but I understood the hurt and it really hit me what sort of impression Elise had made on these women.

'They were about halfway through when I ... now I don't know if I imagined this or what, but I swear I saw Elise standing next to the coffin. She was watching the women singing. She had a very intense look of concentration on her face.

'When the women finished singing the silence flowed into the church to fill the space left by the music and Elise looked away from the women for the first time since I had seen her. She looked across at me and she had that strange smile on her face, the same smile she had when they shot her. She was cradling something in her arms and I realised it was a child. Her eyes moved from me to the child for a moment, then she looked up again and held the child out towards me, offering it to me.

'I wanted to reach out and take it, but Danny was whispering in my ear. "You all right?" he asked. I looked up at him and then back to where Elise had stood, but she was gone. I looked back at Danny and shook my head. No, I was not all right. I was seeing things. That's what I kept telling myself – I was seeing things. Elise was dead, this was just me wishing her alive. I held my head in my hands and I guess I stayed like that for the rest of the funeral. I knew if I looked up she would not be there. That was her parting gesture. She was telling me what I know she had wanted tell me the night she was killed. She was telling me that she had been pregnant.

'Danny was magnificent, he just put his arm round me and held me for the rest of the funeral. When it was over and they took the coffin out the church I followed it, but I was a zombie, in a trance. I don't remember anything else about that day. Danny tells me I was quite normal and chattered politely to all those offering their sympathy, but me, I haven't a clue what I did. I don't remember a thing.

'I still don't know what I saw in the church. I reckon it was all the emotion of the moment that caused me to hallucinate like that. I don't know.'

Deon paused now. It was more than the weight of the emotion, but he didn't want to say that. He had probably said too much already. What would Simon think about this talk of ghosts and spirits? He had got so caught up in the story that he had not realised how it might sound to someone else. There was a reason why he had never spoken of this before, it all sounded too weird. No-one would understand. So why had he told Simon, or had he told Simon? Perhaps he was telling the darkness with ears. Simon just happened to be there to overhear. He held his breath for a second, waiting for a response from the voice in the dark, waiting for the laugh or the mockery.

But Simon was disturbed by this story. As a small boy he had been brought up to believe in and respect the spirits of his ancestors, but this belief in the spirit world only applied to black people. White men didn't have spirits, well at least he had never thought about it until now when he was confronted with a story of white spirits. He shook his head trying to clear it so he could think about this issue, but he didn't want to deal with this now, especially as thoughts about the woman he had shot came back to him.

'Marie Stander,' he said. He had only meant to say it in his mind, but the words slipped out into the lift.

'What?'

'Marie Stander,' Simon said again, 'she was the woman I shot.'

MARIE STANDER 2

The Rubicon was crossed. A proud grey-haired messiah stepped out from behind bars to rescue his people. The revolution had come and fear gripped at the stomachs of the country's whites. *When Nelson Mandela is free, your maid will be given your house, you will be left with nothing.* Whispers in the air, making it thick with dread.

Marie Stander was just one of the millions who sat watching, waiting on that warm February day, a mixture of intrigue and terror eating away at her. Who was this man Nelson Mandela that all the fuss had been about? Who was this man who was going to cause her to lose her house? Would all hell break loose now? Would she be murdered in her bed?

'I can't believe that they're letting that bleddy terrorist free,' Wessel was sombre.

Terrorist? Freedom fighter? Take your pick. And most South Africans did. Among the whites opinion was divided. There were those who believed that apartheid could and should go on forever. Why spoil a good thing? Others were tired of the imbalance, the injustice, the wrongness of it all, but never quite knew how to change it. Marie Stander didn't know how she felt. She never really liked the inequality the system brought, but didn't want it to change.

With Mandela's release, a new violence came to the country. But it was black-on-black, nothing too much to worry about for the Standers. Mandela was free, but they still had their house. If the blacks wanted to kill each other that was fine.

'The more they kill each other, the less there are of them,' Wessel observed philosophically while watching a news broadcast which contained some quite brutal images of the violence.

Marie looked away from the television, a wave of nausea passing over her. Still, this was far enough away from her family for her to worry.

Then slowly the violence began to seep out of the townships and into the leafy white suburbs. It began to take on a life of its own as it twisted its way into the heart of the white psyche.

Did you hear about the O'Connors? Well their neighbour was killed the other day driving to work. Someone just shot him at the stop street near the Roodepoort offramp.

... they broke into the house, raped her and killed him.

... and for what? A hundred rand, that's all. Killed for a hundred rand.

Marie Stander began to worry. She worried about the kids, she worried about Wessel.

Where were they? Why was Kleinjan late getting back from rugby? Suzette was going to give them a lift. *What's happened to Wessel? He's usually home by now. What does the traffic report say? An overturned lorry is blocking the M1 north. Please God let him be caught up in the traffic.*

Then she began to worry about going out at night. *No I don't want to go to the movies, let's just stay in and watch TV, there's a good film on tonight.*

She watched the walls go up around the neighbours' houses and began to bug Wessel. *We need a proper fence with barbed wire on top. I don't care how much it costs. And electric gates. I don't want to have to get out of the car to open the gates.*

But still the violence crept closer. There was a car-jacking three blocks away. The guy had been shot, but luckily survived. Then the robbery occurred four doors down. Cleaned the place out, but fortunately no-one was at home at the time.

Marie Stander lay awake at night. *What was that noise? Wessel are you awake?*

The house popped and crackled as it cooled down and she jumped at each sound.

Then a drastic step. *Wessel I want a gun.*

What for?

Just in case. A small gun that I can carry in my handbag. You never know when I may need it.

Wessel sighed. He was worried about the violence, but you just had to get on with life. Marie was getting paranoid. But if it made her happy …

So Marie went off and did the paperwork for a gun licence. She went for a few lessons to learn how to use it, then felt safer driving around at day.

But still the violence was there, ever present, ever threatening and still it played on Marie's nerves. She struggled to sleep and this made her less able to cope with the stress.

The violence that had crept closer and closer to her door began to leak into her home and one night she threw a plate at Wessel who was taunting her for being paranoid. Despite the shock at her reaction, she continued to be anxious and went to ridiculous lengths to ensure that the violence didn't harm her or her family.

THE LIFT 10

Deon was struggling. He was still reliving Elise's funeral and her strange spectral appearance. What did it mean? Did it mean anything? Now here was this voice talking about another woman, a Marie. He wanted to carry on talking, telling his story, but didn't know where to take it. What more could he say? The story was spent, but the emotions continued. He knew he would never be able to talk about this again.

His silence prompted Simon to go on.

'I was working as a security guard at Eastgate. It was a Tuesday afternoon and the mall was quiet. I was working there near the Standard Bank, you know the place?'

Deon reluctantly shelved the ghost of Elise as he now needed to keep up with Simon's story.

'Ja, it was round the one side, near Woolworths wasn't it. Hey do you know that in England they also have a Woolworths there, but it's not nearly as posh as ours. Ours is more like Marks & Spencer's there. A friend of mine who moved over to London told me.'

Simon grunted. This was all irrelevant. What did it matter what Woolworths was like in England. England was a land far away that had nothing to do with his life here on the other side of the world. It had nothing to do with life in Langa. There was no violence in England as far as he could tell; there was no Marie Stander in England. She had been in Eastgate on that day.

Simon went on, slightly annoyed with the interruption and tried to convey this in his voice. 'Ja, that's right, that side, near the Woolworths that's not like the England Woolworths.'

The talk of England had thrown him and he needed to build up again to tell his story so he sidetracked. 'This was about a year after Nelson Mandela was released. What a day that was. Do you remember where you were when Madiba was set free? I remember we had to wait and wait. But then we had waited so many years for him that a few hours more didn't matter. I was in a bar in Soweto. We were all sitting around a small TV screen. The place was full. Everyone wanted to get a first look at the man.'

Deon shifted his position, folding his arms across his chest. His hands shook slightly at the annoyance he felt about the sudden change of subject, veering off in a direction he didn't want to go. But he couldn't muster the energy at that moment to steer it back to where his interests lay.

'There was a guy next to me, an old man. He must have seen a lot in his time. He was straining to see the TV because the crowds were pushing and shoving, there was a lot of excitement you must understand. Anyway this old man he couldn't see the TV and he was getting quite upset. He had tears in his eyes, I remember that well. He had greying hair on his temples and these lines, what do you call them wrinkles? Yes wrinkles by his eyes. It was like he had smiled so much in his life that he had grown lines round his eyes, you know the ones you get from smiling? Well those were now permanent features on his face. But the tears were coming out and he was panicking that he would not see Madiba.

'I felt so sad for him. We were all excited and we had waited so long, but this old man had waited longer than any of us. So I began shouting and saying to people to let the old man through. It was hard to get myself heard as everyone was making such a noise, but eventually people around me started to see why I was shouting and they took pity on the old man and moved aside. Soon the old man was seated right at the front of the room as close to the TV as anyone could get. I'll never forget the look on his face. It was one of pure happiness. The smile that had made those marks next to his eyes came back, in fact he had the biggest smile in the whole room.

'And then the moment arrived. We didn't know what to expect. There had been some illegal photos of Mandela which were taken before he went into prison that I had seen somewhere, but those were over twenty-seven years old. At last we could see the man as he was now. We were amazed at how much dignity he had when he and Winnie walked out of Polsmoor. He was so smart in his suit, waving and smiling. All the world was looking. So many press photographers were there. And then he gave the salute, the fist in the air. Amandla! Power! That was when we knew we had won, the struggle was over. We were no longer powerless. We had the power.'

Simon paused as he relived that magnificent moment. Some of the euphoria came back to him now in the dark lift. They were no longer powerless. He felt that the lift and its darkness no longer had a hold over him. He was a free man even though he was stuck in a lift. Even though he had to do this menial job just to survive, just to scrape a living. In the day to day struggle to exist, he had forgotten that he was free.

'So how did you kill her?' Deon didn't want to talk about Mandela and his release, that was old news, he knew all about it. He wanted to know whether this man sharing the lift with him was a cold blooded killer, like those who killed Elise.

A strange feeling suddenly took him. If Simon had casually killed a white woman as casually as those men had killed Elise, then maybe he could extract some revenge for Elise's death by killing Simon in the lift, overpowering him and beating him to death.

It was a quick uninvited thought and Deon shuddered and sobered from it as quickly as it had arrived. But a nagging thought remained; what if Simon had been one of the gang? What if by some strange twist of fate, Elise's killer had been delivered into his power to do with as he pleased? What would he do? How could he face that voice? *Let him tell his story*, he said to himself, *then we can see*. It was the sensible thing to do.

Simon was annoyed. He had begun to feel happy again. Forgetting for a minute the horror of having killed that woman, and remembering the good times when he had felt like a man, like a human for the first time when he had first tasted true freedom.

'What? Oh that.' This was the best response that he could give and he felt the irritation reverberate in his voice.

Deon noticed the annoyance, but didn't care, he was after blood now.

'Yeah that,' he said almost sarcastically, 'how did you kill her?'

Simon rubbed his face with his hands and sighed. There was no getting away with it; he would have to tell his story. He began to regret ever opening his mouth about the incident. He had only mentioned it because he thought that somehow it would help Deon, but obviously not. He wondered briefly what had even made him think that, but dismissed the thought as quickly, under pressure to continue his story.

'Well I was at Eastgate on duty; the mall was quiet, not too many people around. I was walking there near the Standard Bank when these three guys walked past me. I thought they looked a little suspicious, but then they walked on round the corner and I didn't worry anymore about them.'

'Were they black?'

Simon resented the question, resented that the automatic presumption was that suspicious looking people had to be black. But the sad truth in this case was that, 'Yes, they were black.'

He hesitated a second wondering if he should have lied just to get a reaction. *No Deon they were white. Don't you know that all criminals are white? They stole our dignity, they beat us and killed us. They are all criminals*. But the old hatred did not flare and catch as it used to.

'Anyway, I walked on past and then when I got to the escalators I turned round, just in time to see those three guys going into the bank. I wasn't certain, but I thought I had seen them holding guns. I immediately called for back-up on my walkie-talkie, then ran towards the bank just to check.

'I was right. Every day since then I have wished that I could have been wrong, but those three *black* guys were robbing the bank.' He injected the word 'black' with as much sarcasm as he thought he could get away with. 'As I got to door of the bank I heard the shots. They had hit the security guard inside the bank and from what I could see he was dead, there was blood all over. They shot him straight through the head. Of course the customers in the bank were panicking and began to scream. These three guys began shooting at the customers then, that's when I reacted.

'I ran into the bank waving my gun and shouting. It was a stupid thing to do as there were three of them and I was only one. They were ruthless killers and I had never fired my gun other than during training. But I had to do something; they would have shot all the customers if I had not done something. And that was my job; I was supposed to protect the shoppers in Eastgate.'

He stopped, drew a deep breath again, trying to cover over what he perceived as his failure to do his duty. It didn't help stopping, it would not change the past, so he went on.

'I was lucky. Those guys were surprised, and stopped shooting at the people for a second. During that time, most of the customers either ran out of the bank or hid behind things. The big problem then, was that I was now their target. I realised this just before they started to fire at me and dived for cover behind a small wall.

'I grabbed my walkie-talkie and screamed into it, demanding someone come and help while the bullets went flying past. I had to shoot back or I would be killed, so I took a deep breath and …'

He paused while he took a deep breath, re-living the moment by re-enacting it.

'… and then peeked round the side of the wall I was hiding behind. I noted where one of the gunmen, the one closest to me, was standing. He shot at me, but fortunately his aim wasn't too good and he missed. I took another deep breath, then jumped out from behind the wall.

'It all happened in action replay then. You know like in the soccer when they show a goal being scored but slowed down? It was like that. I aimed and for just a fraction of a second I realised I was about to kill another man. It was a terrible mistake, stopping and thinking like that, because in that very short time between when my brain told me that I must shoot before he kills me and actually pulling the trigger, this woman, this Marie Stander starts running towards the door of the bank. She was screaming madly as she ran. I suppose she was just trying to get away. She was scared and didn't really know what she was doing. It was too late for her to run though. I had already pulled the trigger and she fell straight away, right between me and the robber. We both stared at her as she fell. I had hit her in the head. The bullet that should have killed the gunman killed this innocent white woman, and I had shot it.'

Simon tried to push on with the facts from that day. He didn't want to dwell on the image of Marie Stander dying.

'The robber was the first to react, aimed his gun and …' but these memories were too painful for Simon and he had to stop for a second. He tried to shake the mental image of Marie Stander falling, blood gushing out of the side of her head where the bullet, his bullet, had hit her, but it came back as it had often done in his nightmares, clear and in slow motion.

'And what?' Deon wanted to hear what had happened. He was now caught up in someone else's story and he could leave the pain of his own behind for a while. All the strange revenge thoughts of earlier were forgotten.

'What happened?' he persisted when Simon remained silent.

'Ag, my boss and the back-up arrived and they shot the guy who was about to shoot me. There was a bit of a gun battle, but eventually the other two gave up and were arrested.' Simon was almost dismissive about the conclusion of his story. His own life being endangered and saved in a split second was not important to him. He had never really thought about how close he had come to being killed. The fact that he had killed an innocent woman was what played most heavily on his conscience.

Deon felt let down by this ending. He had been hoping for a *Die Hard* finale where a bloodied Simon had raised his gun, drawing on his failing strength, and shot the last of the baddies before falling into unconsciousness. He wanted a Hollywood ending where Simon woke up in the hospital in the final scene, a hero surrounded by his colleagues.

But this was a let down. Simon hadn't been shot; he hadn't even got one of the baddies. What sort of a story was this? All he had done was kill a panicking woman who ran into a crossfire.

'So you survived without a scratch?' he asked, almost petulantly.

'Not a scratch physically, but a big scar on my life. I have never forgotten Marie Stander. I found out her name later when the newspapers told the story. They didn't mention my name in the papers. I was just *a security guard*. It was early days for the new South Africa; we blacks were still without a name. We hadn't yet had our say in the elections so I was just *a security guard*. Nowadays I am still a security guard, but if I shot someone like that again I would be Simon Tshabalala (42), a security guard. We have names now.'

Deon grunted. What a strange thing to say. *We have names now.*

'Ja, I suppose things have changed a lot since then. I vaguely remember the story in the papers. Didn't they try and say that you had shot her deliberately?'

This was something that Simon did not particularly want to remember, but it was true.

'Ja, her family, what was her husband's name again? *He* was mentioned by name in the newspapers. Willie or Walter? I think, I can't remember for sure. Anyway he was the one that accused me of deliberately shooting his wife. He came round soon after it all happened. Someone told me that he worked nearby and the police had contacted him quite quickly.

'I remember, I was sitting having a cup of tea that my boss had organised. It was calming my nerves when suddenly this white guy was in my face and shouting at me. *You fucking kaffir, you fucking murdered my wife you murderer you.* Those were his words. I'll never forget them. I don't know what was worse then, being called a kaffir or being called a murderer. I think it was worse being called a murderer as I was used to being called a kaffir, but had never been called a murderer before.

'I really thought he was going to hit me and he probably would have if my boss hadn't come and taken him away. He was a good man my boss. Sean Botha was his name.

SEAN BOTHA

Thickset and tough, Sean Botha was one of those strange anomalies that the apartheid system threw up. He was openly racist amongst his friends, having no time for the blacks and vehemently opposed to allowing them any freedoms, let alone giving them the vote. Yet he would fiercely defend any member of his team, black or white, whenever they were accused of misdoing and he knew they were innocent.

Every Christmas he would invite all his staff over to his house for a Christmas party where he provided the booze and meat for the braai from his own pocket. This would include all the black staff who, for a few hours on that one day a year, he would treat as equals, almost friends.

He knew everyone by first name and would address them by this whenever he saw them. He also knew most of their personal circumstances and would often ask after a son or daughter or wife. He would tease some of the younger guys about their girlfriends and generally treat his staff with the greatest respect.

Most of the black staff would have been horrified if they had heard him talking to his friends and the racist comments he would make. None would have believed it if they had been told he was like that. They all saw him as a New South African, someone who saw no colour.

Sean himself never recognised the duplicity in his life. He had been brought up to treat people with respect but also that the blacks didn't quite qualify as people. Somehow in the transition from the old to the new South Africa, these two values had blurred and the greater humanist value took a slightly stronger hold.

These value sets seemed to exist quite happily in the big frame that he had. There were two distinct parts to his life – work and play. Work was where he was the humanist and play where he was the racist. An outsider would probably have accused him of toeing the line at work, going along with the new system to gain advantage in the workplace as one could no longer show racist tendencies openly for fear of not being promoted, or even litigation.

However with a beer in his hand and surrounded by his like-minded white friends, there was no-one who would report him and even if they did who would they report him to?

THE LIFT 11

'Mr Sean, he saw what had happened. He got to the bank just as the robber was taking aim at me. It was another guard who shot the gangster, but Mr Sean saw what happened, how Marie Stander had panicked and ran just as I shot.'

Unaware that he was doing it, Simon reverted to the old way where the system had made him address Sean Botha as Mr Sean, not Sean or Mr Botha.

'Mr Sean came and took Mr Stander away before he hit me. He was a very big man Mr Sean, lots of muscles, but he was very gentle with Mr Stander. He knew that Mr Stander was only angry his wife had been killed. It was his grief that made him act like that; he didn't really know what he was doing. Mr Sean took him away so that he could no longer see me, the man who had killed his wife. She had a gun you know.'

'What?'

'Marie Stander, she had a gun in her handbag. Mr Sean told me later.'

'What did she have a gun for?'

'Mr Sean said that it was for her protection because she was scared. He spent a long time talking to Mr Stander and Mr Stander told him that.'

'So why didn't she use it instead of running between you and that other guy like that?'

'I wish I knew, although sometimes I think that if she had used her gun, she may have shot me instead of those tsotsis. I was also black and had a gun, she may have thought I was one of the killers. But Mr Sean said that he thought that she was so scared that she forgot that she had a gun. She just wanted to run away to get away from the bullets. If she had only stayed where she was she would still be alive today.'

Simon let that thought hang while Deon nodded a sad agreement.

'I was given the rest of the day off. To recover, they said. I went back to my house and just sat on my bed staring at the floor. I couldn't believe what had just happened. I don't know whether I was more in shock from nearly being killed or from killing Mrs Stander. I was so worried that I would get into trouble for it, Mr Stander really scared me. I thought he was going to complain and say that it was my fault. I think I was sick, but don't remember too much more about that afternoon. I do know that that evening I went to the local shebeen and drank far too much.

'Nothing happened to me though. I went back to work the next day and Mr Sean told me that everything was okay. I had done the right thing and that I shouldn't worry about Mr Stander, he had explained everything to him and he was okay with it.'

Simon put his head between his knees and closed his eyes for a moment, breathing deeply, hoping that the stale lift air would somehow cleanse him of this memory. He felt drained. The reliving of that day brought back too many bad thoughts.

Deon waited. He thought of Elise and wondered if he would have felt any different had she been killed like Marie Stander, by accident. Would it make a difference to him if Elise had not been brutally murdered in cold blood in front of him, but rather had gone off shopping and never returned, cut down by a stray bullet meant for someone else, someone who was committing a violent crime.

He was not sure. He knew that he would have preferred not to have seen Elise being killed, not to have seen that strange smile on her face, and certainly he would have preferred not to find out afterwards that she had been carrying his child. But the question he now asked himself was how would he have felt had Elise's death not been a deliberate and vicious act.

The loss would have been no easier to bear, he knew that. The pain would still be as acute and would continue to carry that spike that pricked him all too often. It was the sense of wanting revenge against the faceless person who had caused the loss that may have been different. What if he could put a face to Elise's killer? Would that make a difference? Would he be burning with hate towards that face, desperately be wanting revenge?

How would he have reacted if he had been in Wessel Stander's shoes being confronted by the person who had killed his loved one, albeit by accident? Would he have been angry with Simon? Would he have wanted revenge, or would he have accepted the horrible truth that it had been an accident, that Elise had just been in the wrong place at the wrong time?

'I went to her funeral.'

'What?' Simon's words banished his unanswered questions.

'Marie Stander. I went to her funeral.'

'You did? Why?'

'I felt guilty. Guilty because I had killed her and she was innocent. She had done nothing wrong, never harmed me, yet I had killed her. I wanted to try and explain this to Mr Stander; to tell him myself what had happened, that I never ever meant to kill his wife, that I was sorry, but it wasn't my fault. I wanted to explain to him that she had run between me and that gangster at just the wrong time. There was nothing I could have done to stop it. I know Mr Sean had told him, but I wanted to tell him myself.'

'So what happened?'

'I ... well, I got to the church and it looked pretty full. Whites only. I didn't go in, I just looked through the door. I felt out of place, not wanted. I was about to go when this priest came round the side of the church. He greeted me. I greeted him back, then as I was not moving on, he asked me what I wanted. He was a bit suspicious of me I guess. Anyway I thought that since he was a priest he would understand so I explained to him that I had come to the funeral of Mrs Stander and that I was the security guard that shot her and that it had been an accident. That I only wanted to tell Mr Stander that I was sorry. I thought he would chase me away, but he was a kind man. He understood why I was there.

'When I had finished explaining he nodded quietly then said to me, "You can't go in there, you will not be welcome. Come with me." I followed him round the side of the church and he led me through a small door and up some stairs. These took us to a gallery where I could see the whole of the funeral yet no-one could see me. "It will do no good talking to Mr Stander," the priest told me. "He is in mourning; he does not want to see the man who killed his wife, even if it was an accident. He needs to find someone to blame for what has happened and he blames you. That robber that you were trying to kill, he is the real cause of Mrs Stander's death. Mr Stander knows this, but that guy is dead so he cannot target his anger on him, he will take it out on you as you are the next best thing."

'I was very grateful to that priest. He was kind and I guess he was right. Mr Stander would not want to see me at that time. He was too upset. Maybe he has forgiven me now. I would like to know. I would like to meet him now and see if he has accepted that it was an accident. I would hate to think that he still holds me responsible. But I will never know.

'Anyway I sat and watched the funeral from that hiding place. It was very different to the funerals I was used to. With black funerals there is a lot more ... wailing, is that the word? And singing. We make a lot more noise about seeing off our dead. These white people were very quiet. I could see some were crying, but they were doing so quietly into their handkerchiefs. The service was solemn, the hymns were very sad.

'I felt sad, not only for Mr Stander and his family, but also sad that it did not seem to be a proper funeral. To me it was not the right way to say goodbye to the dead. I watched as the coffin was taken from the church. There were these really big Afrikaaner guys, like rugby players, Francois Pienaar and his type, that carried the coffin. I remember thinking about whether Marie Stander had a spirit. You know like we blacks believe in the spirits of our ancestors. I had never thought about whether white people also had spirits. It was only now when you told me about seeing Elise at her funeral that I realised that white people also have spirits.'

Deon was surprised by this. He had never really thought about the issue and, even after seeing Elise at the funeral, he still never believed in spirits or ghosts. He just assumed that his vision was an aftershock; that it was his mind conjuring up these images to try and fill the gap left by Elise's death.

'I was sort of hoping that I would see the spirit of Marie Stander …'

He let the sentence hang for a second then went on, 'I was hoping she would give me a sign that she understood that I meant her no harm. But it never happened. They took the coffin away and all the people walked slowly out of the church. I was crying as I watched them go, especially when I saw the little ones who I was sure were her children. It was strange I wasn't mourning for the dead, but for the living. I was sorry for their loss.

'Where I was sitting was near where the sound from the organ came and it was really loud at the end when they played the music as the people went out of the church. I remember how the music stopped suddenly and how quiet it seemed. I suppose the silence filled the space left by Marie Stander. Where she was a mother and a wife, there would now be no sound when she talked, no movement when she moved, and even if she was sitting still and not moving there would be a silence in her not being there. But now all that sound was gone for the Stander family. They were left with nothing but silence.'

Deon listened and was impressed by the insight shown by a man who he had thought would be quite simple due to his station in life. The idea of the silence filling the void was particularly poignant to him. He had felt that silence acutely in the first few weeks after Elise was gone. Even now, despite the presence of Sharon, there was still a lot of silence in his life that could never be replaced with the joyful noise of Elise again.

Yes Sharon had eased some of the pain and had removed the physical silence that had engulfed the house, but she had never, and could never fill that mental silence that ate away at him. This was an unfillable silence.

'It's strange,' Simon's voice filled the silence that had taken over the lift.

'What's strange?'

'You'd think that in killing someone you would not have a feeling of loss, but I did. I had a terrible sense of loss. It was not the loss of Marie Stander that worried me so much, although that was terrible, it was the loss of the innocence that I had had until then. I was never guilty of killing anyone before that, but here I was, a killer of another human being. It was like when things were getting really bad in the townships after Mandela was released and before the elections. The black man lost his innocence then. Before that we did as we were told. Yes there were a lot of unjust laws and unjust behaviour that was directed at us by the police. We lost many young people …'

He stopped. He had not realised that this line of thought would lead to where it had, to another memory, a sharper memory that dug into his flesh like a barbed thorn. A memory for which there was no cure, no ointment that could relieve the pain.

He pushed hard against it and with an effort went on, '… and we also lost many old people, but back then it was the whites killing us. When we started killing each other, we lost our innocence. It's a bit like your virginity. When you lose it, you can never regain it.'

Deon was startled at having his loss of virginity compared to killing someone. It was a strange comparison, but it made sense in an odd way. You did feel a change had occurred when you had crossed that threshold, and killing someone undoubtedly created that same feeling of having moved on in your life, moved to another level, albeit an entirely different place you moved to.

His mind went back to the evening when he had first had sex, proper sex, not just a quick grope. He was sixteen, quite old by today's standards he knew, but back then he was one of the first in his class to have gone all the way. Sally, that was her name. He felt a strange sense of relief that he could remember her name. He always did feel guilty when he forgot a woman's name in the morning and that had happened quite a few times in his life.

It was not that he attached something hugely important to a one-night stand. He had always been quite particular to ensure that the girl was after the same thing as him, a night of sex, no emotional strings attached.

Before Elise he had been somewhat promiscuous, not as bad as some of his friends, but he certainly had slept around a bit. After Elise, after a suitable time of mourning, he had become almost reckless in his sleeping around. It was as though he wanted to exact some sort of revenge on womanhood for having been deserted by one of their number. He had even gone to a prostitute once where the sex had bordered on violent. But that phase had soon passed as it gave him no solace for his loss, and, his conscience began to kick in, telling him that he was defiling Elise's memory, that it was not her fault that she was gone.

This sobering up didn't stop him sleeping with women, but his motives changed. He now sought out the motherly comfort that only women could give and it became important at least to remember their names. That was the polite thing to do. He did recall once when he had remembered a girl's name without any difficulty and had been quite hurt when she called him Dave when she left. He laughed about it later but at the time it had stung.

Sally. She had been an attractive girl although nothing overly special. There were far prettier girls in his class, but Sally was the only one that he got close to who was prepared to go all the way. He had groped various breasts and occasionally had managed to get his hand up a skirt in his quest to satisfy his adolescent curiosity, but most of the others had stopped him before he got too far.

It had been at a party. He and Sally had danced for a bit, then she said she was tired of dancing and wanted some fresh air. They went out to the back yard which was dimly lit by a bright moon. Once outside he searched for her hand which she willingly gave. Slowly he brought her closer and began kissing.

When she responded with more enthusiasm than he had hoped for he got quite excited and, thrusting his tongue into her mouth as he had heard other boys talk about doing, he had groped at her young breasts. 'Not here,' she had gasped and leading him by the hand guided him to a secluded place behind the garage. On that balmy evening, on the grass behind the garage of Glenn Davies' parents' place he had fumbled his way awkwardly to manhood.

Afterwards, to his surprise Sally had just tidied herself up and walked off. She had ignored him for the rest of the evening and, despite his trying to reconnect with her the next week at school she remained aloof. The thought of using a condom, or of her getting pregnant never entered his mind. Aids was something that would not rear its ugly head for a little while, so safe sex back then meant finding somewhere to do it without getting caught.

It was only years later that he realised that Sally's disgust with him had been because he had finished up too quickly without a thought for her needs.

'I can never get that innocence back.' Simon's voice roughly pushed Sally and her needs aside. 'We can never get it back.'

Deon nodded in the dark, more from a feeling of a need to agree rather than actually understanding what Simon was talking about.

'You have lost a loved one,' Simon continued, 'but you have never been the cause of a loved one to be lost.' Deon's head jerked round to the direction the words came from as a different memory suddenly boiled up in his mind. He sat quietly trying to keep a lid on the new emotions that had been stirred up.

Simon meanwhile continued, 'It is hard losing a loved one, but it is also hard to be the cause of someone else to lose a loved one. It would have been easier I suppose if I had not met Mr Stander face to face and even easier if I had not gone to the funeral.'

The conversation had taken a strange turn and Deon was still pulling up his trousers after being with Sally. He was not sure what Simon was getting at and his new thoughts confused him, but before he could try and figure it out, Simon took off in another direction.

'How long have we been in here?' The lack of light was beginning to annoy Simon. The talk had become dark, and like Deon he now felt powerless, powerless to change what had gone before.

'Let's talk about something else,' he said before Deon could even speculate as to how long they had been in the lift. It was a cease-fire, not a peace. More had to be said, more lives were to be lost before the night was done. But for the moment, they needed a breathing space. This was a climbing out of the trenches to play a game of soccer on a muddy pitch.

'What has been your best moment in the New South Africa?'

This threw Deon. He had never been asked such a question, let alone ever thought about it. Still he was glad that Simon had made the move to bring the talk round to something more cheerful.

'Gee, I don't know,' he answered buying some time to think. 'I guess there was winning the Rugby World Cup the first time around. That was pretty special. After years in the sporting wilderness we came back and won straight off. It was like we had been saying all along during apartheid, we had the best rugby team in the world.'

Simon chuckled, 'Ja and then what happened? They couldn't win anything for ages.'

'Hmmm, you've got a point. We didn't really do too well after that for a good while. Our cricket is not so hot sometimes either. We keep finding the most heart breaking ways of going out of the World Cup. I don't know. I guess there haven't been too many great moments in the New South Africa.'

Simon shook his head, a wry smile hidden by the darkness. He clicked his tongue. 'You whities,' he said, 'you just see the bad. If the rugby team is doing well, then everything is just fine, but as soon as we don't do well at sports, then there is nothing good happening. Let me tell you about a few of the highlights of the New South Africa for me. Firstly there was Nelson Mandela being released, now that was a great day. Then, probably the most exciting day of my life was when I voted for the first time.'

'Huh? Voting the most exciting day of your life.'

'For sure! Hau! You whities! You grew up knowing you would vote when you were old enough, knowing that you would always have a say in the country. You have no idea what it was like to be without the vote, without a voice. You talk about having been powerless to stop those guys from killing Elise. Well you try and live in a country in which you were born yet have no say in how it is run. Where you are treated as a second-class citizen, no not even second-class, treated as though you aren't even a citizen of your own country. Were you powerless to stop people treading on you, pushing you down everyday? Where you are denied any of the riches you see those around you enjoying? Imagine then what it was like to finally have a chance to change that. That is a special time. That is exciting.'

There was no venom in what Simon was saying. He was trying to teach, trying to explain something that he was surprised that this educated white man could not see.

'I cannot begin to describe to you the feelings I had on that historic day.'

27 APRIL 1994

It was a crisp morning when Simon woke just after five o'clock. He washed his face in the small enamel dish, the pungent odour of the Sunlight soap he used permeating the dark little shack that was lit by a single white candle. He put on his shirt and peered out of the small, dirty window into the gloom outside as he buttoned himself up.

'Hau!' he exclaimed, his eyes widening as he stared out at the line of people who stood in the dusty road outside his home. 'Surely they cannot be queuing already,' he said to himself, but quickly fumbled for his shoes and put them on without bothering to look for his socks. Then, snuffing out the candle, he hurried outside.

'Hey Simon, you planning to sleep through the election?' It was Ezekiel, his next door neighbour who was standing in the queue which, to Simon's dismay, stretched down the road and round the corner. It was a light-hearted jibe and those around Ezekiel laughed good-naturedly. Simon stared at the queue then back at Ezekiel. Suddenly a big grin flashed across his face.

'All good things come to those who wait,' he replied, picking up on the party mood of the queue.

'Well you'd better be getting a move on or we will have used up all the votes before you get there. You never know with the whites, they have probably rationed our votes.' Ezekiel grinned at him. Simon panicked and started running towards the end of the line.

'Hey Simon, you got your ID with you?' Ezekiel called after him.

'ID?' Simon stopped. 'There are no more pass laws.' At this most of those listening to the banter burst out laughing. Simon grinned nervously not quite sure what the joke was that he had just made.

'You need your ID to vote with remember?' Ezekiel said. 'Didn't you see all the adverts about voting?'

'Oh shit!' Simon dashed back towards his shack somewhat embarrassed, but this quickly passed, today was too big a day to worry about a small humiliation. Once inside he fumbled in the gloom for the matches and lit the candle, then found his identity document and snuffing out the light for the second time that morning hurried outside again, holding the little green book aloft and, enjoying the cheers that the crowd gave. He ran along the line of people till he eventually got to the end where he stood panting next to an elderly couple.

They smiled gently at him, their eyes showing their excitement about the day and what it was bringing. The sun was beginning to push up over the horizon while he stood regaining his breath and watched a few other stragglers join the queue behind him. He nodded at them, the excitement of the elderly couple was spreading to those around him and he was catching it too. This was the day when he could finally have a say. When he would get to vote for the first time. His eyes took on the excited sheen that was glowing in those of his fellow first time voters.

Once he had regained his breath he struck up a conversation with the couple in front of him. He recognised them as living in the area, but had never got to know them.

'Eric Ngubani and this is my wife Constance,' they introduced themselves. Eric had worked as a mail room clerk in the city and Constance as a maid to a rich family in the northern suburbs of Johannesburg. They were both retired.

As the sun began to climb, the excitement grew amongst those waiting. The polling booths would soon be open. They listened to the radio reports coming through on a ghetto blaster that someone had brought with. Mandela had voted! A cheer went up. FW de Klerk had also cast his vote. A jeer passed through the crowd, but it was good-natured. They could smell success. Today was the day that the white man lost his power over them officially. Today was the day that Nelson Mandela would be voted in as President. They could all feel it.

A long borne yolk was finally being lifted from their shoulders. Today they were to be set free to become citizens in their own country. The excitement was tangible. It spread like a large blanket over the memories of the past forty years. It covered the many graves that lined the road to freedom and warmed those hearts made cold by many years of hatred. They would not forget those who had died on the way, but today was about looking forward and celebrating.

There was a certain sadness that clung to those who had lost loved ones, a sadness that those dear to them had not lived to see this day, that they couldn't share in the excitement. But there was also the knowledge that they had not died in vain. Their sacrifice had brought the longed for freedom.

The day was now fully underway and some of the initial enthusiasm began to melt as the queue had not moved. Simon was still standing outside the light blue house that he had arrived at that morning. The old couple were still standing patiently in front of him and the line stretched off in both directions, snaking through the dusty streets of the township.

Then news began to filter down the line – there were no ballot papers! Immediately the old suspicions rose in the group. Were the whites sabotaging the process? Had they played this horrible trick on the people, leading them to believe that they would get a say, then taking it all away from them again. Surely not. Where was Mandela? He would sort it out. He was a free man, they couldn't lock him up again, not with the whole world watching.

Voices began to be raised, tongues were clicked and hands began to fly in angry dismissive gestures. It was turning sour. Their great day was being taken from them. What were the officials doing to sort this problem out?

'What's happening? Why are there no ballot papers?'

'What are the whites doing? Do they want a bloodbath?'

'Who is in charge? Where are the election officials? We demand to know what is happening.'

Those around Simon took up the mood and the tensions rose. Simon was angry too, but also nervous. If things spilt over there would be a lot of violence. He glanced around quickly, trying to determine the best way to run if things did turn sour.

Near the corner up ahead a group of foreign journalists were gathering, cameras at the ready. They sensed the growing disquiet and wanted to get the shots should anything happen.

Then an army vehicle rolled down the road, the white troopies stared out with some menace at the queue, guns at the ready, daring anyone to step over the mark. The people stared sullenly back.

Then just as things were close to boiling over, word came through that the ballot papers had arrived and by way of confirmation, the queue began to move slowly. A large cheer went up and the mood switched again.

The press disappeared and the army vehicle rolled back up the road, this time the white kids smiled and some even waved. It was going to be all right.

Simon and the old couple began to edge towards having their say. It was late afternoon when they finally moved round a corner and they could see the polling station ahead of them. The old woman was quite exhausted and her husband was not much better, but neither would leave the queue, not even to go and get a drink. They both stood stoically waiting for their turn. They were now outside Simon's house and he negotiated with those behind him that he be allowed to pop inside quickly and get something to drink for the old folk.

He returned quickly with a jug of cold water that he kept in the fridge, some glasses and a loaf of bread. He shared the water out amongst those around him, ensuring that the elderly couple got first before handing it on to the others. He then did the same with the bread. The old couple accepted this small gift gratefully.

'Bread and water,' Simon laughed, 'this is like people in prison. All they get is bread to eat and water to drink.'

'Ah yes,' the old man grinned, 'but this is our last meal as prisoners. That there,' he pointed up towards the polling station, 'that is our gate to freedom.'

Freedom. The word tasted good on the tongue and Simon looked towards the small brick building that was slowly allowing people through to that wonderful world beyond, a world where he would be regarded as a human being.

THE LIFT 12

Deon listened to Simon tell his story about the day he finally got to vote. He had never really thought much about it. For him it had been like a normal voting day. A public holiday was called and it was nice to have a day off work. Yes the queue and the wait had been longer than usual, but in the nice clean white suburbs, it was sort of business as usual.

It was a bit strange having blacks in the line with him. Most of those voting in the white suburbs were live-in maids so it was a bit like they were there only to look after the children while the white parents went to vote. The excitement that these maids must have been feeling was suppressed where he was because they were in the minority at this polling station, he supposed. They would have felt they could not show too much joy for fear of upsetting their employers. The small bit of chatter that did pass between them was full of smiles, but he could not understand the Zulu or Sotho or whatever it was they were speaking.

There had been a slight sense of being part of an historic moment, but when all around you seemed normal it was difficult to get a real sense of making history. Deon had stood with Sharon in the queue. He couldn't really recall what they had talked about. He did remember spending a little time thinking about Elise and how she would have felt on that day. She would have been smiling, no doubt about that. This would have been as much her day as it was for all those black maids around them. She had made her sacrifice years back when she left her father's house, refusing to succumb to his racist ways. She would have felt vindicated, perhaps she would even have been laughing at the discomfort Mr Swart would be feeling going off to vote in an election that he knew his people had no chance of winning.

He had tried to imagine what it would have been like standing in that queue with Elise beside him. There would have been a small child with them, he had realised with a slight shock.

These thoughts were short lived as Sharon's voice had broken through them, offering to pay a small entrance fee to be privy to what was happening in his mind. This annoyed him and he dismissed Sharon's request along with the memory.

'You know I never really thought about what that day meant to you guys. Remember this was the old days, I didn't know any black people back then who I could talk to about how they were feeling. Come to think of it, I still don't know any black people who I could talk to about their feelings. Times have changed, but some things still stay the same I guess.'

Simon smiled quietly to himself again. He still didn't get it, this rich white business man. He was educated and had money, yet he could not see what was sitting right under his nose. What had the two of them been doing for the past hour or so? It was quite shocking to Simon that someone could seem so important, yet be so oblivious to the obvious. He decided not to say anything, let this man work it out for himself.

'But it was a pretty special day in the country's history. I mean we were all expecting a bloodbath. Things seemed to be heading that way and then suddenly we were a democracy and there was no bloodshed.' Deon carried on, suddenly feeling the pressure of political correctness and the need to make out that, yes that had been an exceptional day, but in reality for him not much had changed. Elise was still dead, and that was all that seemed to matter.

'Oh, but there was bloodshed,' Simon said. A touch of venom was injected into his voice as memories came back to him. 'There were people dying all the time in the townships, lots of blood flowed on those streets then. We have even been talking about blood having been shed in our own lives. You with Elise, me with Mrs Stander.'

'Ja, but they weren't political deaths.'

'No, they weren't directly political deaths, but the politics of the country had created the environment that caused them. What was it you talked about earlier, indoctrination by environment? That was what was happening. We were sucked into a world where crime and violence was normal. Killing someone to steal a car means nothing, robbing a bank using guns means nothing to people these days. Life is cheap.'

Deon was surprised at the insight shown by his companion and had to remind himself that this was a security guard, someone who supposedly had little education. Yet here he was talking about life and showing a great deal of wisdom. Wisdom doesn't always come with wealth, he thought.

'I suppose there was a political element to Elise's death,' he said. It didn't make it any easier to accept. Political or not, she was still dead, nothing could bring her back. His mind stretched across his life and he realised that the comfort and luxury he had enjoyed had come at a high cost and that cost was the loss of Elise. But there were other ways in which he had paid. As his thoughts flittered over the landscape of his life, there was another jagged intrusion on the otherwise smooth terrain. Elise was a big blip, but there was something else that stuck out, something he did not like to remember.

Like the Elise story it was one that he didn't want to revisit. It was one that he had pushed back even further into the recesses of his mind than the vicious killing of his girlfriend. When Elise had arrived in his life, she had helped him to forget about the incident, not by telling her the story, but by her positive presence.

Simon took note of his reply and smiled quietly to himself as he realised that Deon was beginning to learn. It was a good feeling being able to teach a white man something. For so long it had always seemed as if the black man had everything to learn and the white everything to teach. He liked this role reversal.

'Of course there was a political element to her death. South Africa is a country built on politics. It is a complicated country with many different people. Madiba calls us the Rainbow Nation remember? There are people of all colours and cultures so everything will be political.'

Deon nodded. 'Ja, I suppose you're right.'

It felt a bit strange admitting that a black man knew more about something than he did. He was slightly embarrassed by this because it was he who had had the privileged upbringing and therefore should have known more about these issues, but he had not. He had rather let the aim of accumulating greater wealth become more important.

Now he was beginning to feel uncomfortable with the conversation. It was making him feel inferior and he didn't like that. He was used to giving the orders, being the one in the know, the knowledgeable one. He wanted to move the conversation on and decided to try and put Simon on the back foot again.

'You know earlier you were saying that it's as hard to cause someone to lose a loved one as it is to actually lose a loved one yourself. Surely it's harder to lose someone than to kill someone.'

Simon lifted his head in the direction that Deon's voice was coming from. 'I have been the cause of a loved one being lost and I have also lost a loved one. I know the feelings I had each time and believe me, they were both as bad. Different in many ways, but in both cases I felt terrible. When I killed that Marie Stander I felt terrible. I had taken away the loved one of someone else. I lost someone close to me, so I knew how that felt. Knowing I had caused others to feel as bad as I felt then was a horrible feeling.'

Simon didn't want to talk about these things anymore, but Deon was determined to move the conversation that way, he felt safer, less threatened by this.

'You have never caused a loved one to be lost, so how can you make the comparison.' Simon threw the comment at Deon and it hit him hard

He was just about to respond when Simon went on. 'I will always remember the pain, how it seemed to drive into me like an ice cold spear. No matter what I did I could not shake that cold. Whenever I think of

Mr Stander coping with the loss of Mrs Stander, I always believe that he has those same feelings that I had.'

'Tell me about losing your loved one. When was is? Who was it?'

Deon's voice sounded slightly hoarse but he had the outlet he needed to change the direction of the conversation, change it to put him in charge again. He was controlling while trying to control the emotions that were bubbling up in him again.

Simon hesitated. He didn't really want to share his story with this white guy, but he reasoned that since Deon had told him about Elise he should talk about his own loss. It would give substance to his argument.

'It was a political killing.' His voice was neutral, it held no hatred for the killer, it was matter of fact. 'Straightforward, not like Elise, or Mrs Stander. They were victims of circumstance, of the environment. This was outright political.'

'Who was it?' Deon repeated the question, his tone was aggressive. It was as though he wanted Simon to re-live the pain of loss, the way he had just re-lived Elise's death. He realised this and quickly asked in a gentler tone, 'someone very close?'

Simon sighed and shook his head as the memories came back. 'Yes, it was my brother Peter.'

PETER

As youngsters, Peter was slightly taller than Simon, but not by enough. He was the eldest and that had to show in a superior height, the mere half-inch he had on his brother failed to do the job and consequently he would walk with his heels raised to try and give him that extra elevation. At first he would only do that when others were around, relaxing and sinking back that half-inch when he and Simon were alone together tending their father's cows. But the part-time habit slowly became the norm until he got his first pair of shoes. He took them to the local cobbler and had an extra half-inch added to the heel.

But the shoes took a long time coming into their lives so the two boys would run around barefoot behind the lumbering cattle that fed lazily *en route* to the river to drink each day. The intense blue of the skies would bake the earth and a hard crust quickly formed on the soles of the young feet. Shoes were for cities and cities were far off magical lands that existed only in the stories of the village elders. The buzz and activity of those spoken of places were hard to imagine for the boys as they spent their days lazily guarding the beasts that practically took care of themselves.

Other than the height issue which Simon was completely unaware of, there was a strong bond of kinship and friendship between the boys who played well together, seldom quarrelling. They once lost a cow when out tending the herd and while it was beyond doubt that it was Peter's fault, Simon stood beside his brother in accepting the blame and insisted on going first in receiving the blows from their father's switch, thus allowing Peter to have the slightly less severe punishment from a tired arm.

Schooling, an erratic activity for the boys, came courtesy of the missionaries. The sisters were stern teachers, but with class sizes approaching the hundred mark, little control could be exercised and absenteeism went unnoticed. Simon's superior skills with the little schoolwork they did were not a source of conflict or competition between the boys with Peter placing scant credence in the work, seeing little use for the strange language the sister spoke and what did multiplication have to do with cows, they only added to their number.

Life was quite idyllic for the boys. The days were warm, their parents loved them and, even when food was scarce, their mother made sure that they were well fed, even at the expense of her own sustenance. But fate has a nasty way of upsetting things and an outbreak of an unknown disease wiped out the family's herd of cows and they had barely come to terms with this loss when their father fell ill and quickly followed his cows into the world of his ancestors.

The teenagers buried him as tradition dictated and after a time of mourning, Peter said to Simon, 'I am going to go to eGoli, they say that there is work there in Johannesburg. I will make money to send back to you and mother to help. Then when I have enough, I will build a house for you to come and live with me.'

But Simon answered, 'I will come with you. If both of us go, then we can make two times as much money and the house will be built quicker. Then we can send for mother to come and live with us there. She will live like a queen.'

Their mother cried when they told her of their plans, but she knew it was the best thing. Without a husband, they would struggle to make enough to make ends meet in that harsh land. The rains seemed to be coming less often and she didn't want her sons to starve. So while she cried many tears, she let them go with her blessing and told them not to take too long to build the house so that she could live with them again.

Once in Johannesburg, the boys soon discovered that it was not the place of gold that the name eGoli suggested. They struggled to find work or somewhere to live, but luck was on their side and they met a man from their region who allowed them to sleep on the floor of his shack. He was a security guard who worked nights and rented the shack out to the boys for a small fee. They could stay while he was at work, but during the day they had to be out of the house so that he could sleep.

It was through this man that Simon eventually got a job as a security guard. Peter, however, held out for a mine job. 'They pay better at the mines and I don't want to be a security guard,' he said. Simon nodded, but did not agree with his brother's decision.

Unfortunately the mining industry was going through a bad patch and jobs were scarce so the boys had to survive on what little money Simon brought home. Driven by his promise to build a house for their mother, Peter swallowed his pride and managed to get a part-time gardening job where he worked hard and impressed his white employer. One day as a reward for his work, they gave him a large box of sweets on top of his salary. Instead of eating them, Peter sold off the sweets separately when he got back to the township and made a small sum of money. The next week, when he went back to work, he asked his employer if he could buy another box of sweets, explaining what he had done with the previous one. He showed them the money he had made and was delighted when they told him he could almost buy two for that amount.

They were impressed with his ingenuity and entrepreneurship and agreed to help him set up a small business, where they would buy things for him wholesale and he could then sell them on retail in the townships where shops were scarce.

The business took off and Peter slowly built up enough capital to rent a shack which he turned into a small shop, selling sweets, cold drinks, cigarettes, matches and other such items to passers-by. The shack was big enough for him to live in the rooms at the back, so he moved out of the room he was sharing with Simon.

Simon was also doing well out of his guard duties and their savings towards a house for their mother grew. But the political situation in the country was getting tense and violence spread through the townships. Peter and Simon managed to keep out of trouble, but the violence had a tendency to strike anywhere without notice.

THE LIFT 13

'Your brother?' Deon's tone held more sympathy. He had been an only child and could not relate to the death of a sibling, but he did appreciate that Simon's loss must be something akin to his loss of Elise and he tried to convey that in his voice.

'Yes, my brother Peter.'

'What happened? You said it was political.'

Simon closed his eyes in the dark of the lift, an image of Peter's dead body floated up in front of him and he half gasped at the intensity of the image. The talk of violent death had sharpened his visual memory, and he opened his eyes again, hoping the image would go. It faded slowly.

'Yes, it was political. My brother Peter owned a small shop in our part of Soweto. He was a good man who never harmed anyone. He was honest and did not cheat people when they came to buy from him. People liked him, he was friendly, always smiling.'

'Sounds like a nice guy.'

'Yes he was,' Simon gave a small laugh as he remembered the good things about Peter, forcing the painful memory aside. 'He was my best friend as well as my brother. We came to Johannesburg together from our village and we didn't know anybody else so we stuck together.

'Anyway, Peter owned this shop and he had a lot of good customers. They would come in everyday wanting sweets or cigarettes. He was a good salesman and remembered what everyone liked – Twenty Marlborough for Big Man Maloi, a can of Cream Soda for little Jimmy Duduzile and a Kit Kat every day for Mama Mazibuko,' he chuckled at the last name, 'No wonder she was so large Mama Mazibuko, Peter used to say she was Kit Kat Fat.'

Deon laughed loudly at this, almost too loudly and too forced. He desperately needed this commercial break. 'Have a break, have a Kit Kat,' he chuckled, 'Maybe she should have had a break from eating Kit Kats.'

'Ja,' chuckled Simon. 'She was a lovely lady though, Mama Mazibuko. You know she was the only one of Peter's customers who came to his funeral. I guess people were too scared back then, but she came. She was a woman with great dignity.'

The laughter that had been set off by this dignified woman subsided as Simon remembered his brother's funeral, his mood went with the laughter.

'Hau!' he said, 'that was a sad day that.'

'You're jumping the gun a bit my friend,' Deon said, consciously using the word *friend* to try and coax more out of Simon, but not thinking that using the word *gun* might not be the best choice. 'You have not told me how he died yet and you're already at his funeral.'

This was insensitive but Deon didn't see it. He had started to build up a mental image of the set up that Peter had operated and, given all those names that Simon had mentioned, the people he imagined were decidedly black. At times in the dark lift it had been a little bit difficult to remember that Simon was black, but now that Deon had these images in his mind, he behaved with less sympathy towards Simon. It was an entrenched reaction to black people that Deon was completely oblivious to.

Simon sighed inwardly as the subtle old ways showed through in Deon. He knew it was not being done deliberately, that Deon was unaware he was doing it, but he was saddened that it was still there to be felt, to be endured. His mind flickered over his two children and the hope he had that they would not have to put up with these things when they grew up.

'Yes, you are quite right, I have not told you about how Peter was killed. It is not an easy story to tell, so please be patient with me. Have a break, have a Kit Kat.'

They both chuckled although inwardly Simon was hoping that the lights would suddenly come on and the lift continue its descent. Then there would be no way he would have to recall this episode in his life as the harsh lights would show up their differences. But the dark and silence persisted.

He took Deon's silence as a tacit agreement to be patient and was grateful for this and went on.

'As I was saying, Peter ran this little shop and lived in the back room. He had been looking to buy his own place when he was killed. He had saved up enough money to go and live somewhere nice.

'I remember he opened an account at a building society, you remember that ad that went "John's joined the building society"? Can't remember which building society the ad was for. Can you?'

'No, I can't think which one it was just now. I remember the ad though.'

'Well anyway, I used to tease him and say "Peter's joined the building society" in that voice that they use in the advert. I wasn't being horrible or jealous, Peter knew that as he would laugh at me every time I said it.

'He had saved up all this money in this building society account, nearly enough to buy a house with.'

'Did you inherit the money?'

Deon's question was once again brash and insensitive. Simon shook his head in the dark. What did the money matter? This was typical of the white businessman. Nothing but money mattered. They didn't care how many lives they trod on to get more money, how many people had to live in poverty so that you could live a life of luxury.

'A little bit, most of it went to pay for the funeral,' he let his voice ignore his thoughts.

'Didn't he have an Avbob policy.'

'An Avbob policy?'

'Yes, you know, the insurance. You pay a small amount into it each month and then if you die, it pays for the funeral. You've never heard of Avbob?'

'Ah, yes. I remember hearing about it a long time ago. Some white man tried to sell us a policy. We didn't trust the white man back then so we didn't buy one.'

'Do you trust the white man now?' Deon asked, feeling a little impertinent, but at the same time intrigued.

The pause was short, almost imperceptible, but it was there.

'Nowadays it is easier to trust the white man,' Simon said diplomatically.

Deon opened his mouth to ask, 'Do you trust me?' but thought better of it. It was a stupid question to ask even though he did wonder if his companion did trust him enough to open up the way he had, however he feared that the answer would be no.

The question played on Simon's mind. Did he trust Deon and what exactly was meant by trust? He and Peter had not trusted the white man to be honest about the Avbob policy, but Deon was not asking if he could be trusted to look after his money. It was more a general trust, a trust that he could tell his story without being ridiculed or worse, using the information against him in some way.

But what could a white man do with the information about his brother being killed? It was unlikely that he would have any political affiliations that could cause trouble, whites were never ANC or Inkhata. Anyway that was all in the past, the old animosities were not so sharp anymore. On top of that, Deon had told his whole story about Elise and had even broken down and cried. Surely he had a greater hold over Deon than Deon would over him if he told his story. No man would want others to know that he had cried.

He was in the clear over the Mrs Stander story, Mr Sean saw to that. There was nothing he could think of that Deon could use against him. So yes, in this case, he could trust Deon.

'He lived at the back of the shop as I said,' Simon decided to go on. He had no choice really; it would be rude to tell this white man it was none of his business.

'This was when all the trouble was happening in the townships. We were quite lucky as there wasn't too much trouble where we lived to start with, but every now and then things would spill over and we'd have to run and hide in our houses as the ANC and Inkhata guys would be fighting in our street. Do you have any idea what it is like to live where there are gunfights going on?'

The question took Deon by surprise. There had never been gunfights in his quiet, white suburban street. This was a silly question. Of course he had no idea what it was like. Gunfights were things that happened in the townships and on TV in war torn zones or in cowboy movies. Nothing like that would ever happen in his street. He realised that Simon was not asking the question to get an answer, he knew the answer already. Still he went ahead.

'No, of course I don't,' Deon tried to make the answer not sound too dismissive, but failed horribly. Simon laughed quietly to himself at this reply. He knew he had put Deon in an uncomfortable position and revelled in the feeling of power that it gave him. It was not often that he had the upper hand with a white man.

'Well we had to live with it. You would be going about your business and you would hear the Blam! Blam! Blam! of gunfire getting closer. Then you would rush to get home before they reached your road. You could hear it getting louder and louder. BLAM! BLAM! BLAM!' Simon shouted the last sound affects causing Deon to jump slightly.

'Geez, I get the idea, you don't have to shout. You gave me a fright there.'

'Sorry. But you can now imagine what it was like for us.' Simon smiled in the dark, still enjoying the hold he had over Deon. If you weren't close enough to home you would dive into the nearest house you could. We all knew each other in the area and often when the fighters came you would find shelter at someone else's place, or have someone come running into yours. It was the way we lived back then.

'I remember one day I ended up running for cover into Mama Mazibuko's house, you remember the Kit Kat woman. That was a bad day, there was heavy fighting all around the township. The Inkhata people were running away from the ANC people I think. I was too far from my home so I ran into Mama Mazibuko's which was nearby. She had just got home herself, but had not yet heard the guns. She was a bit deaf. As soon as she saw me she realised what was happening and we both ducked down beneath the windows, waiting for the fighters to go past.

'They came nearer till we could hear them just up the street. The gunfire was heavy; there must have been lots of fighters out that day. Anyway, they came closer and closer until they were just outside and then suddenly a bullet came through the window shattering the glass. Mama Mazibuko screamed and I think I must have shouted in fear. It all happened so fast, I can't remember all the details.

'I calmed down when I realised that we had not been hit, but Mama Mazibuko would not stop screaming. I was so scared that the fighters would hear her and come into the house so I moved her away from the window and put my arm around her patting her like a little child to try to calm her down. "It's okay, it's okay," I kept saying till she was calm enough not to scream more when another bullet came through the broken window and smashed a glass that was on the table. She jumped but made no sound. I think she nearly suffocated me then as she squeezed me hard.

'We were sitting there waiting for the fighting to pass as it usually did when suddenly the door of the house flew open and a man stepped in. He was one of the fighters and was holding a gun. My hand went up over Mama Mazibuko's mouth to stop her screaming again.

'We stared at him and he stared back at us. My heart was pounding I was so scared. I couldn't tell if he was ANC or Inkhata, it was often difficult to know. I was sure he was going to ask us who we supported and if we got it wrong he would kill us. It seemed to take forever that moment when we were just staring at each other. But then I noticed that his eyes were not seeing us. He was staring but not seeing. It was then that he fell to the floor. It was like his legs had melted.

'I knew then that we were safe, that this guy had been shot and was probably now dead. We watched him fall, slowly, slowly, slowly. But then suddenly, as he hit the floor, his gun shot off a bullet BLAM! It just missed us but did make a hole in the wall near my head. It was my turn to scream. We sat there for a long time, me and Mama Mazibuko, hugging each other and staring at the gunfighter lying on the floor. I knew that he was injured and maybe dead, but I couldn't make my legs work to go over and see.

'Then another bullet came through the open door and hit the wall on the other side of the house. This made me realise that I had to do something, so I made Mama Mazibuko let go of me, that was not easy as she was holding on so tightly, but I managed to break free and then crept over to the door and shut it. Then I moved slowly to where the gunman lay.

'He was lying face down and I could see the blood coming out of a wound at the back of his head. So much blood. It was making this great big pool on the floor, all over the place. I ...'

'Enough about the blood,' Deon interrupted rudely. He was getting flashbacks of Elise's head wound and this was unsettling. 'Get on with the story,' he growled.

Simon was surprised by the outburst, but quickly realised the reason and held back his own anger at the interruption. 'I looked over to Mama Mazibuko and her eyes asked the question. I nodded. Yes, he was dead. She lowered her head and crossed herself. She was a good Christian woman. We didn't know what to do. They were still fighting outside so we could not go out, but we were also scared that someone might burst in, see the body and think we had shot him. We sat there for a long time, just worrying and staring at the dead man, hoping and praying that no-one would come in. At last the fighting moved off and I left Mama Mazibuko, telling her I was going to get help. Peter's shop was nearby so I ran over to him. He was just looking up over the counter checking to see if the fighters had moved on when I got there.

'He was frightened, but that was not unusual back then. We all feared for our lives. One of the windows of the shop had been shot out and later he told me how the bullet had just missed him. But we had more important things to deal with just then. What were we to do with the body?

'I quickly told him what had happened. "Was he Inkhata or ANC?" Peter asked me. Of course I didn't know, they never wore uniforms. He was in torn jeans and a T-shirt, there were no badges or anything, just normal clothes. You generally didn't want to give away which side you were on, especially if you were out on your own.

'Maybe if he had spoken I could have guessed. If he spoke Zulu that would mean Inkhata, Sotho would mean ANC although that wasn't always the case. But he never said a word, just came into the house and died. Anyway I didn't want to hang around. Mama Mazibuko was alone in her house with the body and the fighters could come back at any moment. We had to do something.

'Peter knew the urgency of the situation and came with me back to the house. When we got there, he turned the dead man over and looked at his face. He sighed and shook his head sadly. "ANC," he said.

'I was a little surprised that he would know any of the fighters. "Do you know him?" I asked. He said that he had seen him hanging out with the ANC boys, but he didn't want to talk about it. He told me to stay where I was and that he would be back soon. While we waited, Mama Mazibuko made us tea. She had calmed down, but was still very worried about having the body in her house. We sat drinking the tea waiting for Peter. He was gone for hours and I began to get anxious that something had happened, that he had got caught up in the fighting wherever it had moved on to.

'Neither of us wanted to look at the body. We talked about other things, trying to ignore the dead man lying on the floor. The flies were coming in to investigate, but we didn't even want to go over and chase them away. "Maybe we should cover him with a blanket," I suggested, but Mama Mazibuko shook her head. "I don't want his blood on my blankets, this is bad blood, blood caused because we cannot live together in peace. I don't want this blood in my house." She looked slightly embarrassed when she said this, maybe she was worried that I would think that she was not a caring woman.

'I understood what she was saying so I said, "I understand Mama, let's not let this bad blood contaminate us." She smiled sadly then.

'Eventually, just as it was getting dark, Peter returned along with two other men. They were fighters and still carried their guns with them. Mama Mazibuko didn't like having guns in the house, I could tell, but she didn't say anything, she just watched them.

'Without a word, these guys picked up the body and dragged it out to a car that had pulled up outside. They never said a thing, not even Peter. They just went about their business then disappeared. Peter went with them. At the time I couldn't figure out why he did, that didn't seem normal.'

Simon paused slightly as the answer to that question flashed up in his mind and he quickly re-directed his thoughts back to its safe compartment.

'As soon as they had gone Mama Mazibuko was on her knees scrubbing the blood from the floor. It was not long before all signs of what had happened had disappeared. I heard later that she burnt the cloth she used to clean up. She really didn't want any trace of the violence in her house. I remember walking home wondering to myself if I had really seen what I had. It seemed so unreal to me.

'Things were very tense round there for the next few days. The dead man's funeral marched past my house. There were a lot of ANC supporters there carrying guns and pangas. They looked angry, like they wanted revenge.' Simon stopped, the weight of the story had suddenly become too much. 'I don't want to talk about this anymore.' He said and sank further into his corner of the lift. The memories had tired him and the dark was now oppressive.

Deon was annoyed. 'Why start telling a story if you're not going to finish it?' He half muttered under his breath, then immediately regretted this and hoped that Simon had not heard.

But Simon was wrapped up in his own thoughts and he was hurting. He pushed himself as far into the corner of the lift as he could, hoping that it would somehow swallow him and all the pain he had. He did not hear Deon's mumbled protest. The memory of the bad times in the township had opened up a wound that he didn't want opened. He did not want to approach the story of how Peter had died now. It was too painful.

Deon breathed in deeply. The air in the lift was stale. It smelt of grief and pain, of blood and tears, of violence and fighting. And yet there was also a smell of things untold, of stories to be shared. There is more to come, the air seemed to say. You are not finished yet. He wondered how long the powercut would continue. Would there be enough time for everything to be told? Would the darkness last long enough to hear them out? Suddenly Deon realised he was powerless over how long they would be without power and as this thought struck him he snorted a quiet laugh at the irony.

This interrupted Simon's thoughts and he looked up, not realising what had snapped him out of his grief. He peered into the blackness which was still as impenetrable as when the lights had first gone out. He reached out his hand, trying to touch the darkness. It was all around and there was a physical presence to it. It felt thick and tangible. His hand waved awkwardly in the air and he let it hang motionless for a while.

'I only got to wave to him.'

'Huh?'

'Peter. I only got to wave to him, I never had a chance to say goodbye properly.'

LUCY 3

She knew she couldn't come right out and ask him, Simon would not respond to that. She needed to gently cajole him into telling the story, let him want to tell it. She had grown to know him well in the time they had been together and had sensed that he was holding back on some things, holding back a part of his life that he did not want to talk about. She had sensed this even before his mother had mentioned the incident of the shooting. Before this, she was not able to put a finger on what it was about him that was withheld, but now she knew.

How to get him to open up was the problem. His mother had struggled, and she was probably closer to Simon than anyone else. Lucy decided to try and approach the topic by talking about the violence and the tsotsis who had affected Anna. Anna was now safely ensconced at Jonas' place and, Lucy suspected, getting on rather better than the formal arrangement suggested. From there, she could build up to getting Simon to talk about the shooting.

One evening after he had finished working, the two of them lay in bed together. Simon was reading the paper, taking note of the horses due to run that weekend. He always liked a little flutter, never anything serious, money was too tight to throw away like that.

'Anna is happier now,' Lucy started.

Simon grunted his agreement but didn't put the paper down. Lucy was a little disappointed, but continued. 'She and Jonas seem to be getting on really well.'

Another grunt, although Lucy detected that it was a slightly more interested grunt and took heart from this.

'She's so happy to be away from those tsotsis.'

A third grunt but the paper did not stir. Lucy sighed and wondered if it was worth continuing. 'Apparently they killed someone there, a young man, it was very near to where Anna used to live.'

The paper lowered slightly. 'Yes, a young man was shot. They say he was a university student and was doing well in his studies, that he was going places. He was just home for the holidays. Oh, there is too much violence these days.' He continued to study the paper as he spoke. Tanzanite in the 3:30 at Turfontein was a good bet at 13-1.

Lucy clicked her tongue and shot a furtive glance at her man to see if there was any reaction. She didn't like this being indirect, but knew she wouldn't get any response if she was not.

'Yes, you are right, there is too much violence but what can we do?'

He was shutting himself off again, immersing himself in the horses. Lucy needed to act quickly. 'How can a person kill another?' She asked trying to sound free of the information that was weighing her down, 'I don't know how I would feel if I had done something like that. I would always think of the family and friends of the person and how they would be suffering.'

She was pushing it.

The paper shook slightly and then lowered slowly. Simon's eyes were ablaze and Lucy realised that she had gone too far.

'You have to be a very hard-hearted person not to be affected by someone being killed,' he fairly hissed this between gritted teeth.

Lucy could see he was struggling to remain calm, but she had struck the nerve she was after. Where to go from here? She struggled to think of something further to say. 'Hau! Simon, you say that like you know someone who's been killed.' She deliberately didn't say *like you know someone who has killed,* that would give the game away.

'She told you didn't she?' Simon growled.

Lucy panicked. She had just about got him where she wanted, but she did not want it at the expense of blowing the confidence Simon's mother had placed in her. She didn't want to get the old lady into trouble so she shook her head and said, 'Told me what? Who told me what?'

Simon was angry now and turned on his side quickly grabbing Lucy's wrist. 'She told you didn't she?' He was almost shouting.

'You're hurting me,' Lucy squealed, trying to release herself from the strong grip. 'Please. Yes, she told me.' Lucy crumbled not because of the sudden violence but because of the look in Simon's eye. She knew he was not a violent man, but he was hurting and lying to him would only make things worse.

'She had no right to.' Simon dropped Lucy's wrist and grabbed up his paper again wanting to escape from the mental pain that had risen suddenly and quickly within him, wanting to escape from the guilt he felt at causing physical pain to one he cared for. But there was no solace in the inky print. He threw the paper aside. 'I'm sorry.' He said it quickly, embarrassed by his actions. He took her hand gently and rubbed her wrist where he had just caused the pain. 'She had no right to,' he said it again, this time softly and without anger.

Lucy put her hand over his and said, 'She is concerned, like me. We are concerned that this is eating you up inside. You can't keep it locked inside you, it will just drive you crazy.' She lay her head onto his bare chest and gently stroked his stomach. 'I care for you very much and I hate to see you suffering. I want to share your pain. If you divide pain between two people, then each only have to carry half of it.' She raised her eyes to his face.

Simon looked down at her, then away. He didn't want to tell her about this. He didn't want to show his hurt, but he saw in her eyes a willingness to share the pain. Keeping quiet would put a strain on their relationship. She would not want him keeping secrets from her. It would break down their trust, drive a wedge between them. But this was not a secret, it was just something he did not wish to talk about.

Lucy didn't take her eyes off his, her heart pounded as she hoped that she would make the breakthrough she desired and get Simon to talk. For a moment, the story hung between the two of them, untold and raw. Lucy felt she could almost reach out and grab it, but she held back, she knew it had to be given, it could not be taken.

Simon sighed and lowered his eyes. 'Okay, you win,' he said, a note of resignation in his voice. 'I'll tell you, but remember that this is a very painful memory for me.'

Lucy nodded her eyelids. 'I'm here for you,' she said and reached for his hand which she squeezed gently.

Simon cleared his throat and began, 'I only got to wave to him, I never had a chance to say goodbye.'

This was not the story Lucy was expecting. Mama had definitely said it was a woman Simon had shot. She was confused now. 'Who?'

'Peter, my brother of course.' Simon didn't register on her confusion.

THE LIFT 14

Deon waited for him to continue. The silence hung like Simon's out-stretched hand. *Was he going to continue?* He had no idea that Simon was sitting with his hand suspended in a half wave, half salute to the departed, or perhaps he was reaching out for help. It was too dark to see. Deon did not even sense that Simon was doing anything, he just assumed he was sitting huddled in his corner of the lift.

You in your small corner and I in mine. Now where had he heard that before? There was a tune that went with it. He searched his mind, waiting for the music to come. It would help pass the time while Simon decided if he wanted to tell his story. *You in your small corner and I in mine.* The tune formed slowly in his head and eventually forced its way down to his vocal chords.

'You in your small corner and I in mine,' he sang softly, but only that one line came so he sang it over and over again. It comforted and frustrated him at the same time.

Simon was still staring at where he thought his hand was. He was wanting to see that final wave again, as if seeing his hand waving goodbye to Peter would somehow conjure up his brother, raise him from the dead and bring him back so that he could say a proper goodbye. He looked intently into the blackness trying to make out any shape or form that looked like his hand. But the darkness was too thick, too complete. His arm began to ache and somewhere in his dazed conscience he could hear singing.

He shook his head slowly and gently lowered his arm. As his mind re-focussed he realised that Deon was singing. He recognised the tune and smiled sadly. He and Peter had sung that song together as little boys.

'Jesus bids us shine with a pure clear light, like a little candle burning in the night,' he prompted Deon, his voice a rich baritone. Deon stopped singing and listened.

'Oh, you're back,' he said.

Simon nodded, then remembering the dark said, 'Yes, I'm back. You remember that old song, did you sing it in Sunday School?'

'I guess. I was trying to remember it. I could only remember that one line – "You in your small corner and I in mine." It's coming back to me now.

Jesus bids us shine, with a pure, clear light,
Like a little candle burning in the night;
In this world of darkness, so we must shine,

You in your small corner, and I in mine.
The two men sang together as Deon's memory of the song was restored. 'We could do with a few candles in here, hey?' Deon said looking around at the gloom. 'Hell, I haven't sung that song for ages. There was another one, how did it go?' He thought for a second then broke into song again, the words flowed freely this time,
Jesus loves the little children
All the children of the world
Red and yellow, black and white
All are precious in his sight
Jesus loves the little children of the world.
Simon didn't join in this time. He knew the song well but was intrigued listening to this white businessman singing old Sunday School choruses. As the words unfolded he started to chuckle quietly. *Red and yellow, black and white, all are precious in his sight*. Did the white kids really sing those words during apartheid? Surely not. It seemed odd that they would teach the white children to sing those words and yet also teach them that, actually the whites were certainly precious, the yellows semi-precious and the blacks were a dime a dozen. As for the reds, well if you're talking red Indians, they were too far away and too few to be any threat, but if you're talking about communist red, well that was evil personified so they could never be precious to Jesus.

Similar thoughts started going through Deon's mind as he reached the end of the song. He sat silent for a second, then said, 'Ironic hey?'

'What's that?' Simon asked, not too sure what the word ironic meant. Deon misunderstood the question.

'That we were allowed to sing that song. I mean *red and yellow, black and white, all are precious in his sight*, that certainly didn't fit in with the spirit of apartheid now did it?' He began to laugh softly. 'Geez, there were tons of things that never made sense under apartheid. You know I'm sorry, but I've just got to laugh sometimes when I think of how we used to … I mean how the government made us do things and we wouldn't even think about it. How could we sing about all people being precious in God's sight and claim to be good upstanding Christians, yet we would then go out of church and treat black people like dirt?

'You know we never thought about those things. We weren't allowed to think, we just had to obey. If the government said blacks were not equal, then they were not equal. If the government said we could sing that all are equal in God's sight, then we would sing that. *Opfok*, that's what we called it in the army. *Opfok*. That's what they did to us there. Fucked up. They fucked us up. Messed with our minds so that we would obey every stupid order they gave us. They wanted us to be fighting machines, hell bent on killing the *swart gevaar*, the black danger. And they did. Fuck us up that is.' He stopped suddenly. The army was not something he wanted to talk about.

Simon laughed aloud unaware of Deon's discomfort at his thoughts about the army. 'I knew you whities were crazy. Some of those apartheid laws never made sense to me. The whole of apartheid never made sense. You remember "Whites Only" park benches, what was all that about hey? The Reservation of Separate Amenities Act they called it. And all those Acts, Acts of Parliament. There were so many of them, we had more acts than a Shakespeare Play. Prohibition of Mixed Marriages Act, Immorality Act, Population Registration Act, Group Areas Act, Suppression of Communism Act, Bantu Building Workers Act, Separate Representation Of Voters Act, Bantu Authorities Act, Native Law Amendment Act, Bantu Education Act, Prevention of Illegal Squatting Act.

'Hey do you think we are violating the Prevention of Illegal Squatting Act now squatting in this lift? Or maybe this falls under the Group Areas Act?' He laughed his loud booming laugh.

Deon stared into the darkness to where he thought Simon was sitting. He was astounded at the way the Acts of Parliament had just flowed. He had heard of some of them by name, the Group Areas Act had been mentioned on TV often. He knew that there had been "Whites Only" park benches but didn't know that this was set out in a piece of legislation called the Reservation of Separate Amenities Act. He also felt embarrassed by the lack of political correctness in the way Simon talked so openly about these things. There was an unwritten agreement between blacks and whites in the new South Africa not to talk about such things; it was embarrassing to the whites and painful to the blacks.

He laughed nervously out of politeness rather than with any humour. 'I don't know,' he said not very sure of the ground he was on. 'All those laws are gone now so we don't have to worry, do we?' He wanted to get off this thin ice, he was too uncomfortable to make a joke about those laws.

'Ja, they are all gone, thank goodness,' Simon's humour faded. 'But what if this had happened during apartheid. If we had been stuck in the lift together, then what. Would we be in breach of those laws?'

'We probably wouldn't be speaking like this, that's for sure.'

Deon was sure that they wouldn't be in breach of any of the apartheid laws, how could they be? It was not their fault that they were stuck together here. But he didn't want to continue this particular conversation.

'You're right about that. What would we be doing do you think? Would we have talked at all?'

112

Deon thought about this. It was a strange question. Well, not really that strange *per se*, it was the feelings and thoughts that it provoked that were strange. If this encounter had occurred a little over a decade ago, would they have been able to talked so candidly? Of course Elise would not have been dead then, so the story he had told would not have yet happened, but that was not really the issue was it. Would they have talk so openly? 'I don't know. We would have had different stories to tell I guess. The things we have been talking about would not yet have happened, but we would have talked about getting out of here, like I did earlier.' He shook his head slightly as he remembered his behaviour when they had first got stuck. 'Then, I don't know, maybe we would have just kept quiet, probably fallen asleep.'

Simon was disappointed with this answer, but resignedly accepted that Deon was right. What would they have done? The gap between black and white back then was huge. He would have been completely subservient while Deon would have been absolute master. It would have been very awkward to talk. Sleep would have been the easiest option for both of them. Things had changed, he thought and brightened slightly.

'Yes, I think you would still have asked what was happening when the lift stopped and the lights went out?'

'Ja, I would have done that.'

'Then what?' Simon was pushing. Despite being pleased with the change, he still wanted something to be different with the past. He wanted the past to change. He wanted them to have talked freely in that imaginary lift, hidden in the past. A different past would be good, a past where Peter was not dead, where Marie Stander had not been caught in a crossfire, where even Elise, this woman he had only just heard of, would still be alive.

'Ag! I don't know. Look does it really matter. We're here in the present. In the rainbow nation, not the apartheid nation. This is the New South Africa, things are different in the New South Africa. You guys are in charge now, remember?'

Simon realised that Deon was agitated by this talk. Was he thinking of a different past where his Elise was still alive? Or was he agitated that the blacks were in charge now? This thought crept up on Simon, surprising him. He had begun to accept Deon for what he was – a human being. This was not something he was comfortable with. This *was* the New South Africa. A new approach was required. 'I suppose you're right.'

The lift fell silent again.

A CONVERSATION

'You never told me about Peter.'

'Peter? Who told you about Peter?'

'Simon. I was trying to get him to talk about that woman he shot but instead he told me all about Peter.'

'He told you about Peter?'

'Yes. He must have thought I was wanting him to talk about that.'

'Hau! That is a painful memory, more painful to both of us than the shooting of that woman. Simon told you about Peter?'

'Yes.'

'About how he …?'

'Yes.'

'And that he never got to say goodbye?'

'Yes.'

'When did he tell you this?'

'Last night in bed. Why didn't you tell me about Peter, Mama? Oh no, I'm sorry Mama, I didn't mean to make you cry. Here, here's a tissue.'

'I'm fine now, thank you.'

'I just want to be part of Simon's life. I want to share everything with him. Share the good times and the bad. I need to know what is causing him pain. I want to help him.'

'I know my daughter. It will take time. Be patient.'

'I am trying to be patient Mama, but I love him so much. I want to heal his pain.'

'You will. He has never talked about Peter to anyone, you are the first that he has said anything to. When Peter … when Peter died, he just went into a shell. Like a tortoise. He didn't speak for a week, just sat on the step outside staring at nothing. We had to drag him in one day because there was gun fighting going on nearby. He didn't even notice it.'

'Hau! Poor Simon.'

'He has suffered a lot, but you are so good for him. You will heal his wounds. Talking will heal the wounds. Like Madiba did in this country. He talked and the wounds were healed. Come here my daughter. Don't cry now. You will heal him.'

THE LIFT 15

'So tell me about your brother then,' the silence had become too much. 'What was his name again?'

'Peter.'

'Peter?' Deon noted the sullenness of the answer with surprise. He quickly reviewed the previous conversation but could not find anything wrong with it. Surely Simon was not upset that he had dismissed the fictitious lift of ten years ago.

'Yes, Peter.'

Deon willed him to go on. To show that there was nothing wrong between them, but Simon stayed silent. Suddenly he had no wish to talk to Deon, let alone talk about Peter. He knew it was irrational, it wasn't Deon's fault that years back they would not have talked, but it still irked him.

'Eish!' He expelled the word with his breath. It was a popular word, one that didn't really have a meaning, but expressed much. It could indicate pain or surprise or could just be used as a general tsk! tsk!

Deon smiled to himself. He loved that word that was initially a 'blacks only' word, but had been seeping into use amongst the whites. Deon loved the way it showed a melding of cultures. He loved the fact that the whites were beginning to use, and enjoy using, the word. Not only that but it had a great sound to it. Eish! A strong 'ay' sound followed by a long shhhh that flowed from the mouth and was often accompanied by a shake of the head.

'You know it is painful to talk about Peter.' The reluctance was slowly seeping out of Simon. He felt obliged to tell his story, sort of a repayment to Deon for opening up about Elise. Also, if he refused, then maybe he was still sitting in that ten year old lift where they would have nothing to talk about. If he chose to remain sulky about not being able to talk back then and not open up and talk now, was he not being a hypocrite? His mind wandered to the night he had told Lucy about Peter, recalling how difficult it had been and yet strangely how good it had felt once the story was told.

'Peter owned this shop and, like I said, he lived in the back part of it. There was a small bedroom where he slept. He was doing well, making lots of money. But you remember the story I told you about the man who had been killed there by Mama Mazibuko's house? Mama Kit Kat? You remember how Peter sorted it all out? Well back then I didn't realise it, but Peter was involved with the ANC. He was caught up in all that … all that politics. I didn't know, he never told me. I think he was trying to protect me by not saying anything. He didn't want me to get involved because he was scared I would get hurt. But I did get hurt, it hurt me when he was killed.'

Simon lapsed into an introspective silence which Deon respected, giving his companion space to grieve.

Eventually he continued, 'I saw him that morning. It was a hot day, I remember. I had come back from work, the night shift, and was getting ready to sleep. I was very tired and about to get into bed when I heard a knock at the window. It was Peter. He saw that I was getting ready for bed so he just pointed to town to show he was going to collect some supplies for the shop. I nodded, waved him goodbye, then got into bed. I never knew that it would be the last time I would ever see him.'

Deon shifted his position slightly in the ensuing silence. He knew this was difficult for Simon. Not saying a proper goodbye – that hurt. He had often tried to recall his parting with Elise on that horrible day, that day she was killed, but he could not remember his last words to her. It bugged him. He imagined that he had said something like *I love you* but that was a romantic view as he had hardly ever said that despite having felt it. It was more likely that his last words to her had been *don't forget to get milk*. He cast his mind back, picturing the shopping bag that had spilled as Elise had fallen. It was remarkably clear in his head. There was no milk there. Had she forgotten to buy some? Did they need milk that day?

He concentrated on the spilt groceries, focusing his mind's eye on the contents. There had been a loaf of bread, some eggs if he recalled correctly and … Cremora. Yes, Cremora. Suddenly the bottle of coffee creamer became ultra clear in his mind and the famous advert for it followed right behind.

There was the guy frantically searching in the fridge for the Cremora. *It's not inside, it's on top!* Now there was an ad that people remembered. Cremora was so good that the poor bloke thought it was kept in the fridge like normal milk. He remembered the pineapple being thrown over the guy's shoulder as his search inside the fridge became more and more desperate.

Helen, there's no Cremora in the refrigerator, he eventually bellows in despair. And then that screechy off-screen voice delivers the famous catch phrase – *It's not inside, it's on top.*

The man in the ad looks confused as he repeats, *It's not inside, it's ooooon … top!* He turns his head and comes face-to-face with the bottle of Cremora on top of the fridge as he says *top!* What a great ad. Every South African knew this ad; even years later people still remembered the catch phrase. Cremora, that was what they called old whatisname in the army. What was his name again? He looked just like the guy in the ad, Frik that was his proper name. But Deon didn't want to think about the army, or the grocery bag, or Cremora.

'Anyway, Peter went off and I went to sleep. I didn't sleep well as it was so hot. I kept tossing and turning. I was restless. It was like I knew something bad was going to happen.' Simon's voice relieved Deon of his thoughts.

'A premonition?'

'What?'

'Premonition, it's the word for when you feel something is going to happen.'

'Premonition.' Simon tasted the word. It was right for what he had felt. 'Yes, a premonition. But I did eventually fall asleep. I had a strange dream I remember that.'

THE DREAM

There were two men. A black man in a white suit and a white man in a black suit. They stood next to each other, not saying a word. They were just staring at me till I began to feel uncomfortable.

'Stop staring,' I shouted but they did not hear.

'Stop staring, you are making me uncomfortable.' I shouted again, but they carried on staring. I walked up to them and shook them. First the black man, then the white man but they took no notice of this, they just kept staring.

I slapped the face of the white man. There was no reaction. I then slapped the face of the black man. Nothing. I stood in front of them staring back, trying to outstare them, but they did not even blink.

Then suddenly, without warning, they both pushed me really hard. I fell backwards, landing heavily. The force with which they pushed me left me dazed. When I focussed again I saw that the two men were fighting.

It was a great struggle, they fought hard, punching and grabbing, pulling and throwing. They fell to the floor and rolled around together, still fighting, always fighting. Then I saw the black suit start to turn white and the white suit stared to turn black. The white man started to turn black and the black man started to turn white. Then they changed back. Then one suit changed and the other man changed. All the time they fought furiously.

They kept changing colour, the suits and the men. One moment black, one moment white.

Soon I didn't know who was black and who was white. I didn't know which suit was black and which was white. The fighting got so violent that I couldn't tell one man from another. It was like a ball of human, with legs and arms flying in all directions. I am sure that at times there were more than four arms and more than four legs sticking out of that jumble.

The two men and their suits became a blur as they fought harder and harder, the blacks and whites coming together to form a grey mass. Then slowly, as I watched, I began to see colours. At first it was just small dots of colour. A red here, some yellow there and a bit of blue over there.

More and more colours appeared and soon there was no more black or white, only colours – reds, yellows, greens, purples and oranges. And the fighting was slowing down. There were no more legs flying, or arms waving. I realised that there was now only one man, not two. He was rolling around in a brightly coloured suit.

Slowly he stopped rolling till at last he lay very still. Then with a lot of effort he climbed cautiously to his feet. He was an old black man in this colourful suit. He smiled at me, a warm friendly smile.

I stared at him for a long while, all the time he was smiling. Then he suddenly burst into flame, a wild colourful fire. He burned intensely for a short moment, all the time he smiled and stared at me. Then as quickly as the fire had started he collapsed into a heap of ash on the floor.

I stared at the pile of ash for a long time, then walked away slowly.

THE LIFT 16

'A loud knocking on the door woke me up. It was an urgent knock, a knock that said hurry, there is bad news. I jumped up and shouted to the person to wait a minute, I had to put my clothes on. "Come quick! Come quick! Something terrible has happened to Peter," the person said. I knew the voice, it belonged to Peter's friend Albert.'

Deon was still puzzling over the dream when he was suddenly transported back to Simon's story. There was an urgency about it now, like it was rushing to be told. The floodgates were opened and there was no stopping it.

'I could hardly breathe as I dressed. Albert's voice said so much, I could tell that he was in a panic. I put my clothes on as quickly as I could and ran to the door. Albert grabbed my arm shouting, "Quick! Quick!" As we ran over to Peter's shop I tried to ask Albert what had happened but he just kept running saying "Come, come."

'When we got to the shop I saw a crowd of people standing outside. Albert pushed his way through them, pulling me with him. He opened the door and that was when the smell hit me. Have you ever smelt burnt human flesh?'

The question dropped innocuously in the lift. Simon's tone had not changed with its asking and although it had been rhetorical it had changed things. Deon drew a sharp breath as the implications hit him. He had been expecting Peter's death, but not like this. His nostrils were filled with the powerful smell of a human being burning. Smell is a very powerful memory stimulant and a scene immediately formed in his mind, a scene he had witnessed during his army days. It was one that he had never wished to recall.

'Yes. Yes I have.' It was a whisper.

Simon looked up and peered into the darkness. Had he heard right? Had he heard this white man say that he had actually smelt someone burning? Surely not. This was something that only happened to black people. Necklacing they called it. Had Deon witnessed a necklacing? It did not seem right.

'Really?'

'Yes, a long time ago when I was in the army. But that was … anyway it's another story. I don't want to talk about it.' His voice was stronger now, but he was not. A sickening nausea had gripped his stomach.

Simon fell silent. Should he push Deon to tell more or continue with his own story? Deon's tone said that he definitely didn't want to tell that story, but Simon was intrigued now. He wanted to hear what a white man's view of this barbaric way of killing 'traitors' was. He remembered the young white soldiers in the township. They looked more scared of the township dwellers than the black inhabitants were of the soldiers. There had been some soldiers nearby the day Peter was killed.

He decided not to press Deon just then. Maybe he would tell the story later. Simon had to finish his story first.

'Well the smell hit me and I knew straight away what had happened.'

'Necklace?' Soft and respectful.

'Yes.'

Simon paused, accepting the unspoken respect that Deon was offering to the dead, then he went on. 'Albert told me the whole story later. Peter had been walking home with the goods for the shop when a group of Inkhata supporters had spotted him. They were men out to cause trouble. They saw Peter and recognised him as an ANC man. Because he was walking alone they started to chase him.

'Peter dropped his purchases and ran for his life. He got back to the shop and tried to close the door behind him but the group was too close. One man pushed the door hard and Peter fell backwards. The men ran into the house. One found a tyre while another ran to a nearby car and began to siphon off the petrol.

'That was when Albert ran to get help. He had been walking nearby when it all happened. He was scared now that the group would see him and kill him too, so he went looking for a local group of ANC boys who could help. All the time he was praying that he would not be too late. Unfortunately the ANC boys were somewhere else that day. Albert was frantic, running around trying to find them. In the meantime, the men had grabbed Peter, poured the petrol over him and thrown the tyre around his neck. Then they lit a match …'

Simon stopped. He had so often envisaged his brother's last minutes, the horror and fear of the impending death and the pain, Peter's desperate shouts for mercy falling on deaf ears and hardened hearts. He had tried to imagine what was going through Peter's mind, he had tried so hard to put himself in Peter's place, to take Peter's place. But he couldn't.

Deon knew the practice of necklacing. He had first heard about it on TV and then seen it first hand during his military service, part of which had been spent in the townships. It was an horrific death, being burnt alive while your persecutors kicked and punched you. It was barbaric in the extreme, a good example of mob mentality.

The word *good* seemed out of place in that last thought. There could be no good in such an act. Deon wondered if any of those who had carried out a necklacing were walking free on the streets of the townships as they sat trapped in the lift. He wondered if those who had killed Simon's brother were still free. Did they regret what they had done? Had this act in anyway sickened them once they had walked away from the scene and the anger of the mob subsided. Or now years later, did they feel any remorse? It was highly likely that there would still be a large number of those guilty of this offence walking free, never having had to answer for their crime. He shuddered. Maybe those who killed Elise had murdered others using a necklace.

He recalled the faces of those who did the necklacing that he had witnessed. He remembered realising that they didn't really know what they were doing. They were trance-like, caught up in the frenzy of the moment. *Forgive them for they know not what they do.* The words learnt in Sunday School suddenly came into his head. Jesus' words from the cross as he suffered an equally horrific and undignified death: 'Forgive them'. Could Peter have uttered those words, or even thought them in the panic and shock of his own impending death? Unlikely. That would take an exceptionally special man to do that. Did Simon forgive those who killed his brother? Did he, Deon, forgive those who had killed Elise? Could he?

He tried to imagine what he would say if he ever came face-to-face with those killers. Could he even begin to show them mercy of any sort? As he thought this, an anger welled up and he knew the answer. He could never forgive those who had taken Elise from him. It would always eat away at him, but he knew he did not have it in him to forgive. He closed his eyes.

ELISE 3

She was there. Elise. It began as a feeling, then as he opened his eyes he could see her. He sat up quickly in bed, his eyes adjusting in the dark. This cannot be, he reminded himself, she is dead. The scene of her getting out the car, the smile on her face as she struggled with grocery bags, and then the bullet entering her head played through his mind in slow motion. Was that a dream? Is this a dream? he asked himself.

Her pale, naked body cast a dull glow in the room as though it were giving off light rather than reflecting the dull streetlight that sneaked in around the curtains. She stood quietly at the end of the bed looking at him, looking into him. Then he remembered that it was not the first such vision. Since her death he had had a number of these 'visitations'. Were they just aftershocks, a recurring dream brought on by the severe pain her death had caused? Or was this really some paranormal phenomenon? He had never believed in ghosts and even now he still didn't quite believe in them. But these appearances were so real, so intense.

He watched silently as the spectral figure walked slowly round the side of the bed and sat down beside him. There was no sinking of the mattress to suggest that there was any weight to this being. There could be no words, there were never any words.

He looked into her eyes, imploring her to be real, to be alive. He wanted to say something, to talk to her, ask her questions. But his tongue stuck in his mouth as her piercing blue eyes stared back at him. There was love in her eyes, but also a question. She was trying to ask him something with her eyes, but he could not grasp what it was.

Then slowly, as she realised that he did not understand, the light in her eyes dulled and a sadness replaced the question. Eventually she lowered her gaze. He wanted to reach out, to gently lift her chin to make her look at him again. He ached for her eyes to be on him, but he could not move.

She sat staring at her lap, her hands demurely resting there. Then slowly she lifted one hand and began to gently rub her belly. As she rubbed, it began to grow. He could see her beautiful soft skin begin to stretch as the belly began to show the growing life within her. He could almost hear the creaking of her body as it changed shape.

Her breasts began to get heavier too, more round as they filled with milk, the nipples dark and swollen. It was not long before she sat there, a fully pregnant woman ready to give birth. She looked up at him now, her hands cradling her belly.

He wanted to reach out to touch her belly, to feel the new life inside her.

He leaned forward with his hand outstretched.

THE LIFT 17

'Hey! What are you doing?'

Deon fell back into his corner, dropping his outstretched hand quickly. He was a bit dazed, not sure where he was for a second and blinked furiously trying to clear the darkness from his eyes. Then he panicked for half a second as he thought he had gone blind. His wits returned as quickly as the panic had arisen. The dream fell away as the dreadful reality hit him, he had tried to feel Simon's belly.

'Sorry. Sorry.' He slumped back into his corner of the lift, drawing his legs up, trying to put as much space between him and Simon. 'Sorry,' this time with less confusion and more contrition. 'I ... I was dreaming.'

Simon nodded. He had had the feeling that he was talking to a blank wall for the last few minutes and this annoyed him a little. He had been describing his feelings at seeing the burnt out remains of his brother. Was this not of interest to the white man? Did it not arouse the same sense of sympathy that Deon's story of Elise had aroused in him? Under apartheid a black person's life was certainly worth less than that of a white's. But apartheid was gone. We should all be equal. Whether it was a black life or a white life should not matter. It was still a life.

Deon was settling down again. 'Sorry, I am very tired. I dozed off. I was thinking about whether you could forgive those who killed Peter and if I could forgive those who killed Elise. I must have dreamt of Elise. I keep seeing ...' He stopped. Could he really go into detail about those visions? He had already mentioned the incident at Elise's funeral, but would Simon think him mad if he spoke further of these sightings?

'You keep seeing Elise?' The voice was neutral, no judgement.

'Ja,' resigned. He may as well admit it. It was just possible, he thought, that this black man would understand better than his white friends would.

'I see. Sometimes this happens. The dead people want to talk to us, give us a message,' Simon replied.

'I don't think it's the dead trying to communicate with me. I don't believe in that sort of thing. I think it's just my mind still trying to cope. It wants her back so badly that it refuses to let go of her. The nature of her death and the fact that she was pregnant makes it worse.'

'I see,' Simon felt a bit foolish now.

'Have you ever seen Peter? I mean do you have any really intense thoughts about him, so intense that you actually believe you are seeing him?' Deon was hoping. Hoping it was not just him who experienced these things.

'No, I have never seen Peter again, not a ghost or even an intense vision. You are lucky to see Elise. I want to see Peter to say goodbye to him properly. I also wanted to see Marie Stander to say I am sorry, that it was not my fault, that I never meant to kill her. But I have never seen anyone who has died.'

Deon was disappointed. He did not feel lucky to keep seeing Elise, it haunted him. He could not really move on in life while she kept appearing. It was as though there was unfinished business between them. Maybe it was the child. She was trying to let him know she was pregnant when she had been killed. Maybe that's what the recent dream was about. But he already knew, so why did she keep appearing?

He sank back further into his corner, not wanting to face Simon's voice. Embarrassed that he was now perceived as mad. He dared not close his eyes either as he did not wish to face the spectral Elise of his dreams. He didn't know where to turn.

Simon sensed his companion's discomfort but was not sure what caused it. He decided to try lighten the atmosphere. Things had turned pretty serious and he too felt uneasy at the direction the conversation was taking, it threatened to bubble over into areas he didn't want to go.

'So?' It was a general comment, with as much weightlessness thrown in as he could muster, but it fell heavily in the quietness of the lift and clanged to the floor.

Deon didn't stir.

Simon wracked his brain, trying to think of something else to say. He had hoped that Deon would respond to the light-hearted 'so?' and come up with a happier topic to talk about, but now he realised it was up to him to provide the diversion from their respective turmoils.

'Do you have a girlfriend now, or a wife?' Still the silence. Was this a good topic? He panicked immediately after saying this, but to cover up he went on casually, 'I have a girlfriend, her name is Lucy. We met when we had an accident in a taxi. Not a serious accident obviously. She had a bit of a cut and I got a few bruises, but nothing too bad. She's a lovely woman who looks after me and my children and my mother.' No response. He decided to continue anyway, even if Deon had fallen asleep, or was just not going to answer, talking about Lucy was making him feel better.

'She is especially close to my mother. Sometimes the two of them gang up on me in the house. And what is a man supposed to do then, huh? What can he do when the women in his life gang up on him? Just the other day they hid the newspaper from me, the part with the horses in. I was wanting to go and place a bet but couldn't find the form sheet. I searched everywhere but couldn't find it. They just sat there laughing at me hunting all over the house.

'You know where it was?' He didn't expect an answer, but paused fractionally just in case. 'My mother was sitting on it. They pretended that they never knew, but I saw the looks they gave each other. There were big smiles between them. I acted like I had not noticed. I am the man of the house, I must keep my dignity I thought.' He gave a small, warm laugh which revealed a lot about his relationship, the love, the care and the happiness that existed in his home.

It was a simple story, but such a contrast to all the talk that had gone before, the talk of death and violence. Despite his current slump in mood Deon had been listening and Simon's laugh, that warm, deep laugh, had eased his mind somewhat. Despite this he did not smile, he still felt depressed.

'Sharon.'

Simon stopped laughing. 'What?'

'Sharon. She is my girlfriend now.'

'Is she a good woman?'

Deon thought about the question. What did 'a good woman' mean? One who did as she was told in the old fashioned sexist way? Or good as in how Elise was a good, philanthropic person who cared for others? Sharon was certainly the former, a quality that he liked as it gave him comfort, but also one that irritated him at times as it was not … well it was not like Elise.

Sharon wasn't a *bad* person philanthropically speaking. She was more philanthropically neutral. Now there was a good politically correct way to describe her. She never went out of her way to harm others, but equally would not go out of her way to see to the wellbeing of others, except of course for her man and her family. He could not imagine Sharon working in an Aids orphanage for example, or doing any other charitable work that would demand some of her time, but that didn't make her a bad person, did it?

'She is a good woman,' he said almost surprising himself with the feelings he suddenly felt towards Sharon as he realised that yes, she actually is a good woman – good for him.

'She looks after me and we enjoy each other's company. She may not be an Elise in terms of her gestures outside of her immediate family, but her heart is in the right place.

'Yes, she is a good woman.' He repeated it, marvelling at the sensations they brought out in him.

'You're a lucky man,' Simon said, his voice carried the seriousness of what he was saying along with the joy he expressed at Deon's good fortune in finding *a good woman.*

'We are both lucky men,' he added, remembering his own luck in finding Lucy.

Deon nodded in the dark, his mind churning over thoughts. He had been too busy comparing Sharon to Elise, trying to find a perfect substitute for the woman he lost, that he had not realised what he really had in Sharon. Without knowing anything of the tragedy in Deon's life, she had slowly nursed his wounds with her simple kindness and unquestioning love. He realised now how good she had been for him.

He reached out and found Simon's arm which he tapped, a broad grin on his face. 'Here my friend, a glass of champagne to toast our good women.'

Simon accepted the imaginary glass while a shudder of joy raced through his body at the words 'my friend'. He had never thought a white man would ever call him that.

'To our good women,' Deon said raising his glass in the dark.

'To Lucy and Sharon,' Simon replied. 'May they always keep us on the straight and narrow.'

'Steady on now, let's not go too far.'

They both laughed. This was a good tonic for Deon and he felt his mood lighten.

The laughter subsided.

'How's your champagne? It's the best. JC Le Roux.'

Simon took a sip from the imaginary glass which he was holding as if it were a tumbler. 'I've never had champagne before, but this is very nice.'

'You've never had champagne before! We will have to put that right. When we get out of this lift I will buy you a bottle of JC Le Roux.' The champagne had gone to Deon's head.

'Thank you, I would like that very much. That would really impress Lucy if I came home with a bottle of champagne. I might let my mother have some if she doesn't hide the racing form again.'

They both laughed, although it caught slightly in Deon's throat as he pictured the scene in Simon's house, the excitement at getting a small share of the white man's opulence. It somehow didn't seem right that such a small gesture on his part could cause that much pleasure. He thought of Elise and then understood why she had worked at the Aids orphanage. His smile faded and he made a mental note to ensure he fulfilled his promise of getting Simon some champagne.

Simon's voice broke into his thoughts. 'Now it's my turn. Here is some home brewed beer my mother made. She was the best beer maker in the village where I grew up, and now in Langa Township she is highly regarded. There is no beer around that compares to my mother's.' He held out the round pot to Deon who tried to take it in one hand.

128

'No, no. It is a calabash you need two hands to hold it properly. It's not a glass and you don't want to spill any.'

Deon chuckled, felt for Simon's other hand and took the calabash. He lifted it to his mouth and drank then smacked his lips. 'No offence, but I think I prefer my champagne. My taste buds are not used to this home made beer.'

He could almost smell the strong yeasty brew and the sentence was out there before he realised what he had said.

'Is it too strong for you my friend?' Simon's voice showed no offence.

'Yes, also it is not what I have grown up with.' Deon knew he was safe now.

'Did you grow up with champagne?'

'No, not really. More red wine and beer.'

'But not homebrew?'

'No. Castle Lager mostly.'

'And now that you are an important business man, do you drink a lot of champagne.'

Deon laughed. 'I'm not such an important business man. I still have a boss to work for.'

'Hau! You have a boss. I thought you were the boss.'

'No. My boss is Mr Anderson. Do you know him? Tall man, grey hair, always well dressed?'

'Yes, I know Mr Anderson well. He is a good man; he always greets me when he goes past reception. He even knows my name.'

Simon paused. This may have seemed to be a slight on Deon who had never greeted him, let alone knew his name. He had not meant it like that and he waited for a rebuke or a sulky silence.

Deon immediately picked up on the unsaid, unthought implication, but realised that it had not been intentional. Besides even if it had been intentional, it was deserved.

'He is good like that, remembering names. That is why he is the boss, all our customers like it that he remembers their names. It creates good client relations.' It was an excuse and an apology which Simon accepted silently, glad that his offhand remark had not caused another rift.

Despite avoiding this potential problem, the two men lapsed into silence again. Deon began to reflect on the different worlds that they moved in. He often had champagne, usually at company affairs with clients; the bubbly aimed at making a good impression and getting deals signed. Even as he had been moving up the social ladder it had been good red wines that he had enjoyed, a drink that was regarded as having much higher standing than homebrew. Homebrew always had the image of being a nasty, possibly unhygienic concoction, a witch's potion. Even common old Castle Lager had far more credibility, certainly amongst whites anyway.

'In my culture you are supposed to share the beer around, not keep it all for yourself.' Deon's thoughts were brought back and he realised he was still holding the imaginary calabash in front of him.

'Oh sorry.' He stretched out and gratefully handed it back to Simon who chuckled.

'If only this was real beer. I'm getting quite thirsty. Hopefully this powercut will end soon.'

A strange feeling passed through Deon. He did not want the powercut to end. Despite the stories that had been told in the dark, he had found some comfort in being able to talk freely to those unseen ears. He drew the darkness around him like a blanket, trying to hold on to it, suddenly fearful of the bright light that would eventually come and reveal his companion's face. That would shatter the comfort they both took in talking to the dark. He suddenly feared the time when he would no longer have the cover of darkness to hide under while he told his tales. Besides which he still had one more story to tell.

LUCY 4

She sat quietly in the lounge watching Simon's mother who was sitting knitting. She had always admired the old woman, her skill with the needles, the love she had for her family and the wise way she handled the family's affairs, especially the way she took care of Simon and nursed his troubled soul. She hoped that she would turn out as wise when she got to that age.

The old lady looked up from her knitting and smiled, 'What are you thinking my daughter, you look troubled.'

'Oh, I was just hoping that one day I will be as wise as you.'

The old woman laughed, a warm friendly sound. 'You have already shown great wisdom in choosing Simon.' It was not boastful of her son, but rather a compliment of Lucy's ability to recognise a good match for herself.

Lucy nodded and the two women sat silently for a while, only the clicking of the knitting needles and the muffled music from a nearby shebeen could be heard in the room.

'I hate it when he works nights.' Lucy's voice broke the quiet; she was feeling the need to talk. 'I worry about him being alone in that big building.'

'You shouldn't worry. The building is quite safe and he is always careful about locking the doors. There have never been any problems there. Besides he's got the emergency alarm which will bring the armed security people around in seconds.'

'Oh I don't worry so much about his physical safety, I think he is pretty safe on that front. I worry more about him being left alone with his thoughts. He spends too much time thinking about things that have happened.' Lucy deliberately avoided mentioning Peter, or the white woman Simon had shot.

The old woman nodded sadly. She knew exactly what Lucy meant; she had the same worries about her son.

'He needs a friend he can talk to,' Lucy went on, 'someone he can talk to about those things. Working nights a lot means he cannot make friends as most people work in the day and are only around when he goes to work.'

'He has you my dear,' the old woman smiled, acknowledging the difference Lucy had made in Simon.

'Yes, but he has no men as friends. He needs other men to talk to, not just about what has happened but about other things too, I don't know what, but the things men talk about.'

The old woman nodded again. She had tried to get Simon to spend time at the shebeen so that he could make some friends. Since moving from Johannesburg to Langa he had become quite a loner.

'He will not make friends being alone in an empty building,' Lucy said. 'Hau!' she added as the room was plunged into darkness, 'another powercut.'

THE LIFT 18

'Tell me about Sharon.'

'Not much to tell really. We met after Elise died, moved in together a while later and now we live together.'

'Any children?'

'No, no children.'

'Do you want to have children?'

Deon had not thought much about this since moving in with Sharon. He knew that he had not wanted kids at the time Elise was killed, or at least was not ready for them then, and had never really come to terms with the fact that, had Elise not been murdered, he would have been a father now. Kids with Sharon? He struggled with the thought. 'I don't know. Maybe one day.'

The earlier thoughts about Sharon being a good woman were lingering and as he sat in the dark, the idea of kids with her began to appeal. Of course they would have to get married first, her family would not tolerate kids being born to their daughter outside of wedlock. He suddenly found that he was not so anti this idea as he had been in the past. He still didn't like the fact that his life could be dictated by the possible in-laws in this respect, but there was part of him that felt it would be the right thing to do.

'How about you? Will you have children with … Lucy was it?'

'Yes, Lucy. I think that maybe we will have children some time. I only have the two from my marriage, but now that my wife is gone I'm sure that Lucy and I will have some.'

Deon wondered whether to ask where his wife had gone, but thinking it may be another sensitive issue, he let the question pass by unasked.

Simon was somewhat perturbed by Deon's lack of enthusiasm about having children. He wondered if part of the problem was that, because Elise was pregnant when she was killed, Deon was now scared that if he got Sharon pregnant then she would also be taken from him. This view was counter balanced however with the fact that white people never seemed as concerned about having children as the blacks were. For blacks it was an important part of their culture.

Deon meanwhile was beginning to wonder what being a father would be like. He tried to picture his potential offspring. He would want a son to start with, someone to carry on the family name, his father would be happy with that, then maybe a daughter to balance things out. The son would look like him and the daughter would be like Sharon. He conjured up an image of the two kids playing in the garden, he and Sharon standing at the kitchen door watching them – a picture of domestic bliss.

He smiled quietly to himself then suddenly his face changed from one of happiness to one of horror as the two imagined children were mown down by gunfire from an unseen assailant. Both wore the same expression on their faces as Elise had that day. He shook his head as he battled to regain control of his mind. Slightly shaken he muttered, 'Maybe I won't have kids. I dunno, this world is not exactly the greatest place to bring them up in.'

'What about Sharon, how does she feel?'

'Not sure. I've never asked her. We just seem to have fallen into a routine of living together, but have never discussed things like kids yet. Anyway, she'd want to discuss marriage before talking kids. She's a bit old-fashioned that way.'

The imagined scene still rattled in his mind.

SHARON 2

Once *Isidingo* had finished, Sharon moved to the bedroom to freshen up before Deon got home. Like most soaps, it had finished on a cliff-hanger and she could hardly wait till Monday to see how the issues would be resolved.

After a quick shower she spent the next half an hour at her dressing table sprucing up her face and nails and then chose her clothes carefully. She put on her sexiest black underwear and slipped a rather revealing dress over it. She admired the results in the mirror, she looked good. She was now ready for her man. Earlier she had arranged with the maid to cook his favourite – pork chops – for dinner and the smell of the food wafted into the bedroom.

Back in the lounge, she settled down in front of the TV to wait, although her mind was not on the show. She was thinking about her relationship with Deon. His seeming lack of interest about getting married was making her restless, almost concerned that there was something wrong with her. She had waited patiently for him to ask, but so far no request for her hand had been forthcoming and the long fantasised dream of walking down the aisle in a beautiful white dress was becoming more remote where she felt it should rather be nearly a reality. There would probably be some objections from the more conservative members of her family about her wearing white, but she had set her heart on it and nothing would change her mind in that respect.

Tonight she was planning to seduce Deon and then after they were done with the lovemaking she would broach the subject of marriage, in a subtle way of course. A girl never asked a man outright to marry her, that was not the done thing. All she hoped to do was plant the seed. She felt a bit devious using sex to her advantage. It wasn't what a woman should do. It wasn't how she had been brought up, but they had been living together for a while now – surely it was time to take the next step.

The phone rang, pulling her out of her thoughts.

'Hi honey, it's me.'

'Hiya, where are you?'

'Still at the office. I've got some paperwork I've got to finish tonight. It has to be in New York by close of play. They close in four hours.'

'Is it going to take four hours?'

'No, shouldn't be that long, maybe another hour or two. You go ahead and eat, don't wait for me.'

'Okay.' She put down the phone and stared at her beautifully manicured hand that had stayed resting on the receiver. She stood like that for nearly a minute before finally moving. Why tonight, of all nights to be late?

In the lounge she slumped back onto the sofa, feeling slightly sulky. She never understood Deon's work, but knew that it occasionally involved him working late. That was never too much of a problem as he was well paid. But not tonight, not when she really wanted him to be here.

She grabbed the remote control and poked hard at the buttons a few times, eventually deciding that there was nothing worth watching, so she threw it down onto the sofa next to her and sat staring at the screen, her mind far away from the wildlife scene that flickered in front of her.

Maybe he wasn't at the office at all, maybe he was having an affair. What was the name of that pretty girl she had met at one of those work functions? Mandy, that was it. Maybe he was with Mandy right now while she was waiting for him to come home, waiting to seduce him. Waiting for him to ask that question.

But Deon wouldn't be unfaithful to her would he? He was not that type, although even the good guys could be led astray. She had seen that in the soaps she watched. A sudden urge to call Deon back on some pretence came to her. If he wasn't at the office, then she would know. She moved to get up, then thought, *but what if I phone and he has just left his desk to go to the toilet or photocopier? Then I would suspect him of something he is innocent of.* Her eyes focussed on the TV that was showing some ostriches mating. A tinny voice filtered through to her brain, *Ostriches only mate with one partner throughout their lives.* She smiled. Her ostrich was still in the office. She knew that now and her thoughts turned to more pleasant ones about Deon.

The room began to grow dark, only the glow from the TV provided any light. Eventually she shouted to the maid to bring her dinner on a tray. The maid came through, turning the light on and causing Sharon to blink in the sudden brightness. She ate in silence, the sound on the TV a low murmur. It would be too late to do anything when Deon got in. Besides which he would be too tired now for any sort of serious conversation. She contemplated changing into something a little more comfortable.

It was still possible that they would make love. Friday night had become their ritual time for intimacy. It was their way of winding down after the week. Sharon had never really enjoyed the physical act of sex itself, she could never understand what the fuss was all about, but did like the closeness she felt with Deon at the time. Maybe that was what it was all meant to be about. When she had moved in with Deon her mum had given her a brief chat about keeping her man happy and how it was her duty to obey her husb … her lover. Sharon noted, but had ignored the half said word.

As she sat wrapped up in her thoughts her hand gently caressed the remote control. Her mind unaware of the way her perfectly manicured fingers bounced lightly over the knobbly buttons. Slowly her thoughts dissolved back to reality and the TV. She wondered how late it was and just as she peered at the DVD player to read the time the lights, the TV, DVD player and the room all went dark.

THE LIFT 19

Simon was unaware of Deon's recent vision and didn't pick up on his muted tones. He continued to make light-hearted conversation.

'So what would you be doing if you weren't stuck in the lift tonight?'

Deon was still trying to cope with the image of the children being killed and didn't think through the question, didn't register that it was Friday, their intimate night.

'Dunno, maybe just watch TV.'

'You wouldn't go out? It's Friday night.'

Friday. The penny dropped and Deon blushed. Unlike earlier when Simon had asked about the previous power cut and caught him in bed with Sharon, this time the question was not coming from an insolent black security guard, it was coming from the voice that spoke words of comfort and the ears that listened to his story. There was, dare he say it, a bond of friendship forming between them which was too respectable for kiss and tell talk.

He concentrated on other Friday night activities.

'Sometimes we go out on a Friday. We go to visit friends, or just eat out at a restaurant.' The small talk was helping.

'To a restaurant? What kind of restaurant? Do you go to those fancy ones at the Waterfront?'

'No, that's where all the tourists go. There is a quiet place near us that we go to. Does good Italian food.'

Simon was about to ask if the Italian place was like the one he had taken Elise to on their first date, then thought better of it. He didn't want the conversation heading that way again, and suspected that neither did Deon.

'We'd have a nice bottle of red wine. I always have the prawn cocktail for starters, I love that, and then, depending on how I'm feeling, the Rigatoni Amatrciana or sometimes the veal. They do great veal there in a white wine sauce. Man, all this talk of food is making me hungry.'

'Me too. When I'm not working nightshift then Friday night is our treat. I buy some boerewors from the butcher and Lucy is a good cook. She does it just right with *pap* and tomato stew. But this week I'm doing nights so I've got peanut butter sandwiches downstairs.'

'Black Cat?'

'Ja, it's the best peanut butter around.'

'Black belt huh? Uh-uh Black Cat. Remember that ad with the kid that does that judo stuff on the bad guy after eating his Black Cat?'

'Ja, I remember that one, it was really funny.'

'They used to have some good adverts back then. Nowadays they're not so funny. How about that one for Lunch Bar? And what kind of a Mac are yew?'

'A Makathini!' The two men burst into laughter as they visualised the little black man in a kilt pulling over a team of burly Scotsmen in a tug of war after eating his Lunch Bar.

'A Makathini,' Deon chuckled again after the laughter had died down.

The two were silent for a moment and Deon suddenly felt his mood sink again.

'Gladys Makathini.' The name spiralled out of his past and onto his lips.

'Hmmm?' Simon's thoughts had returned to his abandoned sandwich. He was not sure what the time was but did feel it was too early to eat, yet his stomach, having been reminded of the nearby presence of food, suddenly demanded attention.

Deon was surprised by the appearance of the name and didn't respond to Simon's questioning grunt. His mind meanwhile responded to this intrusion by throwing him into a turmoil of emotions. Somehow he had known that this episode in his life would come up before they were released from the dark, and the name, Gladys Makathini had now forced itself to the fore. It was no longer an ominous feeling lurking in the shadows of his subconscious, it was out there, it was real and he knew he couldn't put it back. All that could save him now would be the return of power and light.

He forced his way back to when he was standing waiting for the lift to arrive, hoping this would save him from Gladys Makathini. What had he been thinking then? Certainly not about Gladys Makathini. He wasn't even thinking about Elise. He searched the debris of his mind for the elusive thoughts.

Simon was following his stomach's lead and his thoughts were all around his peanut butter sandwiches. His mother had made them for him while he was getting ready for work. Working nights was always difficult as he didn't get to see Lucy as she was gone when he got in and he left before she got home. When he worked the day shift then Lucy would make his sandwiches. She usually did his favourite – mixed fruit jam, and she spread it liberally. Funny, he thought, they advertise Black Cat but I can't remember seeing an advert for mixed fruit jam.

Sharon. That's what, or rather who Deon had been thinking about when the lift came. Ja, good old Sharon, he recalled wondering if he would end up being too late for the Friday Fuck as he crudely called it when talking to his friends. She had sounded a bit annoyed when he had rung to tell her he would be late. He realised this now, but at the time of the call he was too caught up in finishing the document he was busy with.

Why had she been so annoyed? It wasn't as if this was the first time he had had to call her to say he was going to be late. It was not like he worked late often. Maybe it was just because it was a Friday night, it was unusual to be late on a Friday. That must be it.

He hoped that she would not be too tired or annoyed when he got home, he could do with some loving. He wondered if Sharon would even be awake. Would she try calling to find out where he was?

Why did they never advertise mixed fruit jam? Simon thought. So many people he knew loved its fruity sweetness. He remembered the little shop near the village where he grew up having rows of the brightly coloured tins of the jam and how his mother would buy a tin as a treat for his birthday and another one for Peter's birthday. It never lasted long because they would plaster their bread with it and, when mum wasn't around, they would sneak in and dip their fingers into the tin, licking it up with big grins on their faces. She must have known they were doing this, but she never said. A smile played across Simon's face, this was a warm memory.

Hopefully she's fallen asleep otherwise she'll be in a right panic by now knowing her. Deon continued his thoughts about Sharon. She would probably have tried calling the office and maybe even his cell if she had forgotten that it had been stolen. What would she do next? Most likely call her dad. Good old Mr van Tonder to the rescue. Daddy's little girl's in a panic so here comes superdad to sort everything out. Of course Deon Scott will be the one to blame for causing all this upset, causing all this commotion. But he was completely innocent. There was nothing he could do to prevent this, he was powerless.

Gladys Makathini. Was he completely innocent there? Had he been powerless then? Gladys Makathini. How did that name come into the lift?

GLADYS MAKATHINI

Gladys Makathini woke up at four as she always did. She fumbled in the dark, found the matches and lit the stub of candle that sat next to her bed. The dull light flicked through the room vaguely dusting the furthest corners with a murky gloom. She moved quietly over to a corner and splashed her face with some water from a bucket that stood there.

In her cardboard box crib, Precious Makathini stirred at the sounds and opened her one year old eyes. She was hungry and gurgled to her mother to come and feed her. Gladys lifted her daughter from the box and laid her on the bed, propping her up with a pillow. Precious' eyes watched as her mother moved around the room, preparing her breakfast and getting dressed for work.

She spooned the baby food into Precious' eager mouth and wiped round it to clear the spillage. At four thirty she hoisted Precious onto her back, fastening her into place with a brightly coloured wrap and walked out into the cool morning air. The dark streets bustled with life as the township set about its daily routine of pleasing the white masters.

The air was thick with the smell of revolution and Gladys hurried along the road, watching carefully for any signs of the uprising that had become part of daily life. About ten blocks down the dusty road, she turned into another street and knocked quietly at the door of the second house. Bleary eyed, her sister Mary opened the door and took the infant bundle from Gladys indicating with a nod of her head that her man was home and still asleep.

Gladys acknowledged the nod and left quietly. Mary's man had a temper, especially if he was hung over. He didn't have a job, but always had money. Gladys was sure that some illegal activities were involved, drugs or car theft, but she never said anything. She could not afford to lose the day care services of her sister.

She moved more quickly now that the weight of Precious was no longer on her back. It was a couple of blocks from Mary's place to the taxi rank. People streamed either side of her, all heading towards the mini busses that would take them off to the city or the white suburbs where they worked.

As she neared the rank, Gladys tensed up, glancing round for any sign of trouble. The taxi wars had intensified in the last few days as drivers fought for sole rights to certain routes.

'Morning Gladys.'

'Morning Miriam,' Gladys greeted her friend.

'Things seem quiet today after yesterday's shooting.'

'Any news on Mr Kunene?'

'They don't think he will live.'

'Hau! He was such a nice man, respectable. That will mean ten killed. I was so lucky I missed that fight.'

Miriam clicked her tongue in agreement as the two of them squashed into a taxi heading for Sandton, the suburb of the *nouveau riche* Johannesburg elite. The vehicle trundled out of the township and the tension inside eased momentarily until they were nearing the taxi rank of their destination where it was feared there may be another drive-by shooting.

Relieved, the two women bundled out the mini-bus and quickly moved off down the road, grateful to be away from the commuter war zone. At an intersection a few blocks on they went their separate ways, wishing each other a good day.

The sun was just rising and began to warm Gladys as she reached the large house belonging to the Cartwrights. She let herself in through the side gate that broke the electrified fence and slipped into the kitchen. She could hear the sound of the Cartwright family getting ready for the day.

Mr Cartwright had a senior position in one of the country's big banks and accordingly earned a fortune. Mrs Cartwright was a 'home executive' as she liked to refer to herself. The two children, Greg and Bev were spoilt rotten, given every luxury that money could afford.

Gladys opened the fridge and took out four eggs and some bacon. She made a mental note to ensure that Mrs Cartwright got more eggs when they did the shopping that afternoon. She set about frying the eggs and bacon while popping some bread into the toaster. She had long since grown immune to the smell of the food despite her stomach grumbling that she had not eaten yet, all her resources being used to pay the rent and feed Precious.

Mr Cartwright was the first to arrive in the kitchen, straightening his tie and turning the radio on to catch the morning news. He didn't acknowledge Gladys as she placed his breakfast in front of him, but started eating while studying a work-related document. As the news finished, he glanced up as Mrs Cartwright walked in wearing a long silk dressing gown and fluffy slippers.

'Where's Greg and Bev, I'm going to be late,' he demanded between mouthfuls. Mrs Cartwright shrugged, picked up a piece of toast and took a delicate bite out of it before sliding into her chair. Gladys put her coffee down on the table and she grabbed it, wrapping her hands around the mug to get the warmth from it.

'Gladys, go see what the children are doing.' She didn't look up as she gave the command.

Gladys moved quietly out the kitchen. Bev was just coming out of her room, and heading towards the kitchen. She pulled a face at Gladys and moved past. Gladys ignored the insolence, it wasn't worth losing her job over this, and reached Greg's bedroom door which was still closed. She knocked timidly on the door.

'Greg?'

No reply. She knocked a little louder.

'Greg, your breakfast is ready.'

The door opened and Greg glared at her for a second then stomped sullenly down the passage.

Once the kids and Mr Cartwright had headed off, Gladys cleared away the breakfast dishes while Mrs Cartwright showered and dressed. Gladys then set about cleaning the bedrooms and making up the beds. At ten, she put the kettle on and made Mrs Cartwright her tea which she took through to where she sat in the lounge. Thankfully today there were no guests but still the little digs came.

'Gladys, Mr Cartwright said that his egg was cold today. You must make sure that you cook it just before he comes in for breakfast, you know how he hates cold eggs.'

'I'm sorry madam. I will make sure next time,' Gladys replied putting the tea cup down next to her mistress. The eggs had been straight from the pan when Mr Cartwright had walked in. Gladys suspected that he hadn't said anything and that Mrs Cartwright was just making it up so she could find fault. It was not unusual to get these sorts of comments especially if there were guests.

'Gladys, your dress is dirty, you look a right state.' This was at the last little soiree that Mrs Cartwright had held. Back in the kitchen she had examined her dress but hadn't found the slightest stain. But there was no point arguing, it would only cost her her job.

The rest of the morning was spent finishing the cleaning and other odd jobs, then preparing lunch. While Mrs Cartwright ate hers, Gladys cut a couple of slices of bread for her own lunch allowance. *Always huge thick slices. Why does she need such big slices?* Mrs Cartwright had been heard to ask. She got the jam from the cupboard and smeared it onto the bread. *And she puts so much jam on it, I am constantly having to buy more. I should charge her for it.* She placed the bread onto the enamel plate, *I'm sure she uses my best plates when I'm not around,* and poured herself a cup of tea into which she added two spoons of sugar. *And I think she has about ten sugars in her tea. I think they do this just to spite us.*

Wednesday afternoons were always set aside for shopping so once the lunch things were cleared away, Mrs Cartwright got the car out of the garage and Gladys climbed obediently into the back seat. She smiled slightly, unseen by her mistress. It always struck her as odd that, being black, she was not good enough to sit up in the front seat, yet all the dignitaries she had seen on TV sat in the back seat with a lone driver up front. Often she and Miriam would joke about where their chauffeur had taken them that day.

'Don't forget eggs,' Mrs Cartwright reminded her.

She put two dozen eggs into the shopping cart and waited patiently to continue pushing the trolley around the shop while Mrs Cartwright chattered away to a friend she had just met.

Back home, Gladys prepared and served dinner and after washing up she let herself quietly out of the gate. The taxi back to the township was always a bit quieter at this late hour as all the office workers were already home.

She stopped at Mary's house and collected Precious who was fast asleep and remained so all the way home. Once back in her room, she put Precious down gently into the cardboard box crib, undressed and slid exhausted into bed, knowing that tomorrow it would all start again.

THE LIFT 20

The face of Gladys Makathini floated into Deon's mind. It was not the first time she had visited his thoughts with such clarity, but these recollections were never as vivid as the ghostly visits of Elise. He knew that Gladys was just an imprint on his mind, on his conscience. Her appearances were a reminder of a past event. Elise was something much more tangible. She was part of his conscience, part of the present. She was a part of his mind that was trying to find something.

'Do you ever remember seeing an advert for mixed fruit jam?' Simon was nowhere near Deon's thoughts this time.

'Huh?'

'Mixed fruit jam, do you ever remember seeing an advert for it?'

Deon discarded Gladys' face and smiled at the complete contrast between his thoughts and Simon's. What had led to this seemingly random question? What train of thought had got him there? Deon wondered.

'You mean other than in a supermarket ad like Spar or Pick 'n Pay where they say, *and a five hundred gram tin of mixed fruit jam for only twelve rand?*'

'Ja, has there ever been an ad just for mixed fruit jam?'

Deon thought for a bit. 'No I can't recall ever seeing one, why do you want to know?'

'I was wondering why they never advertised it. I mean everybody loves mixed fruit jam.'

'I don't.'

'What?'

'I don't like mixed fruit jam, it's too sweet for me.'

'Eish! You don't like mixed fruit jam. How can you not like it, it's the best jam ever. I love the stuff.'

Deon smiled at Simon's reaction.

'I suppose it's a bit like you preferring beer to wine. It's a black/white thing. Whites like wine and champagne, blacks like mixed fruit jam and beer.'

'Not together.'

'What?'

'Not together, I don't want my beer with my mixed fruit jam. I think a bit of apartheid is good when it comes to beer and jam.'

They both laughed.

'Strange these differences. Do you think it's a nature or a nurture thing?'

'Huh?'

'Nature versus nurture. It's one of the great psychological debates. Nurture is the way we are brought up. So maybe it is because you were fed mixed fruit jam when you were young that you like it so much, or maybe there is something in your genes that makes you like mixed fruit jam.'

'Something in my jeans? There are only legs in my jeans. Are you saying my legs make me like mixed fruit jam?'

'No, not those jeans. Genes. G-e-n-e-s. It's what makes you up physically, your body, your DNA and all that sort of stuff. So I'm saying that either you were born liking mixed fruit jam, because of something in your physical make up, that would be in your nature. Or you like it because you were fed it as a kid, that's nurture.'

Simon shook his head. He loved learning new things, but this was a bit above him. Nature? Nurture? Genes?

'All I know is that I have always liked mixed fruit jam, I don't care whether it is because of my jeans, or because I ate it as a kid,' he said at length and this stopped the conversation.

Deon's thoughts drifted back to Gladys Makathini. She was not going to go away. It was as though the lift and the darkness were sucking the story out of him, out of the depths where he had tried to hide it.

He knew that he was not alone in hiding that part of his life, few white male South Africans talked freely about their time in the army. Yes, some talked about the funnier times when they were not in action, times when they were mucking about at the army bases. Deon had swapped some peace during wartime stories with his mates, but no-one talked about the war during wartime. Those stories were mostly untold; it was an unwritten code amongst ex-servicemen. Only talk about the good things.

'Ballasbak.' The word came back to him.

'Huh?'

'Ballasbak. That's what we used to call the time in the army when we had nothing to do. We would lie around in the sun baking our balls. Ballasbak.'

Simon laughed at the description, but the laughter faded quickly as the thought hit him.

'You were in the army?'

'Ja, remember earlier I said that I had smelt human flesh burning? That was when I was in the army.'

Simon flinched at the mention of burning human flesh, but that story was told, he didn't need to go back to it.

'Oh ja,' he said, remembering that he had been so engrossed with telling his story about Peter's death that he hadn't really reflected on the fact that Deon had been in the army, had been part of the enemy. He suddenly felt strange. In the few hours they had been in the lift Deon had called him friend and at the same time confessed that he had been his enemy. How times have changed, he mused. One day we are sitting facing each other as enemies in the township, the next we're sitting in a lift together talking as friends, sharing our pain. He struggled to think of Deon as a friend.

'Ja. We all had to go to the army.' Deon continued to explain himself. 'All us white kids, all the boys anyway, not the girls. Two years we had to do, and then camps.'

'Camps?'

'When I went you had to do camps after you finished your initial two years. They could call you up for a month at a time for years after your first stint. It was like going back into the army every time. Hell if apartheid hadn't fallen I'd still be having to do camps now. That's a scary thought.'

'So all the white men had to go to the army?'

'Ja, it was the law, we were all conscripted. When we were at school you had to fill in a form and they sent it off to the army to register you. Then every year after that you'd get call up papers saying you had to report for army duty at such and such a place on such and such a date. Geez I hated those call ups, they always made me nervous. If you were still in school or at university, you could postpone it, but you could never get out of it. That was the law.'

'The law?'

'If you didn't go you could get chucked into prison.'

'You could go to prison if you didn't go to the army!'

This threw a whole new light on how Simon viewed those hated army boys sitting in their armoured cars, guns at the ready every time there was trouble in the township.

'Ja. If you didn't pitch when they called you up, you got six years in prison. There were some who objected. I remember there was this one guy, David Bruce was his name; he made the news for refusing to go. I admire him, his courage. Most of us just obeyed our call-ups; we were all too scared to refuse. Maybe if everyone had refused things would have been different, but you need a leader to do this, and we never really had any leaders.

'Some guys skipped the country, they used to call that the chicken run. Problem with that was that you could never come back because the military police would bust you as soon as you put foot back in the country again.'

'What? You mean there were whites in exile?'

'Oh ja, lots of them moved to England, Australia, America, Canada,

147

anywhere that would take them. A bit like now where a lot of whites have left the country because of the violence here.'

'Eish! White exiles.' Simon shook his head, bemused at this concept. To him there had only been black exiles who had left the country, most of them as wanted men, terrorists.

'Did any of those white exiles come back after apartheid?'

'I don't know. I suppose some did. I never knew any myself. I suspect that most of them built up a new life for themselves wherever they went so probably won't want to move back. I mean they were youngsters when they left, seventeen or eighteen years old. They would have been at least thirty by the time apartheid fell, some even older – in their forties. Probably would have good jobs, maybe got married in the country they went to and such like. Why would they want to come back, especially with the stories they must hear about the violence here. South Africa doesn't have the best reputation for living safely you know.'

Simon nodded sadly, he could understand that.

'So you didn't leave, you went to the army?'

'No choice really. You could object on religious grounds, saying that you were a pacifist. Then you had to do six years community service like working in hospital or prison administration or something like that. But you needed to be able to prove that you were religious. You had to get a letter from your minister and such like, but I've never been a church go-er so there was no way I could get out of it on those grounds. Anyway I thought it was better to do the two years and get it over with than do six years in prison. I wanted to get on with my life.'

Simon was beginning to realise how difficult it had been for young whites to avoid army service. It was quite strange to accept that those fresh pale faces, which he had seen and hated in the townships back then, were not necessarily there by choice. They had to do that. He had always assumed that the soldiers wanted to be there.

'Most guys I knew, my friends, didn't really want to go to the army.' It was almost as if Deon had read Simon's thoughts. 'But some of those I served with were a bit mad. They loved it in the army. They loved carrying guns, the power it gave them. And worst of all there were some idiots that loved killing blacks. Those were the really mental ones, hell they were scary.

'There was one, he was psycho. He had been up on the Angolan border and he was always bragging about how many blacks he had killed. He was so proud of it. He used to tell stories of how he had killed unarmed civilians. I mean he was bragging about it, he had no shame or remorse. When we asked him why he had killed these people he just said, "Because they were kaffirs". Those were his actual words. I couldn't believe the

148

way he said it. He was proud about doing it, like he had done a great service to humanity. There was such hatred for the blacks in everything he did and said. He was really unpleasant.'

Simon was not overly shocked by this story. This was what he suspected about white people. What had shocked him more was the fact that most of the soldiers had not been there by choice, they were forced into doing it. It was strange to realise that a lot of them did not want to be there at all. Deon's latest revelation about that mental guy fitted in better with the image of young whites that he had grown up with.

LUCY 5

She fumbled in the dark and eventually found the matches and candle, then carried the dim light back into the lounge and put it onto the table. Simon's mum settled back slightly in her chair. Secretly she liked these power cuts. Yes, it was nice having the bright electric lights, the stove and the fridge, but whenever they had to huddle around a candle she was always reminded of life in the village. The family would sit around the dying embers of the fire that glowed in the centre of the hut, the pale light catching only the whites of their eyes. It always seemed so cosy, so homely. It reminded her of simpler times, times when Peter was still alive and Simon still had his innocence.

She smiled as she looked round her recollected home and her eyes rested gently on the Simon in her mind.

'He says he enjoys the power cuts.'

'Who mama?'

'Simon. He says he enjoys the power cuts. He likes sitting in the dark at reception when the building is completely quiet.'

Lucy tried to picture the lobby that she had seen once when briefly visiting Simon there. It would be dark now, but there must be some light from the moon to keep him company. There was a big shiny desk that he sat behind. He had a little TV monitor that showed him what was happening in the building. He only had to press some buttons to change which camera he was getting his view from. It was quite a big reception area with some nice blue sofas where guests sat when they were waiting to meet some of the businessmen who worked in the building.

Lucy pictured this scene in that dull blue light that a bright moon would cause. She saw Simon sitting patiently, handsomely behind the desk, alert at his post.

'He's always liked the night.' Simon's mother smiled again and seemed to retreat further from the candle, snuggling up to the dark, drawing strength from it.

'I think he gets that from you,' Lucy laughed gently.

'Yes, there is something comforting about the dark. It hides things that are horrible and nasty so you don't have to look at them. You can be yourself in the dark.'

Lucy thought about this for a moment. She didn't like it herself, too many bad things happened when there was no light. You never knew what was hidden, what dangers lurked there. She didn't want to contradict the old woman, but wanted to lodge some sort of protest.

'Yes, but the darkness also hides things of beauty.'

Simon's mother shook her head, 'Anything that is beautiful you can keep with you, even if it is dark. It is dark now, yet you keep Simon in your mind don't you?'

Lucy smiled at the woman's wisdom.

THE LIFT 21

'Action Man Anton. That was the nickname we gave him,' Deon went on, omitting that they usually added *slayer of kaffirs* to the nickname. He didn't think Simon would really understand the sarcasm that went with the second part of the name.

'He was PF, permanent force, one of those who really wanted to be in the army. He kept telling us about the action he had seen up north on the border and how he had been involved in contact with the enemy a helluva lot. Some of the youngsters looked up to him, admired him for this, they wanted to be like him. But those ous were so young. They didn't really have a clue what it was all about, they just thought that having a gun was somehow cool. They thought that it was all about killing the enemy. It wasn't so cool when some of their buddies got it. Made them realise that war was a two way thing, both sides lost people. It wasn't pretty.

'I remember the way that Action Man went on. He made out like it was really something to go up to the border and kill people. He led those young troopies on and they fell for it. What a wanker,' The passage of time, the darkness and the isolation of the lift gave him the freedom to express what he had thought back then.

Simon was caught between agreeing with Deon and obeying the old rule that had been so drummed into him – you cannot voice negative opinions about the whites in front of them. He gave a half committal grunt.

'A complete and utter wanker.' Deon took some satisfaction in driving home the point that he in no way wished to be associated with this unpleasant man.

'Were there a lot like him?' Simon was curious to know. He wanted to confirm his long held belief that most whites were quite happy to defend apartheid by joining the army.

'No, I only met a few real hardcore ones. There were others that didn't really mind being in the army. Given a choice I think they would still have gone, but they were brainwashed into thinking they were doing the right thing. Protecting us from the *swart gevaar*, you know the black danger, the commies. But even those guys didn't really like it once they were there, especially the ones who had to go to the townships. The border was different, that was a proper war. We were fighting the communists there, a proper war, guns against guns. But the townships …' He left off as memories of his time in the townships came back to him.

Simon waited. This was interesting as he knew very little about the border war. He knew of its existence and that it was meant to be about fighting for his freedom, but it never touched his life directly. He was too busy trying to survive under apartheid, too busy trying to survive the poverty and the police raids to worry about a war happening far away.

The troops in the township though were a completely different matter. This had been part of his daily life not too many years back when things were politically hectic. He had seen them nearly every day, they were in his face, he could never ignore them. Now here was a chance to hear about those troopies first hand. Not only about them, but also what they thought. He gave Deon the space he needed to expand his story.

'Geez, the townships. I mean there we were fresh out of school, wet behind the ears and all that. Hell most of us hadn't even voted, hadn't a clue what we were letting ourselves in for, or what we were fighting for, but hey here you go, here's a gun, off you go. Go point it at some people in a neighbouring suburb. They may throw a few stones at you and if they get really miffed there will possibly be an occasional petrol bomb hurled your way. But don't worry, you've got a gun, just don't use it unless you absolutely have to.'

SHARON 3

Sharon opened her eyes and blinked. It was dark and disorientating. Where was she? What had happened? She sat up quickly, convinced that there was something important she needed to attend to. A slight dizziness took hold of her mind for a second then left. Slowly her thoughts collected the necessary answers. She was still on the sofa in the lounge where she had drifted off to sleep when the power had gone. But there was something else.

Her body ached slightly from having slept in the strange position that the sofa had dictated to her limbs. She stretched cautiously, easing the dull pain from her muscles. What time was it? It felt late. She needed to find the torch or some candles. The pale light from the moon gave her sufficient courage to move and she stood up.

She hated this being alone in the house, even worse now that there was no power. The light was eerie and who knew what lurked in the shadows. Where was Deon? Shouldn't he be home by now? How long had she been asleep? She went quickly through to the kitchen feeling her way along the walls, a sense of urgency taking hold.

Her shaking hands found the drawer and she grabbed at the torch. The beam lit up her confidence and she shone the light round the room. On the wall above the door, the battery-operated clock said it was ten past twelve.

A horrible tightness gripped her stomach and she felt a wave of nausea pass over her. Ten past twelve! Where the hell was Deon! It was not like him to be this late without calling. She searched quickly for her phone and her fingers shook as she dialled his office line.

'Answer, damn it,' she pleaded to the ringing on the other side, her voice filled with panic.

'Hello, you've reached Deon Scott. I can't …'

She stared at her phone for a second then dialled his cell.

'The number you have dialled is no longer available.'

'Where is he?' She screamed at the automated service. 'What have you done with him?'

'Please hang up and try again.'

She took a deep breath, feeling the darkness closing in on her, visions of Deon being hijacked and shot fizzed up in her mind.

Calm down, calm down, she pleaded with herself and slowly rational thought returned. She now remembered that Deon had lost his cell a little while back, so he wouldn't answer that, but why wasn't he at his desk?

She gripped the side of the kitchen table, unsettling thoughts firing through her mind.

Please God, please let him be safe. Surely he was safe. But this is South Africa, no-one is safe.

Her hands fumbled with her phone again.

'Hello? Dad? I didn't wake you, did I?'

THE LIFT 22

Deon went silent for a while after his little tirade. It felt good to have said all that and better still to have said it to a black person. Even this long after apartheid had fallen, people still never spoke negatively about their army stint. Rather keep quiet, it was embarrassing history.

But he had resented those two years of his life 'serving his country'. It was partly the waste of time, the sitting around when he could have been getting on with his life that irked him and partly the injustice of the whole thing.

The fact that it was ultimately a war that his side had lost irritated him too. War always seems more futile to the loser. Not only had the whites lost, but they had done so in a strange manner. There was no great decisive battle in the traditional sense where one side had overpowered the other. It was not the military that ultimately decided who won. The whole war issue had sort of fizzled out as the battlefield moved from the bush in Angola to the jail cells and politicians' offices. Not your everyday armistice.

Having done his time in the army, the final resolution of South Africa's political problems seemed to lack closure for him. Not that he wanted it any other way, he was pleased that things had been resolved in the way they were, surely the death toll was lower this way. But somehow it left him with an acute sense of loss for those two years and that was what he found difficult to accept. Even more so because of Gladys Makathini.

He conjured up the face of Gladys Makathini, so clear in his mind even now despite the time that separated her from him. *They all look the same.* This was a typical racist white statement about black people and it crept into his thoughts. He smiled suddenly at how wrong this sentiment seemed, given his ability to recall in vivid detail the face of Gladys Makathini. She did not look the same as all the others, not to him anyway. Her features would be instantly recognisable; he had seen her face often enough. It was etched in his mind.

'So you ended up in the townships then?'

'Ja.'

'Did you have a choice about that? I mean could you choose if you went to the border or to the township?' Simon was looking for a further excuse for Deon. He sort of knew that if the whities had had no choice about going to the army then there would be no choice about where they were sent. He willed Deon to confirm this.

In his sensitive state Deon bristled. *Simon is angling for a fight, looking for a reason to pick at the scab of my white guilt,* he thought. He sat up straight and took a deep breath.

'Oh ja, we had a choice, either go where you were told or spend some time in DB'

'DB?'

'Detention barracks. Like prison for soldiers. If you didn't obey orders they sent you off to DB and it was marked on your record.'

'I see,' Simon was appeased, but Deon's conscience had been pricked and it was uncomfortable. He kicked back at the supposed threat.

'Well what the hell would you have done?' The anger in his voice surprised Simon, he was almost shouting.

'Go on, tell me. What should one do? Damned if you do, damned if you don't. What would you have done in my situation?' He rose to a proper shout now. His anger was not directed at Simon though, but rather at the system that had put him in the position it had. He wanted someone to stand up and say that it was okay that he had gone to the army. That everyone knew he had no choice, that he had done the right thing under the circumstances. He wanted this black man to condone the course his life had been forced to take.

'I … I …' Simon stammered. It was not just the nature of the sudden attack by Deon that threw him; it was also the question itself. It was a trick question wasn't it?

'I don't know.' He was buying time. He knew the answer was unsatis-factory, not only to Deon but to himself too. 'I need time to think about it.'

'Okay.' Deon's anger was slowly leaving him.

Simon's thoughts raced. What could he say? How could he answer this question? Since the fall of apartheid he had begun to learn what it was like to be proud to be black. In the old days, being black had been something to be ashamed of, you were treated like dirt and felt worth no more than dirt. Despite a strong dislike of and suspicions about whites, being black had never really been something Simon felt he could feel proud of. As apartheid had slowly melted into the history books, so too had his feelings. In its place grew this new concept of being proud to be black. Not only proud to be black, but proud to be South African.

He had spent most of his life being subservient to the white man. Even now as a security guard he was still subservient, but not quite in the same way as it was before. A part of him was instinctively saying agree with the whitie; tell him you would have gone along with the system. Tell him what he wants to hear. It's in your programming to answer this way.

But that was a cop-out. It was selling out his black brothers and sisters, especially those who had died in the struggle at the hands of people like

Deon who had just gone along with the system, taken the easy route.

'Think about it,' Deon was much calmer now, 'it's easy to say that you wouldn't have gone to the army isn't it?'

'Yes. That is what I want to say,' then with conviction he went on, 'I wouldn't have gone. I saw what you white kids did in the townships. I would not have done that.' He relaxed a little; the feeling that he had to kowtow to the white man had subsided and he was pleased with his answer.

'It wasn't that easy,' Deon's voice was resigned, he had had a little time to think. Simon had not been baiting him but rather his anger was a result of pent up feelings and experiences, of bad memories of the time. Things happened back then that he had never really worked through. He didn't begrudge Simon his answer. It was, he supposed, difficult for someone who had never been faced with that stark choice to really understand what the decision was all about. At seventeen years old you are hardly politically aware of what the consequences of your decision are. However, the consequences of not complying with your call up papers were made very clear to you. Few were brave enough to face those punishments.

'We didn't really know what we were letting ourselves in for. No-one talked about what it was really like in the army. You had to go defend your country we were told. Defend the way of life that you had grown up with. A way of life that, because it was always that way, seemed like the natural order of things. I mean as I grew up the world around me said that the white man is superior and the black inferior. I had no other experience to tell me otherwise, no other frame of reference. And the outside voices that did make noises about it were either muted by the government or discredited by the regime's propaganda machine.

'I suppose another thing was that we had a lot to lose, a lot more than you guys. You were at the end of your tether. Tired of being downtrodden. All you had to look forward to was a life of misery. Hell I'm surprised you guys didn't kick us whities out of the country earlier. But us whites had, and still have, a great life in this country. I mean the weather's good, we had all the wealth, we can afford big houses, comfortable lifestyles and all that. We felt we needed to protect that. Wouldn't you want to protect what you have?'

He paused for a second, but the question was meant to be rhetorical.

'Not many would want to rock the boat, risk all this wealth and comfort for a political ideal. Try put yourself in my shoes. If I didn't go to the army that would have been a stain on my record that would stay with me. If I had opted to go to jail instead of the army it would have ruined any career prospects for me. I had a cushy upbringing. I didn't want to give that up for another man's cause. Would you really be prepared to give up a cushy lifestyle to fight for someone else's rights? I don't think many people are that brave to do something like that.'

Simon tried to digest what Deon was saying. It was difficult to accept this excuse. There was too much in his past that had affected him deeply for him to make allowances for any excuses. But if he was honest with himself would he in Deon's shoes have done differently? He tried to forget his upbringing, tried to forget the anger that had been endemic in black people as they grew up in poverty, not only poverty of the physical but also poverty of dignity.

It was hard to forget that. Yes the anger itself had abated but the memory of the anger still lingered.

'It is difficult to say,' he said at length, his voice heavy with thought. 'I cannot easily accept your reasons because my people suffered as a result of your decision, and yet, if someone came to me now and told me I had to leave my family and go and fight a war to free people from a tyrant, people I didn't know, I would struggle to go willingly.'

The unresolved issue hung in the dark between the two men.

LUCY 6

The old woman had begun to snore softly in her chair. Lucy smiled at the sound. She got up and, taking the candle with her, walked to the bedroom. Here she picked up a small blanket and took it back to the living room.

Taking care not to wake her, she wrapped the blanket around Simon's mum then withdrew quietly to her room. This often happened. The old woman would fall asleep in her chair and then later on, usually when the call of nature grew loud, she would shuffle to the toilet, then move on to her bed.

In the early days, Lucy had tried to wake her, but had been reprimanded kindly. 'Let me sleep my child. There are nights when I struggle to go to sleep so when it comes like this I must welcome it and make the most of it.'

In the bedroom Lucy undressed and prepared for bed. When she had settled herself between the bedclothes she let her mind turn again to Simon. She missed his warm body next to her when he did nights, missed hearing his light breathing as he slept. She even missed the way he would turn over in his sleep, dragging the blankets with him. How did he cope on his own in that building, she thought? Does he miss me?

Her mind played over the time they had spent together, going back as far as the day when they first met when the taxi had overturned. She remembered that first night she had spent with him and the slight embarrassment mingled with the glow of new love she felt as she had faced the quizzical look from his mother and the kids the next morning. They had seemed so alien back then. She smiled as she thought of them now and how she loved them and saw them as part of her family.

Her mind then moved forward to when Simon had hurriedly kissed her as she rushed off to work that morning. He looked tired as he readied himself for bed.

She was looking for a clue as she ran her thoughts over their relationship, something that would give her an idea of what could possibly help Simon make it through the night shift without going out of his mind. She pictured him with his kids. He was so good with them, always making sure they did their homework, helping where he could and laughing and encouraging them on to greater things every time his own meagre education let him down.

Maybe that was it, maybe he filled his mind with thoughts of the kids, of their future, a future with so much more promise than he had at that age. The answer worked, but it was not the best fit. There had to be something else.

She moved her mind on to see if there was a better answer but tiredness began to take hold. She was just drifting off to sleep when she remembered something and smiled.

THE LIFT 23

Deon sighed. He accepted that it was not an easy question for Simon to answer. He even felt a bit guilty about asking it, about putting Simon on the spot like that. It wasn't really fair on him. It was as if he was trying to dissipate his guilt, transfer some of it to Simon by getting him to say that he would have done the same. It was underhanded and Elise would not have approved.

'Not easy,' he said at length, releasing Simon of any obligation to answer. 'It screwed a lot of guys up you know.' That was true enough. 'Some guys couldn't handle it, they couldn't cope with the stress of the army. I don't know if it was just the physical and mental demands of basic training or if the politics of the whole situation also played a role. I mean, army life's not for everyone at the best of times. Some just can't handle it normally, but some had the added burden of just not believing in the cause we had to fight for. Some guys had a huge guilt complex about it, and still do.

'There was one guy ...' Deon suddenly remembered the unpleasant episode. 'Hell, I can't even remember his name. Only knew him briefly during basics. Why can't I remember his name now? I suppose it's not too important. Anyway he was a quiet guy, didn't talk much. They gave him a hard time. I guess they picked up that he was pretty anti-apartheid or something. Not that he said anything, but you could just tell by the way he reacted to the whole *kill the kaffir, the kaffir is bad* propaganda that they threw at us.'

Simon winced slightly at the use of the 'k' word, but realised that it was in context. It wasn't Deon using the word.

'Apart from that,' Deon continued, unaware of the slight discomfort caused, 'he wasn't very good with all the physical training we had to do. He was a slow runner so they always made the rest of us do extra PT until he caught up. All done in the name of building us up into a tight unit. But it pissed off most of the guys in the unit big time and they treated him like dirt.

'Blew his brains out eventually, couldn't take it anymore. There was a rumour that someone in the unit killed him and I wouldn't have been surprised, there were some rough ones there. I can't say for sure that didn't happen, but from what I saw ...'

He hesitated for a moment, contemplating the lack of emotion he felt about the whole issue, then went on '... I'm pretty convinced that he topped himself.'

'We were told that officially he *had an accident with his weapon.*' Deon did the two fingered air scratch to indicate the inverted commas around the phrase and then felt a little silly as it was dark and Simon couldn't see him doing so. However his tone of voice conveyed the sarcasm at the euphemism.

'But it was all bullshit. Especially when I heard on the radio a little later that this guy was apparently killed in action on the border. He never went near the border. We were stationed at Potch the whole time.' The memory of this deceit aroused a hidden anger in Deon and the vehemence crept into his voice. 'Makes you wonder how many of those *killed in action* deaths were really *blew his brains out because he couldn't cope with the shit the army was dishing out* deaths. But I suppose that wouldn't make good news, wouldn't help the cause. It's not good that white men aren't tougher than their black opponents.'

Simon was surprised at his companion's sudden anger. He could understand the reasons for it, but had never expected to hear such strong feelings against the army from a white.

'Have you ever had to mop up someone's brains from the floor?'

'No!' Simon recoiled from the question.

'Not pleasant I can tell you.' Deon gave a slight chuckle, but there was no humour in it. 'You know that despite the official line that he had had an accident with his weapon, they knew that we knew, so they made out that it was his fault. That he wasn't good enough, too scared to protect his country and all that. Only real men were good enough for this country. Only real white men.'

Deon sat back. His mood had swung again, he was now resigned to the suicide's fate. It was all part of the growing pains of the nation, a rite of passage. He hadn't really got to know the guy anyway and that was why he never felt any sense of loss. Just like those others *killed in action* in the case of white troopies or *killed in the unrest* in the case of black civilians. Statistics really. It was hard to feel too deeply for them, especially when you had your own deep wounds to contend with.

Deon willed the spectral Elise to appear to him now. He needed something to cling to, to give him strength. But the lift remained dark. He blinked his eyes to ensure they were open, it had become difficult to be sure having been without light for so long.

'Ed.' Suddenly the name came back. 'Ed Stoppard. That was his name. Poor guy, never stood a chance really. Looking back if you had asked me at the start who wouldn't make it through basics I would have said Ed. He was too soft, too delicate a soul.'

Remembering the name brought a realness to the kid and with the name came images of that day.

163

ED STOPPARD

Deon glanced up during the prayers. He didn't feel overly comfortable sitting in the small church listening to the army chaplain prattle on. Most of the sermon was given over to subtly saying that they were doing God's work in the army. He went because it gave him a break from the monotony of basics, and, he had heard, those in charge would treat you slightly better is you were a church go-er.

In the pew opposite sat Ed Stoppard. His slight frame and pale pink skin gave him an almost girl-ish appearance. The blonde stubble on his head was soft and downy. His face was pulled tight in a grimace born out of the stress of being in this hostile place. He was not wearing his glasses and his pale blue eyes stared intensely, almost threateningly at the chaplain.

Deon sensed that something was not right, that Ed was too unsettled. But what could he do? They were all going through a tough time and showing any sort of concern for someone who was the cause of a lot of their problems would only get him in trouble with the rest of the guys. He bowed his head again, glad of the short time he had to relax and let the prayers wash over him.

Generally the unit had Sunday mornings free, only being inspected and made to run after lunch. It was a small break in the otherwise relentless barrage of PT and other degradations. Most sat around the mess tent writing letters home, or lay basking in the sunshine, enjoying the balm that the warmth gave their aching muscles.

It had been Deon's turn to tidy the chapel after the service so by the time all the hymn books were stashed neatly at the back of the small church, most of the guys were already relaxing. Deon walked slowly past the mess tent, not noticing the others there. He had started to compose a letter home in his head.

Dear Mom and Dad, Another day in paradise … No too sarcastic, that would get him into trouble.

Dear Mom and Dad, Another week has gone by, and I still don't feel like I have done anything to help keep you safe from the marauding terrorists. I hope you have not been murdered in your beds. Hell that would get him about seventy hours of PT. What do you write home about when you can't express what you actually think and all you've done is run miles and miles in heavy army kit, been deprived of sleep and forced to eat substandard food while all the time being told what a great service you are doing for your country? Still he had to write something, it pleased those in charge, it showed that you were a fine upstanding citizen who had loved ones to protect.

The barracks were deserted when he got there, the others had already got their writing materials, except for Ed. He sat on his bed fumbling with the lock on his trommel.

'Hey Ed get off your bed, you're screwing up those corners. If there's an inspection we'll all get extra PT'

Ed glanced up momentarily then continued searching inside his foot locker. There was something disturbed and disturbing in his look but Deon chose to ignore it.

'Come on Ed, sort your corners out damn it.' Deon had reached his bunk and started to unlock his locker. He found his writing pad and pen and then stood up and started to go over to Ed to berate him further. But suddenly he had a change of heart. Leave the poor bugger alone for a second, he thought. It's Sunday, he deserves a break.

'Just tidy those corners,' he said in a slightly softer tone and left.

He walked slowly back to the mess tent and sat down. He still needed to think about what to say in the letter home, but his mind kept wondering back to Ed and he contemplated going back to check on him. But the threat of being associated with the weakling of the group and all the hassle that brought made him stay where he was.

Dear Mom and Dad, There is a guy in the unit who is not coping. I saw him in the barracks today and he looked scared. Something is up with him that's for sure. Like that would get past the army censors.

He had just sat down to write his letter when he heard the shot and his stomach tightened in a knot of sickness. Without thinking, he jumped up and ran back to the barracks followed by some of the others who picked up on his urgency.

When he had finished mopping up the bloody mess that Ed had bequeathed his unit, Deon sat down again to write home.

Dear Mom and Dad

It's Sunday again, our one day a week when we get to relax a bit. The P.T. is hard work, but I have made some good friends in the unit. They are a good bunch of guys. I was glad to hear that Auntie Sal is on the mend. Please can you send some more dried fruit. The guys here love it and we have already finished the last lot. Sorry this letter is so short, but I had barrack cleaning duties this morning. I promise to write more next week.

Lots of love

Deon

He re-read the letter then paused while gathering his thoughts. At last he folded it, put it into an envelope and as he stood up to take it to the postmaster he tried to ignore the dried blood that he noticed on the back of his hand.

THE LIFT 24

Simon shifted his position on the floor and sighed. He found it hard to believe that such things had gone on in the army. All the propaganda directed at the whites to make them fear and hate the blacks, that he could understand. He had been on the receiving end of its effects, but to lie about the death of one of their own? That did not make sense.

It was tempting not to believe Deon. The whites had lied before, was it beyond reason to believe that here was one of them lying now? However there had been too much emotion in Deon's voice for him to be lying. He felt he should say something and cleared his throat to speak but couldn't find any words to express his thoughts.

Deon had fallen silent again, going back into a retrospective mood, examining the past. What did all this mean? Where had all this violence and death got us?

He began comparing Elise's death with Ed's, ignoring the potential hurt this could bring. Both of them had been young but where Elise had been free, Ed seemed chained to the norms of the abnormal society. He had desperately wanted to fit in, to be part of the unit, and the disappointment of his failure to do so had ultimately led to his death.

The deaths had been violent, not only in a physical sense, but also in the suddenness with which they had come. The blood that had flowed was particularly vivid in Deon's mind as was the sense of shock.

Although Elise had come from a middle class background, the family rift had meant that she had struggled in those first few years away from home. Ed, from what Deon had gathered, was from a wealthy family and, being an only child had been doted on by his parents, he had never had any financial worries.

Different backgrounds, different circumstances but there was no denying that the cause of both deaths lay rooted in the strange politics of the country. Undoubtedly Peter's death was due to the politics and to a degree the unfortunate killing of Marie Stander had also been touched by the long tentacles of apartheid's legacy.

And then there was Gladys Makathini, still waiting for her story to be told to the dark of the lift.

'I knew someone called Ed once.' Simon was elsewhere.

'What?'

'I said that I knew someone called Ed once. He owned the café near where I used to work. He made the best curry and rice. Five rand would buy you a big plate of it, or you could get the bunny chow. I used to have curry nearly every day when I worked there in Isando.'

Deon chuckled at the mention of the food, then suddenly recalled something he had once read. 'Do you know how bunny chow came about?'

'Huh?'

'Bunny chow, do you know how it all started, you know putting the curry into a hollowed out loaf of bread?'

'No.'

'I read it on the Internet somewhere. Apparently in the old days before we had cardboard plates and plastic knives and forks, people sat inside the cafés and ate off proper plates using proper knives and forks. The white café owners would always worry about blacks breaking the plates or stealing the cutlery, but there wasn't much they could do.

'Then this one café owner noticed that most of his black customers liked to have a slice of bread with their curry and hit on the idea of serving the curry inside the loaf of bread. The bread then worked as a plate to hold the curry and a knife and fork weren't necessary as you could just tear off bits of bread to mop up the sauce. So hey presto, no more worries about blacks breaking plates or stealing the cutlery.'

Simon laughed. 'So something good actually came from apartheid. The bunny chow, apartheid's gift to the world.'

Deon laughed too, relieved at the break from the more sombre topics that had weighed down so heavily on them.

'But why is it called bunny chow? I mean bunnies don't eat curry.'

This brought on another bout of laughter from both men which was slightly more forced than it should have been, both of them needing the release of tension and exaggerating their mirth in an effort to exorcise it completely.

'I don't know,' Deon said eventually. 'There is one theory that the guy who started doing this was called Bunny, otherwise I have no idea.'

'Someone called Bunny? That's a strange name.'

'No, not too strange, we used to have a café near us called Bunny's Corner Café. The man that owned it was called Bunny. I think he was Portuguese. Maybe it was a nickname.'

'Do you think he was the one who invented bunny chow?'

'Maybe. He was old enough.'

'So what's the best bunny chow you've ever had?'

'You know what? I've never actually had a bunny chow before.'

SHARON 4

The car lights lit up the lounge as it swung into the driveway, stopped outside the gates and Mr van Tonder hooted. Sharon peeked round the curtain to check that it was her father before pushing the button to open the electric gates. She hurried to the front door to meet him, her pent up anxiety now ready to spill over into tears.

The air outside was slightly cool and Sharon shuddered at the change in temperature. She stared into the bright lights of the car that still stood outside the closed gates. Why was he still outside? Why had he not come in? For a second her stomach tightened as images of her father being hijacked right outside her house flashed into her mind. Deon's absence had already heightened her paranoia.

She started to run towards the gate when her father leaned out of the car window and shouted, 'The power's off my love, you're going to have to open manually.'

Relief flooded through her as she still ran to the gate, her mind not working properly.

'Daddy,' she said, reaching out between the metal bars of the gate. She wanted his comforting touch, wanted to cocoon herself against his breast as she had done as a child and surrender her anxiety to the warm softness of the cuddle.

'Go and get the key. You'll have to open manually,' he repeated, trying to keep the irritation out of his voice. Being woken up just after having fallen asleep was not a mood enhancer.

Sharon stood for a second, caught between the closeness of her comforter and returning alone into the dark house. Another shiver brought her back to her senses and she turned and ran back to get the key. Her hands shook as she found and grasped it, nearly dropping the torch in the process.

A minute later she was soaking in the comfort of her father's chest, tears falling liberally from her eyes.

'There, there don't cry my love. I'm sure he's okay.' He felt awkward. He always did at moments like these. What could he say? One wrong word could set off a fresh bout of wailing and, although she still sobbed he could sense this easing. He tried not to betray his fear that Deon was not okay. He was not overly concerned about Deon's safety, rather he cared more about his daughter's happiness. He had never taken a great liking to Deon. Financially he was a well placed suitor for his daughter, but Mr van Tonder always felt that there was something hidden in

Deon's psyche that was not quite right, a ghost he had not exorcised.

Sharon was happy with him and that was all that mattered, but if Deon was to ever hurt his daughter, he would kill him. That was not an idle threat. In the lawless wake of apartheid falling, Mr van Tonder genuinely believed that he could get away with killing someone who upset his daughter.

'Okay, tell me all that's happened.' They were seated in the candlelit lounge.

Sharon explained between small sobs how Deon had phoned to say he would be working late, how she fell asleep and then couldn't get hold of him when she woke up. She made no mention of her plan to seduce him that evening. Even if the plan that had long since left her mind had still been floating around she would not have mentioned it. It's not the sort of thing a daughter talks to her father about.

'I see,' he said when she was finished. 'Um …' He bought some time while he wondered what to do. They could try calling again but, he suspected, the likely unanswered call would create further panic for his daughter. 'It must be something to do with the power cut. Bloody Eskom.' Assign the blame somewhere else, always a good tactic.

He had three suspicions about Deon's whereabouts. One, he had been involved in a car accident and was in hospital or dead. Two, he had been hijacked and was either in hospital or dead or three he was having an affair and in which case he would soon be in hospital or dead.

However, none of these options were good suggestions to put to Sharon right now. Inactivity was also not an option.

'Come on, I'll take you to his office, he may still be there. Maybe there's a problem with the phones.'

THE LIFT 25

He had never had bunny chow before as it always seemed beneath him. It was not really white man's food, but he couldn't say that. He loved a good curry and rice, but never bought any from the little cafés that served it. There was a sense that because these places predominantly served blacks, somehow it must be unhygienic, such was the way the whites thought.

Elise had tried once to get him to have one, but he had steered her away from the idea by suggesting a return to the Italian restaurant where they had had their first date.

'You just want to see me running down the street naked again,' she teased.

Deon raised a daring eyebrow, hoping that this would keep the talk away from having bunny chow.

'No. Been there, done that, didn't wear the T-shirt,' Elise laughed.

'Is there anywhere round here that you can you get good bunny chow?' Suddenly the idea of having the previously suspect dish appealed and kept the conversation light. It was not so much the culinary experience he was after, but he hoped that somehow this would help recapture some of the free spirit that Elise had. He felt hemmed in by his life, by the constraints the legacy of apartheid and all the fake morality it thrust on him, hemmed in by the lift and the dark.

'There is Dora's Den in that little mall off Kloof Street. They do a fairly good one. Not as good as that place in Isando though. That was the best.'

Deon knew the small café; he had walked past it quite often in his search for a more upmarket lunch. The place always looked clean and, rather surprisingly, attracted clientele of all races, something still a little unusual in post apartheid South Africa.

'You must take me there one lunch time when you're working day shift.' It was an invitation not a command.

Simon was shocked by this. Not only was Deon reaching out across the racial divide, but he was also breaking down a class barrier.

'It will be a pleasure to … Deon.' He felt warmed by the gesture and added Deon's name as a sign of appreciation and acceptance of the outreached hand of kindness.

Deon suddenly realised what he had inadvertently done and as he fumbled for a way out, a way to rescind the invite he had a flash vision of Elise sitting in Dora's Den, pregnant and eating a bunny chow.

'Yes, we must definitely do that. If only we can get out of here first.' He knocked on the side of the lift, not the hard impatient banging of earlier, but more as a reminder of where he was.

'Well we change shifts at seven so if the power is not on by then Jacob will come in and realise what has happened. He will turn on the generator.'

Deon took some comfort from this and his thoughts now returned to Sharon.

'Please God let her be asleep,' he muttered a short prayer to a god he didn't really believe in.

'Seven? You know I never spent the whole night at the office before. I've worked really late, nine, ten, once even till two in the morning but never the whole night.'

'I often spend the whole night at work, Deon.' Simon smiled at his little joke while Deon grinned partly at the humour and partly at the use of his name.

'Yeah, good one.'

Things were settling down in the lift. The hurt and pain of the deaths of Elise and Peter as well as the guilt of killing Marie had all but vaporised. Simon felt relaxed; he had no more traumatic issues to discuss, but Deon was not fully at ease. He still had to go over the top one more time.

He shut his eyes tight, drew in a deep breath and conjured up Gladys Makathini's face again.

LUCY 7

Her eyes opened and quickly adjusted to the dim light in the room. A pale moon threw a faint glow through the thin curtains. She could picture the night perfectly, it was a year or so ago. She and Simon lay in bed together and she had drifted off to sleep but had woken later to find Simon still awake.

'What is it my love?'

'Nothing I just can't sleep tonight.'

'Is anything the matter?'

'No, just trying to adjust to the dayshift again.' His tone was calm; there was no trace of anxiety in his voice. Lucy relaxed.

'Think nice thoughts, that will help.'

'Oh, I'm thinking nice thoughts already. It's what I do when I'm bored at work, especially when I'm on nights.'

'And what sort of nice thoughts do you think?' She snuggled up to him; her question contained a silent giggle.

'These thoughts are private property. Trespassers will be prosecuted.' He picked up on her playful mood. 'You need to pay if you want to hear my thoughts.'

'Oh, and how much do I have to pay?' She snuggled closer.

'Hmmm. Let me see. I think at least a kiss for the first thought.'

'Phew! That is expensive sir.' The giggle was not silent this time.

'I'm afraid that is the admission price, you can only get a discount if you are a pensioner.'

'In that case,' she pulled herself up, 'I will just have to pay.' Her lips found his and she gave him a long passionate kiss. He responded quickly to this but as his hand moved up her thigh and under her nightdress, she pulled away playfully and said, 'I have paid the price, now you must tell me your thoughts.'

For a second he was tempted to ignore this and continue down the path his arousal had started on, but sensing that there were more games to be played, he started. 'Well I often think about winning the lottery.'

There was a long pause while Lucy stroked his chest. She was expecting more, but when none came she looked up into his eyes.

'And?'

'And what?'

'You think about winning the lottery and what? What do you do with the winnings?'

'That will require further payment.' He had a naughty grin on his face.

Lucy smiled and then gave him another long, slow kiss. This time she let his hand get a little bit further up her nightdress to find her buttock. He started to push her gently into his body and she teasingly let him get away with this almost to the point of no return, then she suddenly broke free.

'I believe that that should get me quite a bit of information about your thoughts.'

Simon stared and re-adjusted his mind with some difficulty. He loved the way the game teased him, the frustration and desire mingling into an intense tender rawness.

'Well, when I win the lottery I would buy you a nice dress and me a good suit. Then we would go and look for a big house there where all the whites live. We would get out of the township.'

'Oh yeah, just one nice dress?' Her hand was moving in slow caressing circles down his stomach.

'You can have as many new dresses as you want,' he grinned and the hand moved fractionally further down his body. 'And shoes. All the shoes you can buy.' She was now perilously close to changing the subject.

'What about your mother?' She kissed him gently on the lips, 'Can she live with us in our new house?' The hand hovered.

Simon was a little surprised that this was important to Lucy but the need to appease her at the moment was too great, so he didn't reflect too much. Besides the answer was easy, 'Of course she can. She is my mother and I love her.' He drew in a sharp gasp as Lucy made contact.

THE LIFT 26

Where to start? Deon felt ready to tell all about Gladys. He had sort of rehearsed the story in his mind a number of times for when he eventually met someone he felt he could tell it to. He had never expected that the time would come in such a situation or with someone like Simon. He had been too busy being happy with Elise around for the story to burden him then, but after she was gone, Gladys came back to haunt him.

In his mind it had always been a white friend whom he would eventually tell. He had never felt that Sharon would be the one, she wouldn't understand, wouldn't give him the release from that episode that he needed. Once he had tried to picture himself telling her. The reaction he had imagined was of her backing away in horror or, in an alternate version, being overbearingly motherly about it. Neither reaction would help.

He had come close to telling Elise's brother Danny about it. After Elise's death the two had become good friends who turned to each other for manly comfort to cope with the shock of what had happened to her. But there was no place to squeeze Gladys into the relationship. Elise was the dominant woman there. Too dominant for another to stand a chance.

But now, here in the dark lift, suddenly there was someone he felt he could maybe talk to about that episode in his life. They had already shared stories of their respective losses and Simon had unburdened himself of the unfortunate episode about Marie Stander.

How would Simon react to his story about Gladys Makathini? Deon was not sure that Simon understood how little choice he had had in going to the army. Their earlier conversation about this had ended unresolved with him feeling that he had not won the argument. Was it an argument he could ever win?

He pushed past this obstacle and thought further about what he and Simon had talked about. Simon had been distressed by being the cause of someone losing a loved one. He knew this was the part of Simon's psyche he should appeal to but was nervous about starting.

He drew in a deep breath and with it the thought that if things went wrong he had the dark of the lift to hide in.

'You remember earlier you were talking about how traumatic it was to kill someone?'

Simon stiffened. He had been moving on, feeling relieved of that dreadful memory and now suddenly Deon was throwing Marie Stander back in his face. He gave a vaguely confirming grunt, suspicious of what was coming.

Deon sensed the reluctance and faltered slightly, but still took another small step on the thin ice. 'I know what it feels like too.'

Simon's earlier comfort evaporated and was replaced with a sense of unease. He had thought all the talk of death was over, but here was another one.

'Huh?'

'Yes, I have killed someone too.'

Simon waited, too surprised to talk.

'An innocent person, like you did.' Adding the last bit helped Deon, it was a touchstone that he could anchor himself to, a common thread. It didn't help Simon, but Deon was once again caught up in sorting himself out.

'Remember, I said that when I was in the army I had to go to the townships?' Simon braced himself, he knew what was coming and he wasn't ready for it. He had gone too far down the relaxing path and was now desperately scurrying back up to the thick of the battle.

'Which township?' He was buying time, giving himself a chance to prepare for another emotional battering.

'Hmm? Oh Soweto. It was while all the problems were happening.'

SHARON 5

The car headlights bounced off the surface of the road with hypnotic force. Mr van Tonder stared intently ahead, his mind mulling over the possibilities surrounding Deon's whereabouts. Sharon sat next to him feeling calmer now that daddy was there, but she didn't know what to say. She had her hysterical outburst and didn't want to prolong that, not only because she feared that her father would get annoyed if she went on too long, but also it made her more nervous and she needed to calm herself.

The silence between them was awkward. Unspoken fears and concerns hovered in the half light of the car, waiting to pounce on the first train of thought that left the mind bound for the vocal chords.

He has never liked Deon, Sharon thought, he is only here for my sake. This only confused her as she was caught between resenting her father's cool non-acceptance of the one she loved, and the warm glow of being daddy's little girl. She sat in her lukewarm puddle of emotions.

After a while she forced her thoughts back to Deon. Where could he be? She could not shake the image of Deon being dragged from his car, shot and left dying at the side of the road.

As if summonsed up by her thoughts she suddenly saw the flashing red light of an ambulance up ahead and felt an ice-cold knife of fear plunge into her stomach.

Mr van Tonder had seen it too and glanced nervously over at her. She pulled herself up in the car seat, trying to get a better view of the rapidly approaching scene, while Mr van Tonder eased up on the accelerator. He had a sudden urge to put his foot flat and speed past, not stopping, not allowing a glimpse of what had happened, then to keep going and never stop, to keep moving on past the scene that everyone dreaded confronting. But he knew that his duty as a father was to ensure that they knew one way or the other whether this was his daughter's lover or not.

Sharon was perturbed by the slowing of the car, not realising that this was done so that they could check whether what was now looking more and more like an accident scene was also the answer to where Deon was. She took the slowing to be an unwillingness on her father's part to face the possibility that Deon could be involved in this crash.

They were nearly at the scene; a car had wrapped itself around a lamppost. A white Audi. There was a tangible release of tension in the car as the image of Deon sitting behind the wheel of his red BMW slid into their minds. The usual sense of sympathy for those involved in accidents was replaced with relief and they both satisfied their macabre curiosity, crawling past the accident scene as paramedics rushed around in an attempt to release the unfortunate people from the wreck.

'I thought that Deon was in that accident.' Sharon felt that she had to say something to break the tense silence.

'Me too. Thank goodness he wasn't.' That was the right thing to say wasn't it?

'Daddy, I'm so worried. Where can he be? It's not like him not to call.' Opening her mouth re-released the flow of emotions that had been damning up.

Mr van Tonder cast a vaguely reassuring glance over at his daughter and she smiled back nervously.

'I'm sure he's okay,' he tried to muster as much reassurance as he could.

Sharon nodded, grateful for the reassurance but didn't believe it.

'Turn left at the next street,' she said suddenly realising where they were.

He turned into the road as directed. It was quiet and without street lighting a certain eerie-ness hung in the air. They pulled up outside the main entrance to the building.

THE LIFT 27

Soweto. The name brought that huge sprawling mass of a township into Deon's mind. It was a place where tin shacks stood piled one on top of the other, jumbled together with the occasional mansion belonging to those few who, against all odds, had amassed fortunes and overcome the chains of poverty. Music, dance, life and death mingled with sewerage, blood, dust and smoke to flow in a lively pulse through the place.

He had been too young to really remember the Soweto Riots of '76. A vague haze of a burning township fogged his memory, just a sense of fear of the place, inherited from his parents, remained. It was only when Elise had told him about the incident that sparked off the riots that he gained any sort of understanding of it. She knew the history, the reasons for the protest, the fact that the police opened fire on unarmed school kids. She even knew the death toll – twenty three. It gave him a better understanding of the place, but the knowledge scratched at the scab he had grown over his experiences of the place and made it impossible for him to tell his story of what had happened.

'I was not best pleased to be given township duty I can tell you.'

Deon wasn't trying to make excuses. Given the history, he had dreaded township duty more than being sent up to the border. The border war seemed to have more legitimacy to it than patrolling civilian streets. Even better would have been a cushy army administrative job in Pretoria, but fate had conspired to send him into Soweto.

Simon grunted his assent. He would not have liked to be sent as a combatant to Soweto during those times, he had lived there and seen what was happening.

Encouraged this time by the seemingly affirmative grunt, Deon continued.

'It was in June. I remember this for two reasons. Firstly it was bloody cold when we set off and then there was that smoky haze hanging over Soweto, all the fires were burning to keep people warm. I remember the smell, the smoke and morning dew mixed together. Normally I love the smell of wood burning, but for a while after that day I could hardly face a braai without tensing up whenever the smoke from the fire blew in my face. I would hang around inside just to avoid that smell. It's not so bad these days. Anyway we headed into Soweto and with it being June and the sixteenth coming up, things were especially tense.'

Simon recalled those times. Every year as the anniversary of the start of riots, that black day in South African history approached, the knots of apprehension pulled tighter in most of Soweto's residents' stomachs. The commemorations got more political and more violent. General strikes by blacks were called for and enforced by political henchmen.

'And to make matters worse, there was a funeral procession for some youngster who had been killed in the violence a few days earlier. You know what those funerals were like, they invariably led to another funeral.' Deon stopped short, as the thought, *Ja, and this one certainly led to a whole lot more,* lay unspoken in his mind.

'Eish! There were a lot of funerals back then. Too many. Mostly the young people. I remember those funerals, they were like political rallies. The coffins had the ANC flag over them and there was always those guys leading the chanting. Veeevaaa ANC Viva.' Simon drew out the words in the chant style that the battle cry had been delivered. Instinctively he raised his fist in the air to give the gesture that accompanied the cry, then, embarrassed by the automatic-ness of the salute, quickly lowered his arm, once again grateful for the dark that hid him from Deon's eyes.

Deon shuddered. Those rallying cries, *Viva Mandela Viva, Viva ANC Viva* added further detail to his current recollections of those times in the townships, colouring the memories with vivid detail. The chants were tightly interlocked with the events of that day. He was about to articulate this feeling when Simon went on.

'Every time you heard that, you would get scared because you knew a funeral or a rally was coming your way. If you got caught up in it you just had to go along with them. Those guys didn't like it if you left a funeral. You were betraying the cause they would say while beating you up. Better to be far away when you heard those cries.'

Deon grinned to himself. He had not thought that some of the blacks had been as scared of those rallies as the whites were. Still, he supposed, Simon was just an ordinary bloke going about his daily business. Like most people, he would just have wanted to get on with his life, not risk it getting caught up in anything violent if he could help it. Not everyone was a hero.

'It scared us whities too I can tell you that. You know as troopies we weren't supposed to shoot. The guns and our presence were supposed to be like a show of power, a deterrent.'

'But some of you guys did shoot.'

'Only in self defence, only if we felt our lives were in danger.'

'So this person you killed, it was self defence?'

There was a long silence then an almost inaudible whisper, 'No.'

LUCY 8

A small groan woke Lucy. She took a moment to orientate herself, then slipped out of bed and, pulling a small blanket round her shoulders, she padded softly through to the lounge. The old woman was trying unsuccessfully to push herself up out of the chair. In the gloom that the moonlight provided she looked old and worn.

'Here Ma, let me help you.'

She moved quickly over to the frail figure and supported her as she rose unsteadily to her feet. Slightly rasping gasps escaped from the old woman's lips at the effort of standing and Lucy realised with a shock just how light and thin she was.

Simon's mother let out her breath now that she was steady on her feet. She shook her head slowly and clicked her tongue.

'Where is Simon?' she asked, her eyes searching the dark room.

'He's at work Ma,' Lucy answered, her tone betraying her concern. Simon's mother was always aware of what was happening, even when she had just woken up. It was not like her to forget when Simon was at work. Lucy peered through the gloom trying to see the old woman's face more clearly, trying to find a tell-tale clue into what the problem was.

The old lady shook her head and clicked again. Something was not right. She steadied herself against Lucy's arm.

'At work?'

'Yes Ma. Are you all right Ma? Do you want to sit down?'

Simon's mother looked at Lucy. In the pale glow, Lucy could see that her eyes, usually bright and alert were clouded with confusion and a hint of fear.

'Sit down Ma,' she said gently easing the woman back to her chair.

The old woman settled back into the comfort of the chair without any fuss, her thin, wrinkled arms resting lightly on her lap as she looked around.

'What are you looking for, Ma?' Lucy scoured the room trying to second guess Simon's mother.

The old lady turned to look at Lucy, her eyes had a childlike innocence to them as she stared up from her chair.

'Where is Peter?'

THE LIFT 28

Simon stiffened. Had he heard right? Did he dare ask the question again?

'No.' This time it was stronger and followed by a sigh. 'No it wasn't self defence.'

'You mean you murd …'

'No, damn it, I didn't murder her. It wasn't a cold blooded killing.' He slapped the floor as he spat out his reply, the anger stemming from his own repulsion at what he had done.

'I'm sorry.' Simon apologised without really understanding what he was apologising for. It seemed a logical question to ask. If it wasn't self defence what else could it be but murder? Unless it was …

He left the thought unfinished as he fought against the image of Marie Stander's bloodied head that threatened to rush back into his mind.

'No. I'm sorry. I didn't mean to get angry like that. It wasn't aimed at you, rather aimed at the situation. It's something that I wish I could erase from my past, but can't, and that angers me – that I can't just dispose of this memory, make it not have happened.

'I guess it's like you and … and what was her name? That woman who got caught in the crossfire during that bank robbery?'

'Marie Stander?' Simon did not relish bringing her name back into the conversation. She had had her time in the limelight. She should now be left to rest in peace.

'Ja, like her. From what you told me you would rather not have that episode in your history. Doesn't it anger you that you're powerless to change your past, especially things like that?'

'I … I suppose so.' Had he ever had an angry outburst about Marie Stander's death like Deon had just had? He suddenly remembered the angry way he had reacted to Lucy when she had broached the subject of Peter's death. It was not the asking that had angered him, but rather the sharpness of the remembrance and the sense of helplessness it brought back that had caused his temper to flare.

Deon's explaining his outburst gave Simon an understanding of his own emotions surrounding both Peter's and Marie Stander's deaths. He made a mental note to try and explain it all to Lucy when he got a chance. He wanted her to understand that he had not been angry with her that night and as he thought this, he unconsciously rubbed his wrist gently.

Deon was relieved that he had managed to relate his anger to something that Simon would understand. He could now move his thoughts and story on.

'Gladys Makathini was this woman's name, but she didn't get caught in a crossfire.'

Gladys Makathini. This time Simon heard the name and it rang a bell. Where had he heard it before? He immediately connected it with the struggle, with those unsettled times. So many had been killed, but there was something about Gladys that made him remember the name. He searched his mind for an answer.

GLADYS MAKATHINI 2

It was cold that June morning. Gladys felt the sting of the air on her face as she left her shack. She hoisted Precious higher on her back and adjusted the blanket used to tie the child there. It was still dark and her breath hung in wispy white clouds as she moved quietly towards the main street. She heard the mumbled lives waking in the surrounding shacks and smelt the sharp tang of fear in the air.

Was she early enough to beat the 'political activists' who would prevent anyone leaving the township today? It was the same every year these days. A stayaway was called and the heavies were deployed to enforce it.

She turned onto the main street, keeping a watchful eye out for any signs of trouble, her mind running over the conversation she had had with her employer the day before.

'Madam?'

'Yes, what is it Gladys?'

'They have called for a stayaway tomorrow.'

'Yes Gladys, I know.' A sigh and a slight shake of the head. 'It was on the news.'

'Madam, there is always trouble with a stayaway. Please, I would like to stay in the back room tonight. Just one night.' The back room was a separate small building at the bottom of the garden. It had been used as servants' quarters before, but the Cartwright's had refused to take on a live-in maid because of the paperwork required, besides with the taxis these days there should be no problem for Gladys to commute.

'I'm sorry Gladys, but you know I'm not allowed to have blacks sleep on the property without a permit. It's against the law. You will just have to get up really early before all the trouble starts.'

'Yes madam, but madam the tsotsis are up very early when the sixteenth of June comes near. They are always causing trouble.'

What was it with blacks? Mrs Cartwright thought clicking her tongue in disapproval. Always got some excuse not to work, they were so lazy.

'Well I'm sorry Gladys, but if you don't make it in you know we can't pay you for the day.'

Gladys nodded her subservient nod and mentally calculated if she could afford food for her child and pay the rent on her shack if she had to miss a day's pay.

On the main street things looked quiet. A few people scurried quickly along in the dim light of early dawn. They were skittish, all expecting trouble. Gladys made her way along the dusty street, a sense of fear and foreboding gripped her. She turned down a small alley and found Mary's shack.

'You're not going to work today?' Mary was horrified.

'I have to, I need the money.'

'But the tsotsis will get you.'

'I have to try. The madam says she won't pay me if I don't go in.'

'But it's too dangerous Gladys.'

'I have to go.' Gladys swallowed hard, trying not to let her fear show. 'I must go now or I will have no chance of getting out of the township before the trouble starts.' She gently kissed Precious on the forehead then handed the child over to her sister.

'I may be late getting back.'

'Take care my sister.'

With the weight of Precious off her back, Gladys rushed towards the taxi rank, despair growing as she noticed the number of people milling around. She turned the last corner and saw the empty taxi rank.

'Going somewhere sister?' A youngster blocked her route. His eyes were slightly glazed over with malice. A machete held loosely in his hand threatened as much as he did.

'I have got news that my brother is not well. He lives over there.' Gladys indicated past the taxi rank. If you lived in the townships you quickly learned to think on your feet if you wanted to survive.

The glazed eyes sized her up appreciatively and he started to move slightly aside for her to pass. Gladys took a step forward but the youngster suddenly jumped back in her path, the machete slightly raised.

'What's your rush sister? Why don't you spend a little time with me? Your brother can wait can't he?'

Gladys retreated a step or two and the youngster grinned maliciously. Just then a call came from further up the road.

'There's a taxi leaving! Quick we must stop it!'

The youngster turned to face the cry, then turned back to Gladys with a smile still etched on his face.

'Later sister. Come back later or I will come and find you.' He turned again and raced off.

Shaken by this incident Gladys stood for a few seconds as the realisation that her efforts to get to work would prove futile sank in. She began retracing her steps.

As she turned into the main street, her heart sank. The army ratels were pulling up across the road and beyond that she could hear the sound of a march. She needed to rush to get past the army vehicles before they blocked the road completely.

She got there just before the last vehicle was in place and squeezed through, ignoring the cold white stares she got from the troopies. Now all she had to do was blend in with the mob. It would be stupid to try get past them; they would lynch her if she didn't join in. She walked quickly down the side of the road towards the angry crowd. Suddenly a shot rang out.

THE LIFT 29

Gladys Makathini. A story slowly formed around the name in Simon's mind. There had been so many deaths back then, but not many were shot by the army boys. It was usually the cops or an ANC – Inkhata clash. But why did this one, this Gladys Makathini, stick in his mind. She had been killed around the sixteenth of June, Soweto Day.

'What do they call the sixteenth of June these days? Freedom Day isn't it?' He needed a little distraction because his mind was warning him that he didn't want to look too closely at Gladys Makathini and her death, something there was not right. 'Why didn't they call it Soweto Day when Mandela took over? I mean everyone called it that back then, it was the best name to call it.'

'I dunno. All us whities thought that it was going to be called Soweto Day, but I guess Mandela did a lot of things differently to what we expected. I mean who would have expected the Truth and Reconciliation Commission to be set up?'

Simon nodded in the dark and Deon sensed his agreement.

'Stroke of genius that was.'

'You didn't have to go before the TRC for having shot Gladys Makathini did you?' The brief detour to talk about public holidays had released Deon slightly from the weight of his story but Simon dragged him back with this question.

'No.'

'No?'

'I was half expecting it, but my case was one they never seemed to get round to. I guess everyone accepted that it was an accident.'

'An accident? How do you kill someone by accident?' Simon knew the answer as the question left his lips. 'No, don't answer. I know. But how did it happen?' His feelings towards Deon softened immediately.

'Well, I was really shitting myself. It was the first time I was in the townships you know and we had orders not to shoot unless shot at. Despite all our training, saying to someone "don't shoot unless you're shot at" is not exactly going to put them at ease is it?

'So anyway I was really scared and there I was, standing on top of the ratel looking down at this angry crowd. They were getting closer and closer, toyi-toyi-ing all the way, the women doing the halalalala thing.'

Simon gave a small chuckle at Deon's attempted ululation, but the subject was too serious for him to laugh out loud.

'They got right up close and you could feel the tension in the air. There was real hate coming from the mob, you could see it in their eyes. And we were scared as hell, I could feel it in the guys round me. Closer and closer they came, chanting all the time.

'As they got right up to us I got this really weird feeling. It was like it was me they hated and that they wanted to kill me, me personally. The whole of Soweto wanted Deon Scott dead. That was what was going through my mind at the time.

'I was so scared that I didn't have any idea what I was doing. I undid the safety catch on my rifle and aimed it at the crowd. Fortunately my squad leader saw me lifting my rifle. I say fortunately because I probably would have shot into the crowd and killed a lot more people than just Gladys. He shouted at me to stop. That broke the spell, but my hands were shaking so much and well those bloody triggers …'

Deon stopped to regain his composure as the story threatened to get out of hand. Simon waited patiently for him to continue.

'Well anyway those triggers were so bloody sensitive and … well a shot went off. Damn near killed the squad leader; missed him by millimetres, I'm sure. But it didn't miss Gladys Makathini. It was like a freak accident, one random shot, could have gone anywhere, but it went straight through the back of her head.

'She wasn't even part of the crowd. She was walking, no almost running the other way. She was trying to get away from it all.'

Deon stopped again. The story was over, he had told Simon what had happened and yet somehow something still hung in the air. But what was it? The facts had been laid out on the table. What more was Simon's silence wanting him to say?

'How did you feel?' Simon gave up waiting for Deon to answer what he thought was the obvious question.

'What? Right at that moment or later?'

'Both.'

SHARON 6

The car eased up to the kerb and Mr van Tonder looked around nervously. The dark was menacing, almost as though it was trying to ward them off. He shuddered slightly, but quickly composed himself; it would not do to look scared in front of Sharon.

'You sure this is the right place?'

'Of course daddy, I've been here a few times before.'

'Well there's no sign of life,' he peered at the foreboding glass doors. It was completely dark behind them, surely no-one was about. He began pulling the car back into the road.

'Daddy!'

'What?'

'We can't just drive off. Go and check the door.'

'What!'

'Go check the door. There should be a security guard. All buildings have them. I want to be absolutely sure that Deon isn't here.'

It was unlike Sharon to be demanding like this. Mr van Tonder hesitated. He really didn't want to have to get out the car, he didn't feel safe here. But his daughter needed him now and she obviously cared a lot for this Deon character. He sighed inwardly and moved the car back to the kerb whilst looking around nervously. The coast seemed clear.

'Okay, now lock the doors as soon as I get out and keep your eyes peeled. I'll leave the car running. If you see anyone coming hoot and if anything should happen to me drive off as quick as you can and get help. Understand? I don't want you hanging around if there are any problems.'

Sharon took in a sharp breath. She had been so caught up in worrying about Deon that she hadn't considered that she could be putting her father in danger by sending him out to check. But it was too late to change her mind as Mr van Tonder had already climbed out the car and was striding quickly over to the front door of the building.

She sat up in the seat, her head turning in all directions, peering intently into the gloom, imagining movement where there was none, her mind racing.

Mr van Tonder reached the door and took another quick look round to see that no-one was about then shaded his eyes to see past his reflection. The reception area was quiet, no signs of life. He could just make out a jacket hanging over the back of the chair where the security guard would normally sit. He tried the door. Locked. He rattled it slightly but to no avail. He rattled harder, maybe someone might hear him.

Sharon watched her father trying door and her heart sank. It seemed like the building was completely deserted. She wanted to cry, but knew she must keep her wits about her. She turned back to look for a tissue to blow her nose and, out of the corner of her eye she thought she saw movement. She stared into the dark and a fear grabbed at her stomach. A black man was on the other side of the street. He was still a little way off, but was undoubtedly coming towards them.

'Dad!' she screamed and hit the hooter.

Mr van Tonder jumped at the sudden sound and turned.

Sharon was desperately trying to wind down the window while she pointed frantically up the road in the direction of the approaching danger. It took him a second to see the ominous figure in the gloom.

'Unlock my door,' he shouted as he ran round to the driver's side.

THE LIFT 30

'Was that a hooter?' Deon sat up. The muted sound gave him a glimmer of hope that they might be rescued from the lift. Someone may be out there. It also bought him time to answer Simon's question which was something he wasn't sure he wanted to do just yet. He was not ready to explore the feelings he had had at that time.

'Huh?'

'That noise. Was it a hooter?'

He pulled himself to his feet and listened half heartedly at the door. He didn't want to raise his hopes too much.

'Could be. Probably a taxi, they're always hooting wherever they go.'

'A taxi? Do you get them around here at this time of night?'

'Not often, but sometimes.'

'This sounded different though, not like a taxi. It was more urgent. Maybe there's someone outside the building.'

His mind flew to Sharon. She must be mad with anxiety. He had not had much time to think about how his failure to return home at a decent hour would affect her. He had said he would be late, but he was never this late. She would certainly be worried, panicking more like.

But she would never come down here on her own, that would be madness. Surely she would try and phone. His hand reached instinctively into his empty jacket pocket where he usually kept his cell.

'Bugger!'

'What?'

'No, I just tried to reach for my phone, but then remembered that it was stolen the other day.'

He chuckled humourlessly and Simon gave a reassuring grunt. They fell silent for a while, Deon wondering what he could do to get a message to Sharon to say he was alright, and Simon's thoughts were gravitating back to the killing of Gladys Makathini. There was still something nagging him about the story.

'So how did you feel when you shot Gladys?'

He jumped straight back in, he really wanted to know. This was a rare opportunity to get inside the minds of those young troopies and see what it was that made them do what they did. Already he had been surprised when Deon admitted he was so scared the day he had shot Gladys. He had never thought of them as being scared, after all they had all the fire power.

Deon was caught off balance. He had convinced himself that the hooting had been Sharon, or more likely, Sharon and her dad. He needed to let them know he was okay. Simon's question was swallowed up by his thoughts. The dark of the lift suddenly grew closer, taunting him and he rose to the bait.

'Damn it! Damn this fucking lift, damn fucking Eskom!' He punched the side of the lift again. Simon jumped at the unexpected outburst.

'Hey, hey calm down, calm down.'

He tried to reach out and grab Deon's arm as a gesture of comfort and calming, but ended up pawing the air. He went on in a soft and gentle voice, using it to coax Deon back to serenity.

'Calm down, there's nothing we can do. No-one will hear us in here; we just have to wait for the power to come back. I'm sure it will soon.'

He waited a second, listening to Deon breathing heavily.

'Look, maybe we're both just too stressed. All this talk of death and killing. Gladys, Elise, Marie, Peter. This isn't helping. Maybe we should talk of other things. What do you say hey?'

Deon simmered slowly, his breath coming quickly. He had always battled to understand what brought on these sudden fits of rage. It has to be stress he thought, taking a deep breath to calm himself down.

'You're right, I'm sorry,' he said and eased himself slowly back to the floor.

Simon smiled nervously. Deon's outbursts were quite disconcerting.

'That's okay. Maybe we should talk about something else, what do you say?'

'I suppose,' Deon sighed, feeling his muscles relax as he expelled the air.

But what could he talk about? He thought for a bit. Holidays? Could Simon relate to his trip to the Kruger Park last year? Or the time he had gone to the States? Rugby? The Sharks were doing well, but Simon had said earlier that he didn't like rugby. Soccer then? Simon said he liked soccer, but Deon knew very little about it, especially the local game. He had heard some of the team's names – Kaiser Chiefs, Orlando Pirates, Sundowners – but the players, the teams standing in the league, or even the leagues for that matter, he had no knowledge of these. Even the English football they got on DSTV was not really something he took much note of. Manchester United was big and he vaguely remembered Liverpool as being one of the good clubs, but that was about it.

'Actually I think that I would like to carry on talking about Gladys. It's good for me. Therapeutic.'

LUCY 9

'I think maybe she's had a stroke,' Lucy tried to keep the panic out of her voice. 'Can you take her to the hospital?'

Thomas Morewa looked sleepy. He was wearing a hastily thrown on shirt, trousers with an undone drawstring and ill fitting shoes that he had donned when Lucy had come knocking on his door. As he was the only one on the street who owned a car, Lucy had rushed over there as soon as she had got Simon's mother into bed. She kept looking anxiously back to their house, checking that the old lady had not wandered out.

'Of course,' Thomas said, the sleepiness giving over to shock. 'Of course, for Mama anything. You go back to her and I'll get my keys. I pray to God that she's okay.'

Simon's mother had been particularly good to Thomas and his family, especially when their little Dorcus had been so ill. She had done the baby sitting and had even walked the three kilometres to the doctor's rooms, carrying Dorcus on her back. Thomas had always felt he owed more than the excessive thank yous he had expressed and now here was a way to repay the kindness. He grabbed his keys and hurried out.

Lucy returned home and sought to make the old woman more comfortable and then she fumbled in the candlelit gloom for her cell phone. She was just about to call Simon's number when Thomas's car lights lit up the front room and she hastily dropped the phone into her handbag. She ushered Thomas in and watched him carry the old lady to the car. It took little effort, her slight body somewhat limp in his arms. She was bewildered and muttered under her breath but was not making any sense. Once they had settled her on the back seat Thomas eased the car into the street. Recent developments in the townships meant that it was only a short strip of dirt road that needed to be travelled before they hit the comfortable tar.

As they settled on the tar, Lucy got out her cell. 'I must call Simon,' she said to Thomas who nodded, not taking his eyes off the road. She brought up Simon's number and dialled. The ringing on the other end continued and a worried expression came over her already tense features.

'That is strange, he's not answering. Where can he be?'

Thomas glanced nervously over at her, then returned his concentrated look back to the road. In his head he murmured a short prayer for Simon's safety.

THE LIFT 31

'You wanted to know how I felt that day?' Deon's voice was calm now. He pulled his thoughts closer round him, arranged them neatly, then went on. 'Well at first I was numb, no feelings, nothing. Then the realisation of what had happened hit. I had never killed anyone before.' He pushed the dark away, not letting it oppress him. He wanted this out of him in a dignified manner.

'I put my gun down carefully on the floor of the ratel and just stared at the space where the woman I shot had been. A crowd quickly gathered around her so I could not see the body. I wanted to jump out, to go to her and see if she was okay, but I knew she was dead.'

Dead. The word sounded like what it meant. Dead, a dull, flat, lifeless sound. The two d's buffering either side of it, hemming in the livelier vowel sound, ensuring the life contained therein could not leave.

Dead. The word stuck briefly in Deon's mind and he paused momentarily, then forced himself to go on, to go beyond dead.

'The crowd's initial shock was quickly turning to anger. Not surprising really. They started chucking stones at us and a petrol bomb fell just short of the ratel.'

Simon shuddered at the mention of petrol bombs. He had seen the effect of these and this reminded him too much of Peter's charred body.

Deon continued, oblivious of Simon's thoughts. 'We had to get out of there fast so I didn't really have time to think or feel anything for a few minutes as it was a mad scramble to move the ratels and other vehicles.'

'We got out of Soweto all right but even then I didn't have much time to think as I was getting a blasting from my Sergeant. "*What the bloody hell do you think you were doing back there. You could have got us all killed. You know the procedure, you're not supposed to shoot. Are you a bloody idiot or what? You endangered the men. This is not what we trained you to do …*" On and on he went, the whole journey back to base, swearing and shouting. I felt so small and ashamed because I had put everyone in danger. That was the only thought I was permitted at that time. I had endangered the unit. I was not a good soldier. I was an idiot. I had endangered the unit.

'I could see the others looking sheepishly at me, but I reckon that they were not thinking, "Deon Scott you bastard, you endangered us." They were all thinking, "Thank God it was someone else who had crumbled under the strain and not me." They had all been as scared as me. I was the unfortunate one who had broken under the pressure.

'I was too busy worrying about the consequences this would have for me that I had no time for thoughts about Gladys. It was only when I finally sat down in the barracks after our debrief that I had time to think about her.'

Deon fell silent as he recaptured those feelings, that horrible knot-in-the-stomach that tightened even now at the recollection. 'You know the strange thing?'

'What?' Simon was intrigued by this story, by the opening up of this white man. Here he was about to reveal how he felt killing a black woman. A strange shudder of anticipation ran through him. Surely very few blacks had been privy to the personal feelings of a white man over the killing of a black woman during those politically disturbed times. Yes, there had been the TRC, but that had seemed to Simon to be more about establishing the facts than really getting to the heart of the emotions. He was never sure whether some of the emotions they had seen had been real.

'The strange thing was that I never got into further trouble over it.' Deon was still building up to explaining his feelings and this frustrated Simon.

'Well of course you didn't,' Simon wanted to say, 'which white ever got into trouble over the killing of a black in those days? Besides, was that all you were concerned about your own skin?' The words floated just outside the reach of his vocal chords.

'It was almost as though they were actually happy with what I had done. I couldn't understand why at the time, but later I heard that a rumour had gone round the township that it wasn't actually me who had shot Gladys Makathini, but that it was an Inkhata sniper positioned near us. Quite a lot of people died as a result of this rumour, but I know it was me who shot her.'

This threw Simon. Here was a different development to Deon's story. This hinted at that mysterious *third force* they had heard so much about. The surreptitious dealings of the apartheid government designed to stir up black against black. Divide and rule.

Simon's mind ticked over. The story of Gladys Makathini was coming back to him now. The name had been familiar. It was one of the many names that cropped up in the list of deaths during the struggle. It was, he recalled, as the story formed in his mind, around the time that Peter had ...

He paused in his thoughts. No! That cannot be. He wracked his brain and pushed hard against the thought.

SHARON 7

The shadowy figure drew closer as Mr van Tonder scrambled into the driver's seat. He fumbled with the gear stick, violently shoving the car into first and then with a screeching of tyres wrenched the car from the kerb and sped off down the road. His hands shook as they clasped the wheel.

Between sobs Sharon chanted an hysterical mantra, 'Daddy! Daddy! Daddy!' grabbing at each word for support.

The deserted street fled past them and at the intersection Mr van Tonder paused only slightly to check that nothing was coming before flinging the car round the corner in a loud squeal that momentarily drowned out Sharon's cries.

It was only when they were a good few blocks away that he slowed the car slightly and pulled his seat belt on while Sharon's hysteria subsided to a hiccoughing twitch.

'I'm sorry daddy, I'm so sorry.'

Emotions twirled and twisted within her. She was horrified with herself for putting her father in danger like that and was even more convinced now that something terrible had happened to Deon. She wanted this night to end, she wanted the darkness to go. She longed for the warm sunshine of daylight where things would look better, where she could think clearly again.

Outside the office building, the figure that had caused their sudden departure stood in the middle of the road staring after them. It waited while the silence wafted back into the street, then dismissed them with a shake of the head and a click of its tongue and transformed from a sinister figure into a slightly built man.

He took a few strides across the road and peered through the glass doors as Mr van Tonder had done a few seconds earlier. The reception area was gloomy and empty. He scoured the room for signs of life then clicked his tongue again and chuckled quietly.

'Heh! I bet Simon is stuck in the lift,' he chuckled to himself, then turned and wandered back across the road to the building he had emerged from earlier. Here he locked the door behind him, then took his place at the reception desk to sit out the rest of his night duty.

THE LIFT 32

'I guess that made me feel worse,' Deon's voice pierced Simon's thoughts. 'I mean it wasn't just the innocent woman I had shot, but all the others who died afterwards. It was almost as if their blood was on my hands. I tried not to think about it at the time, I could barely live with having killed Gladys.'

Despite the horror of his thoughts, Simon was struck by the sincerity of Deon's confession and the gentle manner that his voice had caressed his victim's name.

'She had a daughter I was told, about a year old.' Deon was completely unaware of the turmoil in Simon's mind now. His voice was tired and drenched in emotion as the thought of the orphaned little girl came to mind.

'She must be about ten by now. You know I often wondered what happened to her. I sometimes thought, you know after Mandela came into power, that Elise and I could track her down and adopt her, but I had no idea where to begin to try and find her. Besides which, I always worried what people would think of a white man trying to track down a black child, whether that would cause more problems for her if I did. I reckon I would not have got any answers.'

Deon sighed at this. The thought of adoption had genuinely entered his mind when Elise was alive, but he had never built up enough courage to tell her the story of Gladys.

Secretly he had hoped that one day Elise would arrive home with a little girl and announce that she wanted to adopt Precious Makathini. He wondered now what had become of her. Most likely she had been taken in by relatives. The blacks were good like that, they looked after their own.

'Peter was killed in the violence that followed Gladys' death.' Simon dropped his bombshell.

PRECIOUS MAKATHINI

The small figure scrambled up the steep bank of the litter-strewn stream. The stench of human excrement was sharp and overpowering and the muted noises of the township mumbled behind her. At the top of the bank she paused to stare at the twinkling lights of Johannesburg in the distance. She was unaware of the darkness that encompassed a large part of Cape Town, unaware of the man who had changed her life so drastically and who was now held captive by that darkness. She was unaware of the events that day, save for the odd comment her aunt had let slip.

News of the shooting travelled quickly and reached Gladys' sister. Mary ran to the area where she had been told the tragedy had occurred. But the violence following the shooting was gaining momentum and she was forced to seek shelter at a nearby friend's house as the angry mob had blocked her route.

After an unendurable wait, the crowd moved on to another area, leaving a blood trail in its wake and Mary was able to leave her refuge and find the place where Gladys had been killed. All that remained was a blood-stain in the dusty ground. As she stood staring at the dark brown patch of sand, a voice behind her made her turn.

'Mary, it was Gladys. They have taken her body away.' David Molet-swane was a family friend and he stood a little way off, his head bowed slightly in despair at what had happened. He moved to support Mary as the grief thrashed through her body.

Slowly and kindly he led her back home where, in her panic, she had abandoned baby Precious. Promising to try and find out more about the fate of Gladys' body, David left while Mary sat sobbing quietly, rocking back and forth on a small stool. Little Precious wiggled and stretched in her arms, oblivious of what had happened.

It was only when Precious cried out to be fed that Mary was forced to move and she mechanically set about her chores, her mind racing. They would have to keep Precious, there was no other family close enough to do so. But how would she tell her husband? He would not be happy. She fretted about this and the fate of Gladys' body and as the day drew on and no news came from David, her fear for his safety began to build. Eventually he returned.

'I have asked everywhere. No-one knows what they have done with Gladys' body. I will go tomorrow again.'

'Thank you,' she felt too tired to cry any more.

After David left, silence, punctuated only by the occasional whimper from Precious, filled the room. Mary paced nervously. Her husband would be home soon, what would she tell him? She began preparing dinner and was halfway through when she heard the door open.

'Why is Precious still here? Has Gladys not come to collect her?' No pleasantries, just this demand.

'I think Gladys has been delayed. There is a stayaway today.'

'Liar!' he screamed and slapped her hard across the face, the smell of alcohol wafted in the breeze caused by his swinging arm. 'It's all over the township. Gladys is dead. Killed. Why do you lie to me wife?' He punctuated the word wife with a hard slap the other way that sent Mary sprawling. Precious, woken by the noise, began to cry.

'I suppose now we will have to take care of your useless sister's offspring.' He closed in on her, then paused to glance across the room where his own two children stood wide-eyed and frightened.

'Bugger off!' he shouted. 'Go next door, anywhere. Bugger off.'

They ran. They knew from experience not to be at home when he was like this.

A few punches later he kicked the prone figure on the floor for good measure then stormed out.

Slowly Mary pulled herself up and, grimacing with pain, cleaned the blood from her face. Her right eye was badly swollen and her ears rang from the blows. Once she had patched up her wounds as best she could, she found Precious who had eventually stopped screaming. She drew her close to her breast, drinking in the innocence of the new life.

The next morning the door opened again and her husband walked in. He looked sheepish, a look which changed to shock when the light from the doorway lit up his handiwork.

'I am so sorry my love.' He moved closer to her. 'I was drunk last night and the news of Gladys upset me.' He was beside her now, his hand reaching out to gently touch her cheek. He smelt of hangover and last night's woman.

Mary tried not to shy away from his touch. That would just bring more violence, but she could not help glancing over at Precious who was sleeping quietly next to her on the bed. Her husband followed her gaze then said, 'Of course we must take care of Precious. It is our duty.'

Precious stayed, but became a constant source of conflict.

'I already have two mouths to feed and now there is this extra one who isn't even mine.'

Sometimes this was just a complaint muttered between gritted teeth, sometimes it was punctuated with a slap or worse.

Patience grew up learning to avoid this strange man who ran hot and cold with her depending on how he smelt.

When she was six, the man disappeared for a few weeks and the small family basked in the peace that his absence brought. He returned in a subdued and sombre mood, but did not explain the reason for his absence.

HIV was nearly as rife as the violence that gripped the township and a visit to the witchdoctor in his tribal village had revealed to Mary's husband that sex with a virgin would cure the disease. The message that being monogamous in order to prevent was crudely interpreted as sex with a virgin would cure.

There were only two female virgins in the house. One was his own flesh and blood so the choice was simple. Soon after his return, he sent Mary off on an errand and set about being cured.

Precious fled from the house in pain and tears. She ran as far away as she could, eventually joining up with a small group of street kids in a distant area of the township. Miraculously she did not contract the infection of her attacker, but Mary was not so fortune and was dead within six months of Precious' departure.

LUCY 10

The emergency room was quiet as Lucy and Thomas carried the old woman in. They found a chair and, while Thomas went to inform the nurse on duty of their plight, Lucy tried calling Simon again.

Still no reply. During her earlier attempts she could picture the deserted reception area, dark and quiet except for the giggling baby sound of Simon's ringtone. He must be doing his rounds, she had told herself, but now she was worried. Surely he should be back at his post by now. Where was he?

Simon's mother was quickly seen to and Lucy's anxiety about Simon was put aside while the palaver of getting the old woman into the examination area took priority.

She listened carefully to the white doctor as she explained that Simon's mother had had a mild stroke. 'It is too early to tell, but she may lose some of her sight and possibly some of the functionality on the left hand side of her body, but she will survive.'

She was a kind doctor, but busy and moved off to another patient, leaving Lucy staring at Simon's mother who lay sleeping in the hospital bed. She took moments to absorb the news with its mixed messages of survival and incapacity. But soon her thoughts turned to Simon again.

The doctor had said that they would keep the old woman in for a few days so there was really nothing more Lucy could do and she was also acutely aware of Thomas waiting patiently to drive her home. She smiled a sad smile at him when she got back to the waiting room and he acknowledged this with a slight bowing of the head.

'She is going to live.'

Thomas nodded again, but he read Lucy's look and gently guided her out to the car park.

Once in the car she tried Simon's number again, clicking her tongue and shaking her head as the tinny ring continued in her ear.

'Still no reply?' Thomas's eyes were glued to the road as he sat slightly hunched behind the wheel.

'No. Where can he be? I don't know what he could be doing.'

There was a short silence then Thomas asked, 'Do you want to go round to his office?'

'Hau! Thomas it is a long way to go so late at night.' She knew though from the tone of his voice that he had already considered this and had made up his mind. 'You are a good man Thomas Morewa.' There were tears in her voice.

THE LIFT 33

Deon stared into the dark corner that Simon's voice had come from, his mouth hung open slightly as he tried to digest what had just been said. He ran over it again in his mind quickly, trying to assess the tone in which it was said. Was it accusatory? Was Simon angry?

' I … I …' he stuttered, grasping desperately around in his mind for something to say. What could he say?

Simon was also contemplating what he had just said and the implications thereof. He was still trying to process all this information for himself, scrambling around in his mind for the feelings he should be having. In all the time since Peter's death, he had never thought about the events that led to the particular period of unrest that had taken his brother from him. They all seemed to merge into each another. Every wave of violence was like the one before, even the one that killed Peter. It was just another round in a never ending fight.

He ignored Deon's stammering. He needed to work through his own feelings before he could even consider what his companion was thinking. Was he angry with Deon? Should he be angry with Deon? Was Deon directly to blame for Peter's death? His lift companion hadn't physically lit the match, but figuratively he had.

'I'm so sorry.' It was choked, wrapped up in a sob. All the years of carrying this burden suddenly produced a dividend. The death of Gladys Makathini was playing over and over in his mind, like a looped film projected onto the back of his skull. The burning township mingled with this and slowly a dreadful image of a man desperately flailing his arms while the burning tyre around his neck consumed his life began to play centre stage in this macabre movie while tears began to flow down Deon's cheek.

'Please forgive me,' he sobbed.

Simon was slowly finding that he could not bring himself to hate Deon. The wounds so sharp and piercing back then had been heightened by all the bitterness apartheid had brought. But time, the great healer, had been doing its job and in the years following apartheid's collapse, the hatred he may have had had eked out of him, drawn out slowly by the beauty of his new home in Cape Town and the warmth of Lucy's love.

The solid darkness of the lift had filled the huge chasm that existed between them when Deon first climbed in on the tenth floor. They had both taken steps across the gap towards each other and now they were within touching distance. All it needed was for one of them to reach out and grab the other. Slowly, almost in a trance Simon raised his hand, sought and found Deon's sobbing body and gently patted his shoulder.

SHARON 8

A vague light fluttered gently around the room. The candle sat in the middle of the low coffee table and a faint scent of lilac rose from the flame. Mrs van Tonder preferred these scented ones to regular candles.

Mr van Tonder sat uncomfortably in his favourite chair guiltily watching his wife, Almarie, pat Sharon on the back while she sobbed uncontrollably. He was the outsider now, no longer part of the action.

'I just know something terrible has happened to him,' Sharon drew her breath in sharply. The voicing of the thought seemed to make it more real.

They had travelled back to Mr van Tonder's home in virtual silence. It was not even discussed that they should go there rather than back to Sharon's place. Mr van Tonder had reasoned that being away from her home would hopefully mean less reminders of Deon for her to notice and besides there was Almarie at home who could take over. This was not father territory, he had done his duty.

He was still shaken from the close encounter with the sinister figure outside Deon's office and he downed the last of a quickly drunk whiskey. The empty glass now sat next to the candle beckoning him. He was beginning to believe that Sharon was right, something must have happened to Deon. It was not like him to go missing in action. He was after all a decent enough bloke. Mr van Tonder felt a slight twinge of guilt at having wished him dead.

'We could try phoning him again.' Almarie's voice was cracked and held no real hope.

'We tried only a few minutes ago,' Mr van Tonder shifted in his seat; the whiskey was beginning to have an effect. 'No point in trying again. Anyway if he had access to a phone, he would call wouldn't he? He's usually good like that.'

This brought on a fresh bout of crying from Sharon and Almarie shot a withering look at her husband who sighed and gave into the call of the whiskey glass.

THE LIFT 34

Until the connection was made between Simon's grief and the killing of Gladys Makathini, Deon had been in the emotional safe haven of not actually being personally involved with the losses. He had carried guilt at what had happened with him, but it was more a factual than emotional remorse.

The intimacy of the lift had made friends of the men and now his past had become tangled up with Simon's. His sobbing slowed and after a deep breath stopped. He wiped his cheeks with his sleeve and took another gasp of air. It tasted stale and heavy. The lives and deaths that had unfolded in the darkness hung like a cloud above them.

Where did they go from here? Deon struggled for the energy needed to answer that question. The long work week, the dark of the lift and the emotion of the evening had taken its toll on him. He longed for the warmth of Sharon's arms. He wanted to lie next to her, to feel her holding him, to feel all the pain, tension and tiredness seep out of his body as he cocooned himself in that motherly embrace.

Suddenly Elise was there. Her spectral presence cut away the dark, her naked body glowing faintly. Deon stared at the apparition despite her beauty being too painful to look at. She stood completely at ease, her breasts proud, she was truth, she was purity and yet he struggled to maintain her gaze. He turned his face away.

'Look at me Deon,' she said, her voice soft and gentle. 'Look at me.'

She had never spoken before. Deon raised his eyes and met hers. She smiled and he saw the truth. It was over. The long held tensions and worries were gone. There had been forgiveness – he had been forgiven. In the small confines of the dark lift, he had managed to reach out and make contact with Simon, with someone from the other side, someone who had once been his enemy.

They had bared their feelings, blurted out long pent up remorses and now he had been given absolution. He didn't need Simon to say the words, he knew from Elise's smile that it was so and he felt good.

He reached out a hand towards her. He wanted to touch her one last time. He knew now that he would not see Elise again.

SHARON 9

'I want to go back to his office.'

'What? Are you mad? There was no-one there except that …'

'That what?' Sharon's response was almost snapped. 'We didn't even wait to see properly. It was probably just a homeless tramp and he must have gone by now, but Deon must be there. Where else could he be?'

Almarie van Tonder gave her husband a *go on humour her* look. He returned it with a *but you heard what happened* look. A *well you know you're not going to get any peace till you give in* look came back in return. If looks could sigh.

'Okay, but we're out of there at the first sign that things aren't right.'

Sharon smiled a sad appreciative smile. She stood up and took a candle into the bathroom where she washed her face and applied a fresh layer of make-up.

Mr van Tonder fumbled for his car keys on the darkened table next to his seat, a knot tightening in his stomach. He got up and grabbing a torch from next to his chair, moved into the bedroom where he moved the clothes in his cupboard and opened the small safe at the back. He took out the small pistol and a magazine, loaded it and checked the safety catch, then quickly shoved it into his jacket pocket.

As he turned he saw a figure in the doorway.

'Be careful Gert,' Almarie said, her voice slightly tense and shaking.

Mr van Tonder nodded and patted his pocket.

'No, be careful with Sharon, she's really upset. She loves Deon and she could do a lot worse than him.'

LUCY 11

'Turn left here, I think this is the way,' Lucy directed Thomas. She was not totally sure how to get to Simon's work place having only been there once before, but the streets were beginning to look familiar.

Thomas nodded and manoeuvred the car along the dark road, his eyes alert, watching out for signs of trouble.

'I really don't know what could have happened to Simon. Why is he not answering his phone? It is not like him.'

Thomas nodded. He had known Simon since he had moved into the street and saw him as a respectable man. He never got drunk, always looked out for his kids and helped his mother out. Silently he offered up a short prayer for Simon's safety.

'Turn right at the next street,' Lucy interrupted his thoughts.

He swung the car round the corner, the traffic lights standing as useless sentries in their unlit state, and eased down the street.

'It's along here somewhere.' Lucy said suddenly sure of where she was. 'There! That's the building.'

Thomas pulled up outside the office block and they got out of the car. Lucy peered through the door, her breathing steaming up the glass slightly. She could barely see anything in the darkened reception.

'His jacket is still there,' her voice was edgy.

Thomas stood a little bit behind her and was the first to notice the figure moving down the street towards them. He tensed and peered into the gloom. He could just make out the security guard uniform and felt that he could relax slightly.

'Someone is coming,' he informed Lucy who moved away from the door and stood next to him as the security guard approached from the opposite side of the street.

'Good evening,' he greeted them. They returned the greeting and Thomas shook the hand of the man formally.

'How are you?'

'We are well and how is business with you?' Thomas was the spokesman and the pleasantries needed to be dealt with before any questions about Simon could be asked.

'Oh, it has been a busy night tonight, especially outside this building. You are the second lot of people to come here tonight. Hau! Here comes another car.'

SHARON 10

Mr van Tonder turned the corner into the road that contained Deon's office block. He drove slowly now, eyes looking in all directions for any possible attackers. The car's lights pierced the darkness of the street and caught the tail-lights of Thomas' car parked outside the building.

He slowed further, eyeing the three figures he now saw standing outside the door. They did not look threatening. There must be something happening at the building, he thought as they neared it. He drew the car up a little distance from the kerb, ready to move off quickly if need be. He felt the weight of the gun in his pocket and took some comfort from that.

The three people were black and he could see that one of them was a woman and another security guard. Surely they posed no threat? However, he still held his hand near his gun.

'Can I help sir?' the security guard asked as Sharon rolled down the window. He recognised the car and the white man with the woman from earlier and was surprised that they had returned.

'You the security guard here?' Mr van Tonder was unaware of their previous encounter. He spoke in his authoritative white voice that had been honed over the apartheid years. It was a voice that spoke down, a voice that had to be answered with respect.

'No sir, I look after that building over there,' he pointed to another office block a little way down the road, not noticing the authority in the voice. The whites had no more power over him anymore, but he was still polite.

'Do you know where the security guard is for this building?' Lucy and Thomas remained silent as Mr van Tonder spoke; it was rude to interrupt the white man.

'Simon? I think he is stuck in the lift sir. The power went off just as he would have been making his rounds. I was lucky, I had just got out of the lift in my building.'

Lucy sighed with relief and looked at Thomas who stepped forward slightly and said to the guard, 'Ah, thank you very much. We have come looking for Simon. He was not answering his cell phone and we need to speak to him, his mother is very ill. We were worried about what may have happened to him.' The relief suddenly overrode the programming not to interrupt the white man.

The guard nodded.

'Is there anyone else in the lift with him?' Sharon was now more at ease, these people were not criminals waiting to hijack the car, they were in the same predicament as her, just people trying to find out what has happened to their loved ones. She did not care about this Simon character or the fact that his mother was ill. She had just been thrown a lifeline and she grabbed it with both hands.

'I don't know madam,' the guard said, 'I work at that building over there.' He pointed again as if this explained everything.

Sharon turned to her father. 'Deon has to be stuck in that lift. It's the only thing that makes sense.'

Mr van Tonder nodded. He had reached a similar conclusion, but was not as convinced of it as Sharon sounded.

'Is there any way we can get in there?' he asked the security guard.

'No sir, not unless you have a key.'

'So there's nothing we can do?'

'No sir, I'm afraid you will have to wait for the power to come back on. Then the lift will come down to the ground floor. If the security guard is in there, then he will be able to open the door for you.'

Mr van Tonder grunted a thanks and started to move the car off.

'Daddy! Where are you going? We have to wait and see if Deon is in the lift.'

'What?'

'We've got to wait. I'm sure Deon is in there.'

Mr van Tonder sighed. He felt safer now that he knew who the people outside the building were, but did not fancy waiting up all night on the off chance that the power would come back on. A look from an imagined Almarie made him ease the car back to the kerb.

'Okay. Let me just phone your mom.'

THE LIFT 35

'It's like a Truth and Reconciliation Commission in here,' Simon pushed the silence aside, unaware of Deon's vision.

'I suppose it is a bit,' Deon was now just waiting for the words. Elise had confirmed for him, but he still needed to hear it from Simon's lips.

'But for it to be a proper TRC, then I need to grant you amnesty for what your actions have done to me. I need to forgive you,' Simon continued, the decision process going through his mind coming out in his voice. Deon bowed his head, agreeing with Simon, but, not wishing to sound eager for the forgiveness he craved, he remained silent.

Simon considered for a long time before eventually going on, 'We have to move forward. There is nothing to be gained from looking back anymore. It is not easy to just grant amnesty like that, but we have grown to understand each other better and I now know why you were in the township as a soldier so it makes it easier to understand.' His voice was fragile with emotion but there was also a conviction about what he was saying. 'But just because I understand it, it doesn't mean I like it, and it does not take away the pain.' He was silent again for a long time, then said, 'I forgive you.'

The words floated into the lift and seemed to blow away the darkness and misunderstandings that had been there when it had first ground to a halt. All the heaviness of the air evaporated.

Deon breathed in deeply. 'Thank you.' It was soft almost inaudible.

The men sat in silence for a while, Deon dealing with the forgiveness he had received and Simon contemplating that which he had just given.

'You know I never thought I would ever be forgiven for the death of Gladys Makathini. I thought I would have to live with it for the rest of my life. Do you know how much this means to me my friend?'

My friend. There were those words again, so strange in a white mouth. Simon smiled in the dark.

'I am sorry for Elise, what happened to her.' He felt a gesture was needed.

'Hey it wasn't your fault.'

'I know Deon, but I am still sorry it happened. She sounded like a very nice woman. I would have liked to meet her.'

'She is at peace now.' The sentence caught in Deon's throat.

'Yes.' Quiet and respectful.

There was a long silence.

'But now you must treasure your new woman, Sharon? Was that her name?'

'Ja, Sharon. I will …'

The lights snapped on, blinding the two men and the lift's mechanics clicked into life as it resumed its broken descent, oblivious of what had happened inside it.

WESSEL STANDER

'Bugger,' he grumbled as the light in his bedroom snapped on, waking him from his sleep. It was not the first time that he had forgotten to switch it off when the power cuts came. He had sat staring in the dark at the lifeless TV for a while before heading off to bed, remembering most of the lights this time, but not the bedroom one.

About a year after Marie was killed, Wessel moved the family down to Cape Town where the violence was not as pronounced and his job less stressful, giving him time to raise the kids.

In the bright light that now filled the bedroom, he swung his feet off the bed and sat for a minute, rubbing his eyes, adjusting to the brightness. Then he moved silently over to the bedroom door and stuck his head out, checking down the passage. It was just his bedroom light that had been left on as far as he could tell.

He sighed and was just about to turn the light off when he glanced at his bed. The side where Marie used to sleep lay untouched and he felt the familiar knot of despair tighten in his stomach. The pain of her death never really left him. Most of the time he was okay, but every now and then it would catch him unawares. His hand moved away from the light switch and he walked quietly down the passage. He stopped outside Kleinjan's room. His son lay quietly in his bed, the bedclothes rising and falling slightly with his breathing.

Further down the passage, he checked in on Annette. She looked more and more like Marie every day it seemed. He peered into the inky dark of the room, wanting to take comfort from the living.

'Dad is that you?' The voice was sleepy.

'Yes my love.'

'Are you okay?'

Wessel swallowed hard, 'Yes my love, go to sleep.'

'I dreamt of ma again. I miss her.'

'Me too, my love. Go back to sleep.' He turned away, not wanting his daughter to see his tears.

PRECIOUS MAKATHINI 2

She snuggled closer to her friend searching for a bit more warmth from the slight body next to her. The wind was getting up and had a bite. The burnt out shack they occupied offered little shelter from the elements. The stench of her friend's body mingled with her own unwashed and uncared for smells.

Precious felt the hunger pull at her stomach. It had not been a good day. They had managed to steal an apple and had begged a half-eaten sandwich that they shared.

Through her half closed eyes she saw a dull light flare up across the small room. The boys were taking tik again. Hopefully they would not get violent. She felt her bruised arm; it was tender to the touch. A raw hacking cough took over her lungs and her companion pushed her away while she cleared the phlegm.

Her arm throbbed and her stomach cramped in protest at its emptiness. She sat up and coughed again. She knew that she would not sleep tonight. Across the dirty floor she watched the boys as they sat inhaling the tik, their bloodshot eyes starting to glaze over. Precious waited for them to go into their stupor and envied the way the drug seemed to shut out the pain of reality that surrounded them. She shifted uneasily on the floor and coughed again. She was very tired, not just physically, but also mentally. Tired of her scrap of life. In her mind she always felt that she had been destined for better things, but so far that had not happened.

A worn and dusty image of Mary came up in her mind, the mother figure she had had a short chance to get to know. She had no image of Gladys to comfort her. Then the horror of the rape took hold as it always did, but now it didn't seem as bad as it did back then. Perhaps she should not have run away.

She fingered the bruise again and looked across the room at the boy who had given it to her, she was startled to see that he was staring back at her in a strange way. He was one of the older boys, maybe as old as fifteen. He motioned for her to come over.

She hesitated, caught between staying away from the potential violence should she go across and the potential violence should she not. The tuberculosis took control of her lungs again and when the coughing had finished she looked over again. He was offering her some tik. This was a first.

She moved trance-like across the room, keen to sample this thing that shut out the pain for the boys. The broken light bulb used for heating the drug felt strange but she took it anyway and inhaled as she had seen the boys do. Immediately a coughing fit took hold and her small frame spasmed in time to the hacking of her lungs. The boys laughed, but slowly as the effect of the tik spread she felt herself relax and the cares flow from her body.

The boy who had given her the tik reached out and grabbed her arm, pulling her roughly towards him. She felt his warm acrid breath on her face, breath that usually repelled her, breath that she would have struggled against, but now she realised this was payment for the drugs and her hazy mind didn't resist.

Maybe this is the way she thought. The boy always seemed to have food, drugs and money. She knew he had other girls who brought him the money and she had heard them talking about what they had to do to get it. Now it was happening to her.

She lay back and closed her eyes while accommodating the boy between her legs. Maybe this was the way. A slow tear dripped from her eye.

YVONNE 2

Yvonne lay awake in bed, the streetlight backlit the curtains and cast a murky gloom into the room. Trevor was asleep and snoring softly next to her. She had not thought about Deon for a long time and his sudden appearance in her dream had startled her awake.

Why now, after all this time had she suddenly been reminded of a man she had tried so hard to forget? Despite having spent so much effort trying to cleanse her mind of Deon, she did not object to this intrusion into her subconscious.

She thought about the time spent talking on the phone, the laughs they had shared. She smiled quietly as she remembered a particular conversation they had had.

Her mind then moved the relationship forward to when it got physical. She closed her eyes and felt again his soft caress and the hard warmth of his body up against hers. Suddenly she began to ache for his touch. She had not been touched by Trevor since that day when she had scrubbed herself clean, almost as if he knew. But her mind would not let her relive that episode, it preferred to concentrate on the more pleasant aspect of their relationship.

Trevor snorted and shifted position, bringing her out of her thoughts. She sighed and climbed quietly out of bed. In the kitchen she turned the light on, blinking in the brightness till her eyes adjusted, then she put the kettle on, oblivious of the power that drove the light and the kettle. She took it for granted.

The light in the room made it look pitch black outside and as she looked she felt it was too bright for her thoughts. She flicked the switch off and stood for a moment while her eyes adjusted back to the dark. The kettle began to get up some momentum and was starting to rattle. Yvonne moved over to the sink and stared outside into the serene darkness of the garden. Nothing moved.

Her thoughts returned to Deon along with the ache for his touch. She wondered where he was now, what he was doing. She wished he was here with her in the kitchen. A naughty grin flashed across her features as she imagined him sitting at the small breakfast nook, watching her.

Then the grin got naughtier as her fantasy took hold completely. She wanted him to see her naked. She wanted to tell him he was forgiven for that horrible time when he had called out another woman's name.

Before her sensible side could react, she had whipped her short nightshirt over her head and whisked her knickers off. She stood for a second enjoying the cool air on her skin and the freedom it brought.

Then, just as she was about to look up to meet his imagined appreciative eyes, the kettle clicked boiled and she was dumped unceremoniously back into reality. She looked down at her nakedness and embarrassment overrode all other feelings. She covered her body with her hands while a tear leaked out the corner of her eye.

It was a tear of despair, of unhappiness at the emptiness of her life, a life she felt powerless to change. She fumbled on the floor for her nightdress.

OUTSIDE

The florescent lights in the building lobby flickered while the streetlights glowed dull orange in their warm up. Lucy sat up in Thomas' car.

'The power is back on.'

Sharon saw it too and gently shook her father who was dozing behind the wheel, feeling tired by the evening's activities and safer with that security guard across the road.

'Quick Daddy, the lights are on.' She jumped out of the car.

The two men followed slowly after the women who were already at the door, peering through the glass. They felt a strange kinship in their support of the fretting women, but the separation of race so entrenched in their generation denied them the ability to acknowledge it.

Lucy was the first to speak. 'Look the lift lights are changing, the lift is coming down. Please God let him be in there.'

For a second Sharon thought that Lucy was talking about Deon and instinctively reached out and took hold of her hand, as if looking for support against her own concerns. By the time her mind realised that Lucy had not been talking about Deon it was too late for her to let go without feeling embarrassed so she hung onto this stranger's hand, her eyes glued to the flicking lights on the panel above the lift doors. They were after all united in their concern for their respective men and Sharon dismissed her strange feelings about holding a black woman's hand by thinking that this was now a show of solidarity for their womanhood.

Lucy was too wrapped up in her concern for Simon and how he would react to the news about his mother to take any notice of the white hand that now held hers. She moved her head and stood on her tip toes to try and get a better view of what she already had a perfect view of, almost like she had to look over the heads of an invisible crowd in front of her.

What would emerge from the lift? Neither woman thought anything but that their respective men would be in there when the doors opened. It could not be otherwise. To contemplate any other scenario was not acceptable. They did not stop to think that the other woman's man was there, only their own.

THE LIFT 36

The lift companions blinked rapidly as the harsh light threw aside the comfort blanket of darkness. Deon scrambled to his feet, squinting against the hurt of the brightness. He felt acutely aware of himself now, felt that the light would somehow expose him. He did not want to be caught sitting down.

They were almost on the ground floor and Simon was starting to push himself up, following Deon's lead. He did not feel the same degree of self-consciousness as Deon, but was still conscious that the protection of darkness had gone.

Deon looked down at Simon and his self-awareness faded as the gratitude he had felt a moment ago flooded back. He stretched out a hand and helped Simon to his feet, then pulled him closer and hugged him.

'We made it,' he half whispered.

Simon resisted the instinct to step back as Deon moved forward to embrace him. He put his arms around Deon, awkwardly at first, then with more certainty and patted his back tentatively.

'Yes we did my friend.' The word *friend* did not sound so strange on his tongue this time.

www.ingramcontent.com/pod-product-compliance
Lightning Source LLC
Chambersburg PA
CBHW050357030726

47503CB00006B/1906